TOUCHING

THE

SKY

Books by Tracie Peterson

www.traciepeterson.com

House of Secrets • *A Slender Thread* • *Where My Heart Belongs*

LAND OF THE LONE STAR
Chasing the Sun
Touching the Sky
Taming the Wind

BRIDAL VEIL ISLAND*
To Have and To Hold
To Love and Cherish
To Honor and Trust

SONG OF ALASKA
Dawn's Prelude
Morning's Refrain
Twilight's Serenade

STRIKING A MATCH
Embers of Love
Hearts Aglow
Hope Rekindled

ALASKAN QUEST
Summer of the Midnight Sun
Under the Northern Lights
Whispers of Winter
Alaskan Quest (3 in 1)

BRIDES OF GALLATIN COUNTY
A Promise to Believe In
A Love to Last Forever
A Dream to Call My Own

THE BROADMOOR LEGACY*
A Daughter's Inheritance
An Unexpected Love
A Surrendered Heart

BELLS OF LOWELL*
Daughter of the Loom
A Fragile Design
These Tangled Threads

LIGHTS OF LOWELL*
A Tapestry of Hope
A Love Woven True
The Pattern of Her Heart

DESERT ROSES
Shadows of the Canyon
Across the Years
Beneath a Harvest Sky

HEIRS OF MONTANA
Land of My Heart
The Coming Storm
To Dream Anew
The Hope Within

LADIES OF LIBERTY
A Lady of High Regard
A Lady of Hidden Intent
A Lady of Secret Devotion

RIBBONS OF STEEL**
Distant Dreams
A Hope Beyond
A Promise for Tomorrow

RIBBONS WEST**
Westward the Dream
Separate Roads
Ties That Bind

WESTWARD CHRONICLES
A Shelter of Hope
Hidden in a Whisper
A Veiled Reflection

YUKON QUEST
Treasures of the North
Ashes and Ice
Rivers of Gold

*with Judith Miller   **with Judith Pella

LAND OF THE LONE STAR ★ BOOK TWO

TRACIE PETERSON

BETHANY HOUSE PUBLISHERS
a division of Baker Publishing Group
Minneapolis, Minnesota

Published by Bethany House Publishers
11400 Hampshire Avenue South
Bloomington, Minnesota 55438
www.bethanyhouse.com

Bethany House Publishers is a division of
Baker Publishing Group, Grand Rapids, Michigan

Printed in the United States of America

Library of Congress Cataloging-in-Publication Data
Peterson, Tracie.
    Touching the sky / Tracie Peterson.
        p.   cm. — (Land of the lone star ; bk. 2)
    ISBN 978-0-7642-1008-2 (alk. pbk.)
    ISBN 978-0-7642-0616-0 (pbk.)
    ISBN 978-0-7642-1009-9 (large print pbk.)
    1. Texas—History—Civil War, 1861–1865—Fiction. I. Title.
PS3566.E7717T68 2012
813'.54—dc23   2012001270

Scripture quotations are from the King James Version of the Bible.

Cover design by Jennifer Parker

Cover photography by Mike Habermann Photography, LLC

12   13   14   15   16   17   18   7   6   5   4   3   2   1

⤸

To Dr. Josh Knappenberger,
an awesome doctor and friend!

May God guide your work.

⤸

Thick clouds hung low on the horizon. Laura Marquardt studied the sky for a moment, hoping she still had time to make it home before the heavens opened and rain descended. If Mother hadn't been desperate for her nerve tonic, Laura never would have ventured out on such a day. She certainly wouldn't have traveled alone. A flash of lightning far out over the Gulf of Mexico caused her to pick up her steps.

So much had changed in Corpus Christi. The town had once bustled with thousands of people, but the war had reduced that number to no more than four hundred or so. With the War Between the States finally coming to an end, however, the city was once again adding to its number with a great many Union troops—most of them former slaves. Blue was the color of the day thanks to the army's occupation. Unfortunately, many a heart was still gray, and most Southerners weren't of a mind to be ordered about by black troops.

"Well, if it ain't Miss Laura Marquardt! Where you runnin' off to in such a hurry?"

She stopped in her steps, then turned to see two men walking toward her. Their raggedy appearance served as a reminder of the South's defeat: dirty shirts covered by equally filthy coats, and worn trousers with holes here and there. There was something familiar and yet menacing about the men. Laura slipped the ties of her reticule over her gloved wrist, feeling the weight of the bottled medicine that she'd put inside.

"See, I told you it were her," the taller of the two men said.

Recognition dawned, and Laura realized who the men were. "Mr. Edwards. Mr. Riley." She gave a curt nod. The men approached her with a familiarity that made Laura feel uncomfortable.

"My, my, my. You've grown up to be quite the little belle," Edwards declared. He rubbed his tobacco-stained mustache and grinned. "Ain't seen you since before the war when we worked for your papa."

Riley, a dark-eyed man not much taller than herself, nodded. "I'll bet the men are just vyin' for your attention."

Edwards leaned in closer. "If I weren't married, I'd ask for your hand. A fella could have a lot of fun with a little gal like you. Why, I'll bet you can dance a pretty jig."

Laura frowned. She would turn twenty-two in August, and still that made Edwards at least twice her age. Besides, such conversation was completely uncalled for and inappropriate

8

given their stations in life. These men had once worked for her father. Not only that, but she knew they had fought on the side of the Confederacy. Mr. Riley apparently recognized her discomfort and snorted a laugh.

"Maybe she reckons that since her people are Yankee supporters, she can't be speakin' to the likes of us Southerners anymore."

"I think nothing of the kind, Mr. Riley." She looked hard at the men. "Our family has remained friends with supporters of both sides of that horrible war."

"There ain't such a thing as a friendly Yank."

Laura had endured more than enough of the men, and with the first well-timed drops of rain starting to fall, she opened her parasol. It wouldn't afford much protection, but she hoped the action would speak for itself. "I believe it's starting to rain. Good day to you both."

She didn't wait for their reply but instead turned to resume walking. Without warning, however, one of the men took hold of her arm and pulled her into an alleyway. She dropped her hold on her parasol as Edwards slammed her against the back of the building. The hooping in her petticoat pushed forward, but the man didn't care. He pressed into the thick folds of her skirt and held her in place. Leaning forward, with his index finger pointed inches from her face, Edwards leered.

"You need to tell your pa that we don't cotton to his kind down here. He should've taken his place with the Confederacy or gone north. Now he'll pay for bein' a traitor."

Her heart raced. "My father is a good man who believed in the solidarity of the Union," Laura countered. "He wasn't against the South; rather, he wanted unity among the states."

"He chose his side, same as the rest of us," Mr. Riley said, moving closer. "He figured there was more to profit with the Union—that's all."

"That's a lie," Laura proclaimed. She tried to move, but Edwards pushed her back again.

"Maybe your pa needs a different kind of lesson. Maybe he won't listen to a simple message."

Laura began to tremble. She could smell whiskey on the man's breath as he leaned in closer.

"Maybe you uppity Yankee girls need an old-fashioned lesson in manners."

"I was thinking the same of you, Mr. Edwards. There was a time when you conducted yourself in a gentlemanly manner. I see that day is gone."

"The war changes things," he said, leaning forward as if to kiss her.

Laura turned her head to the right only to have the man take hold of her face and forcibly pull it back. Laura squirmed uncomfortably, wondering if she should scream for help. She didn't have to wonder long, however. Two men from the Twenty-eighth Regimented Infantry called out.

"What's goin' on here?" one of the men asked as they approached.

Edwards released her with a scowl. Laura knew the only people hated more than Union supporters were the Yankee Colored Troops. Those who fought for the South found it an insult to be subjected to their authority.

"You boys need to mind your own business," Riley said. "Ain't no war goin' on now . . . or ain't y'all heard?"

Edwards laughed. "I'm sure there's a field of cotton just waitin' to be picked."

Laura fought to control her fears as one of the soldiers stepped closer. "We have orders to follow," the soldier declared.

Edwards laughed at this. "You got that right, boy. Your people ought to be followin' orders, but they went and got uppity. Now they think they're just as good as everybody else."

The man ignored him and turned to Laura. "Are you all right, miss?"

She was surprised by his genteel speech. "I was on my way home," Laura replied. "These men recognized me as a Union supporter and felt it necessary to express their distaste of such things."

"Maybe you two could come along with us and explain to our commander."

"Who's gonna make us?" Edwards asked.

"It'd take a whole lot more than two of you colored boys to take me," Riley said, striking a stance that suggested he was ready for a fight.

"Maybe you boys need a real man to teach you a thing or two," Edwards added.

The soldiers said nothing, but something about their bearing changed. Laura sensed they were more than willing to take on the two older men. Apparently Riley realized the same thing.

"I think they're itchin' for a fight." He grinned. "Well, so am I. I didn't kill enough of you boys in the war. It's mighty obligin' of you to give me a second chance."

Mr. Edwards started to take off his coat and one of the soldiers leveled his rifle.

This caused Riley to put out his hand to stop Edwards. "They ain't worth the effort. They won't fight like real men," Riley said. He punched his friend on the shoulder. "Let's get out of here."

Mr. Edwards muttered a string of curses and insults on the men before spitting at them. "You darkies should learn your place, but I ain't got the time to teach you."

"You ain't goin' nowhere," the armed man declared.

Laura was about to speak when Mr. Riley took hold of her and threw her toward the soldiers before he and Edwards took off down the alley.

"Halt!" one soldier called out as the other steadied Laura so she wouldn't fall.

The men laughed and continued their escape with a glance over their shoulders. If anything, Laura thought they'd slowed their steps in a taunting manner.

"I said halt, or I'll shoot."

One of the soldiers aimed his rifle, but Laura hurried to push the gun down. "Please don't. There's been entirely too much bloodshed already." Edwards and Riley took her actions as a cue to run.

Laura continued to try to reason with the men. "Please don't go after them. They aren't very honorable men and may be planning an ambush down the way." She patted the arm of the soldier. "I wouldn't want anything to happen to the two of you on my account."

"What's going on here?"

Laura and the two soldiers looked to find a Union captain approaching. The man was rugged in his appearance and his broad shoulders bulged under his coat, but it was his striking blue eyes that held Laura's attention.

"The lady was bein' detained," one of the soldiers began, but the captain raised his hand.

"Say no more. I'll deal with this. You two go on about your patrol."

"Yes, sir," the men said in unison. The soldiers nodded and tipped their forage caps. "Ma'am."

The captain turned his gaze on Laura. She felt his eyes studying her carefully, as if he could assess her value. The set of his jaw suggested a no-nonsense manner. Perhaps he was growing weary of rescuing damsels in distress. The thought made Laura smile.

"I suppose you think it funny to argue with Federal soldiers, but I'm not amused," the captain told her. "The sooner you folks learn to accept that the North won this war, the better off you'll be. I will not tolerate rude behavior . . . even from Southern ladies."

"I assure you, sir, I was not arguing with anyone," Laura countered. She felt miffed at his mistaking the situation. Why, he hadn't even asked for a full explanation from his men.

"I won't discuss it with you, ma'am. You would do well to stay off the streets without an escort."

Laura drew up to her full height. "Whether I walk unescorted or not is none of your concern."

"It's my concern, ma'am, when you argue with my men. This town is under occupation for your welfare as much as anything. I realize you Southerners are angry and hostile toward our soldiers, but we have our orders. Orders that, as I have already stated, are for your benefit." He let his gaze travel the length of her and back. "It seems a lady of your upbringing would realize this. Nevertheless," he said, fixing her with a hard stare, "I am not going to argue with you."

"Again, Captain . . . ?" She waited for a name.

"Reid."

"Again, Captain Reid, I am not arguing. You merely misunderstood the situation." Her nerves were finally steadying themselves, and fear was quickly being replaced by anger.

He shook his head. "Rather like the North misunderstood being fired upon at Fort Sumter?"

She opened her mouth to reply, then dropped her head. He wasn't worth the effort. Besides, it was beginning to rain in earnest. She picked up her parasol and marched back to the street. No doubt she'd be drenched by the time she reached home.

"Men," she muttered, picking up her pace.

Captain Brandon Reid was only a month away from mustering out of the Union Army, and yet the future eluded him. He felt directionless . . . uncertain. He could return home to Indiana, where his preacher-father owned a small but well-managed horse farm; he knew his mother would be delighted with that choice. Brandon, however, wasn't sure that God would be.

The heaviness of the Texas air felt like nothing compared to the weight of indecision perched upon his shoulders. When war had been declared, Brandon knew without a doubt it was his duty to enlist and come to the aid of his country. His family had long been abolitionists, and freeing slaves was a cause he believed in—as well as keeping all states united as one. But now that his soldiering days were coming to an end, Brandon couldn't help but feel overwhelmed with the choices before him.

He made his way down Water Street, past John Dix's house.

Rumors ran amuck about the owner. The man was said to be an avid Union supporter and had offered invaluable help during the war. Or so Brandon had been told. As a sea captain it was rumored that he signaled Federal ships in the harbor by hanging lanterns from his house. Brandon had also heard it said that Dix's son had served in the Second Texas Cavalry under Colonel "Rip" Ford and completely disagreed with his father's stand. Sadly, such was often the case with the War Between the States. How many families had been forever divided because of politics?

He continued his walk a block to Taylor Street, where his destination was the same house that had once been assigned as a commissary for Zachary Taylor's troops during the war with Mexico. And, even though the house had been built by a man named R. C. Russell, the place was now known simply as the Ironclad House. The strange title was due to the ironclad oath that every Texan who had not borne arms against the North was required to take. The oath required men to swear they had never given service to the Confederacy and that they were loyal to the Union. This was required if a man were to vote or hold office. In fact, given the demands placed by the North, this oath was necessary for most anything a man wanted to do. Some said it would have been impossible to buy so much as a bag of flour on credit without having taken the ironclad, but Brandon knew this was stretching things a bit.

He paused a moment. Despite its years and neglect due to the war, the architecture of the Ironclad House spoke of money and charm. On the porch were a couple of rocking chairs and a wicker settee. The pieces seemed to suggest a quiet evening spent with friends, but Brandon knew better. Inside, General

Charles S. Russell, no relation to the original builder, oversaw the grave duty of restoring order to this part of the South.

Charles was a good friend from before the war, but now he was Brandon's superior, overseeing the Second U.S. Colored Cavalry, as well as the Tenth and Twenty-eighth Regiments of the U.S. Colored Troop Infantries. Brandon served as a captain for the latter.

They had seen many battles together over the years. Both Brandon and Charles had left family in Indiana to serve with the colored troops, enduring insult and slander for their positions. While the Northerners were all for freeing the blacks, few wanted to associate or work with them. Brandon was frustrated by the hypocrisy.

Neither the North or South had won this war, as far as he was concerned. He'd lost good friends on both sides, and though Brandon and his family had strongly supported the abolitionist movement, he wasn't convinced that the Emancipation Proclamation had done for the slaves all that Lincoln had intended. Already, Brandon had heard from his superiors that many of the slaveholders were ignoring the law. The most cunning found ways around the demands of the deceased president they had abhorred. It was said that in some places the Negroes were forced to leave all of their possessions—including clothing—if they were to be freed. The former owners defended this, saying that while Mr. Lincoln might have freed the slaves, clothing would come at a price.

Of course, none of the former slaves had money. In order to pay for their clothing, the Negroes were required to stay on and work for an allotted time—time that inevitably grew with additional charges for food, housing, work tools, and other supplies the white masters forced their laborers to pay. It didn't take a mathematical genius to see that it would soon be impossible for a former slave to work himself out of debt.

Freedom for the blacks had, in many ways, only served to cause them more pain and suffering. It grieved Brandon in a way he couldn't express. Having grown up in Indiana, not far from the Ohio River, Brandon's family had been active in helping runaway slaves. He knew the horrible conditions many had endured. He'd helped to bury more than one slave who had taken ill or received fatal injuries during his escape. Even so, it was often said by those who survived that it was better to die in freedom than live in bondage.

Brandon entered the house and was immediately greeted by a uniformed soldier jumping to attention. "Sir, General Russell is awaiting you." The man simultaneously saluted and Brandon returned in kind.

"Thank you, Corporal."

He made his way past the man and into the small room where a tired-looking man sat deep in thought. He glanced up and motioned Brandon to his desk.

"Come in, Brandon. How goes it for you here in Corpus Christi?"

"Better than we fared in Antietam," Brandon countered.

The man gave a hint of a smile. "As I recall, we won that one."

"Strategically, yes, but you and I both know the price it cost. I fear we are up against much the same here. Perhaps not in blood, but in hearts."

General Russell sobered. "Sadly, I agree. May we never see

such a war again." He drew a long breath, then leaned back against his leather chair. "Still, you look fit. I believe the town must be agreeing with you."

Brandon nodded. "For the most part. I just had an encounter with a simpering Southern miss who didn't appreciate my men detaining her. She had a sharp tongue, but nothing more dangerous than that. And you, General?"

"Now, Brandon, we've been friends much too long to resort to formalities in private."

Brandon took a seat opposite the man who was only some six years his senior, but looked at least a score.

"I had a letter from my mother, Charles," Brandon said. "She told me to give you her best and to tell you that she's given Annie that recipe for chocolate cake you like so much."

"That woman has been a godsend to my wife," the general replied. He glanced down at the papers on his desk and frowned. "Seems like forever since I've seen Annie and my girls." He paused and sighed. "But this isn't why I sent for you. We must discuss the looting and vandalizing that has been reported around the town. There have been increasing complaints, and some of them from Union supporters."

"Why don't you fill me in," Brandon suggested.

The general picked up a piece of paper. "This one reports damage done to a cemetery." He picked up another sheet. "This one is in regard to our men vandalizing a known Confederate's home." He glanced upward. "There are numerous reports of harassment and so-called indecencies with women."

"You say 'so-called.' Do you think the reports are false?"

"Who can tell? This town is a powder keg waiting to explode.

I had hoped we'd find it easier as time went on. After all, there are large numbers of Union supporters in this city. Not only that, but I'd like to believe my men are honorable. They may be colored troops, but you and I both know the quality of men we've had under us."

"Yes, I agree."

The general got to his feet and paced. He wasn't all that big of a man—certainly nowhere near as tall as Brandon's six-foot-three frame. Putting his hands behind his back, he reminded Brandon of a banty rooster strutting to and fro in the barnyard.

"There are bad apples in every bushel basket, however. I'm not without the ability to acknowledge that my men are capable of such deeds—but I will have proof before meting out punishment. That's why I called you here. I know you're mustering out at the end of July, but I want you to keep your eyes and ears open. I want to be on top of this. If we fail to keep the men in line, we will lose the support of those who remained loyal during the war."

"I'll do what I can," Brandon agreed.

"I knew you would," the general replied and stopped pacing. "I've already discussed this with Major Armstrong. He agrees you will be beneficial to this task. I only ask that you monitor the situation and gather information as you receive it. Should you find men in possession of anything other than army regulated goods, I want you to confiscate them and document the items."

Brandon got to his feet and nodded. "Anything else?"

The general smiled. Shuffling through the papers once more, he pulled a white card from the pile. "As a matter of fact, there is. Tonight, there is a party and I wish for you to attend in my place. It's to be quite a grand affair and only Union supporters will be in attendance. Wealthy Union supporters."

"Me? Why me? Wouldn't Major Armstrong be better at such a thing?" Brandon had no desire to go and make small talk with the socialites of Corpus Christi.

"The major is busy elsewhere. Besides, he's married and our host has two very pretty daughters." Charles grinned. "Annie has been after you to settle down for a long while now. Who knows? You might find a lovely young woman here in Corpus."

"That's highly doubtful," Brandon replied. "Not that there aren't some very beautiful women in this town," he said, remembering the young woman he'd encountered earlier that day. "Still, I will most likely return to Indiana. I doubt these warm-blooded beauties would have an appreciation for the colder climes."

The general laughed and shook his head. "Please don't make me issue this as an order."

"I'll attend, but it's under protest, General Russell."

This made his superior laugh. "Duly noted, Captain. Duly noted." He handed him the invitation. "Make the army proud, Brandon. We need all the positive attention we can get."

Brandon looked at the card and frowned. "Very well."

"Oh, and Brandon, there is an ulterior motive behind this, as well."

Now Brandon was intrigued. He raised a brow in question. "You mean besides finding me a wife?"

"Indeed. We have a man we're watching. He should be in attendance at this party, and I thought perhaps you could observe him and even befriend him. It might help to speed our investigation along if we can get someone close to him."

Brandon sat back down. "Tell me more."

꩜

Brandon entered Stanley Marquardt's house a little later than he'd planned. He handed his card, gloves, and hat to the butler and was then shown to the entrance of a large music room, where the rest of the party was listening to a dark-haired woman play the piano. When she lifted her face to sing, he was startled to see it was the same young woman he'd encountered earlier in the alleyway.

"If you will wait here, sir," the butler instructed, "I will announce you in a moment."

Brandon nodded, his gaze never leaving the woman. Who was she? She played exquisitely and her voice was beautiful in its clarity and range. Brandon stood back in the shadows, hoping she wouldn't see him. He wanted to study her better. He'd already relived their earlier moments together, wondering if he could have been gentler or less caustic. Now seeing her here—at a party for Union supporters—Brandon couldn't help but wonder about the woman.

Her brown hair had a rich sheen that seemed to glisten in the lamplight. He recalled that her eyes were a light, buttery brown. Not quite amber, but far from the dark brown-black of the local residents who were of Mexican descent.

When the song concluded, she stood and gave a brief curtsy while the others clapped. Brandon would have joined in with his approval, but the servant drew his attention.

"Sir, I will announce you now." The butler stepped into the

room as the clapping faded. "Captain Reid," the man said as if they had all been expecting him.

The audience, who only moments earlier had been enraptured by the performance, now turned their attention to him. He gave a slight bow as an older gentleman stepped forward.

"Captain Reid," the man said, extending his hand. "We were sorry to hear that the general couldn't attend tonight but were so delighted that you could come in his stead. I am Stanley Marquardt, and this is my wife."

Brandon looked to the small woman who had swept up alongside the man. Her wheat-colored hair was sprinkled with gray, and a few wrinkles around her eyes and mouth suggested she had reached middle age and then some.

"Mrs. Marquardt. Mr. Marquardt. Thank you for allowing me to attend on behalf of General Russell." He gave a bow.

"It is we who are thankful. Your presence is most welcome. Come and let me introduce you to some of the others," Marquardt declared. He turned almost immediately to his right. "This is James Sonderson and his wife."

Brandon went through another dozen such introductions, knowing he would never manage to keep all of the names straight. He wondered what had become of the young woman who'd played and sung in such an accomplished manner. He didn't have to wonder for long.

"And this is our daughter Laura."

Brandon met Laura's gaze and could see from the fix of her mouth that she was amused. She was all but smirking at him. He bowed and addressed them. "I'm pleased to make your acquaintance."

"Goodness, Father, but are we being invaded by the army?" Laura asked, giving her fan a flick open.

Her father chuckled. "Daughter, Captain Reid is here on behalf of General Russell. He knows very well how faithful we've been to support the Union."

Laura raised a brow and looked at Brandon with an expression that suggested she was enjoying every minute of his discomfort. "I'm not at all sure that the captain understands our faithfulness. Given the fact that so many in this city were Confederate supporters, perhaps Captain Reid believes none of us capable of loyalty to the Union."

Her father looked at her oddly, but Laura only shrugged and continued. "I suppose, however, he wouldn't be the type to jump to conclusions. After all, it's not difficult to ask a person to state their loyalty. Why, there is even an oath being given. I believe you took that oath, did you not, Father?"

"I did indeed. I would take it a hundred times over."

Brandon knew he deserved her words, but they stung nevertheless. "I have been known to jump to conclusions," Brandon admitted. "It has usually landed me in a mud pit."

Stanley Marquardt was momentarily distracted. "If you'll excuse me, I must attend to another matter. Laura, do be a good friend to the captain and show him around."

"I would be delighted," she said, smiling. She waved her fan and batted her eyelashes. "Positively delighted."

Once her father was out of earshot, Brandon leaned down and lowered his voice. "I suppose I deserved that."

"You most certainly did," she agreed. "I've done nothing but think about you all day."

He couldn't help but grin. "Why, Miss Marquardt, I'm honored."

Her eyes widened. "Well, don't be. My thoughts were of torment and torture for you, not pleasantries."

He laughed. "I can well imagine. If looks could have killed, I believe I would have been felled in that alleyway."

"Hardly," she replied. "Perhaps a strong thrashing, but never murder. Especially not when one of our glorious war heroes is involved."

"I can hardly claim that fame, but I yield to your mercy. I do apologize for my hasty judgment." She smiled, and Brandon thought he'd never seen anyone quite so beautiful.

"I suppose it wouldn't be Christian of me to refuse. Therefore, Captain Reid, I accept your apology." She let her fan drop. "We shall be friends."

"Why hello," another female voice greeted from Brandon's left.

He looked over to meet the young woman who approached. "Laura, darlin', you simply must introduce us."

Laura rolled her eyes and snapped her fan shut. "Captain Reid, may I present my sister Miss Carissa Marquardt."

She extended her gloved hand and gave a teasing giggle behind her fan. "Why, Captain, I'm completely charmed."

"As am I, Miss Marquardt." Brandon barely took hold of her fingertips and bowed over her hand in a brief salute.

Carissa took hold of his arm, much to Brandon's surprise. "Now, Captain, you simply must tell me all about yourself. I want to hear positively every little thing."

Brandon caught Laura's annoyed look just before she said, "If you two will excuse me."

She slipped away before he could protest.

Carissa smiled. "She's so very serious. I apologize if you thought her rude and unbecoming. I'm afraid the war has left her an old maid and she is quite bitter."

For a moment Brandon was stunned into silence, and then without meaning to, he laughed. Carissa looked at him oddly.

"I am sorry, Miss Marquardt, but please forgive me. I would never call your statement into question, but I'm certain that if your sister wanted a husband, she'd have no difficulty in getting one."

"Y ou are far too flirtatious for your own good, Carissa,"
Laura chided her sister the next morning as they finished
dressing. "You have a beau, and it's most unseemly that you
should fawn all over Captain Reid and others."

"Oh bother. You have nothing to complain about. You were
able to have a proper coming out party before the war stripped
away all that was lovely. I turned sixteen during the war and
there was no hope of a party or public announcement. Now I'm
eighteen, and I intend for people to know me and to see what
I have to offer." She looked at Laura and shrugged. "Besides, I
think you're just jealous."

"Think what you like," Laura said, not wanting her sister
to know how close she was to the truth. "Even so, you have a
reputation to protect and acting out in such a manner will only
serve to harm your social standing. War or no war, the ladies
of Corpus Christi will not easily forgive impudent behavior."

Carissa plopped down in a chair by the vanity and picked up a brush. Giving her gold-brown hair long, determined strokes, she looked over her shoulder at Laura. "He was quite handsome."

Laura rolled her eyes and reached for the brush. With quick work, Laura plaited Carissa's hair into a single braid. "And rather dashing. But then, the uniform can't help but enhance a man's appearance. Father even said so."

Carissa giggled. "It wouldn't help old Gaston."

Her reference to the butler made Laura smile. "No, I suppose it wouldn't."

Mr. Gaston had been with the Marquardt family for as long as Laura could remember. He was already in his forties when he came to help at the Marquardt house, and that had been nearly twenty years earlier. He had once mentioned having been born in another century, so Laura figured him to be approaching seventy, if not already there.

She quickly pinned Carissa's braid in place. "There. You are as pretty as a picture."

Carissa jumped up and pressed a kiss on Laura's cheek. "Thank you, sister." She all but danced to the door.

"Don't forget that after breakfast Mother is hosting a gathering of church women to discuss the needs of the less fortunate."

"Oh bother," Carissa said, turning at the door. "I don't have to attend, do I?"

"I know Mother would be greatly disappointed if you didn't. She wants to show us supporting the cause as one."

"Well, I haven't any desire to support her cause. I care about the less fortunate, but in my own way."

Laura narrowed her gaze. "And what way would that be? By flirting with them? By parading around in your finery?"

"What finery?" Carissa countered with a harsh laugh. "I haven't had a new dress in well over a year, and even then it was only a gown remade from one of Mrs. Sonderson's. I hardly call that finery." She puckered her lips. "What I wouldn't give for a wardrobe full of Worth gowns."

"Oh, cease with your pouting." Laura checked her hair in the mirror. Their maid Carlita had done a good job in sweeping it all into a manageable bun atop Laura's head before hurrying off to help their mother. Carissa had been more than a little miffed to be neglected, but she knew better than to say anything.

"Mother will expect us both to be there, so don't be late. The meeting starts at ten."

Carissa shook her head. "I shall just speak to Mother about it. Malcolm plans to come calling today, and I think that much more important. She will, too. I'm certain." She flounced out of the room.

Laura sighed. She knew the war years had been hard on her sister. Carissa wanted big things out of life: a wealthy husband, a palatial house with plenty of servants, and at least a half-dozen carriages at her disposal. Laura was never really sure why the numerous carriages were important. As she had once pointed out to Carissa, a person could only ride in one at a time—to which her sister had countered, "You can only wear one gown at a time, but a responsible woman of means will have several."

At breakfast Carissa picked at her fruit and complained that the tea was too strong. Laura could see her mother and father's displeasure at their younger daughter's complaints, but still they said nothing. She supposed they felt guilty for all that Carissa had missed out on because of the war. Never mind what Laura had lost. Some of the same men whom Carissa pined for were the very ones Laura had eyed with matrimony in mind. Not only that, but there were concerts, plays, and other wonderful entertainments Laura never had the chance to enjoy. She could still remember lectures she'd attended with her friends . . . friends whose families had quickly evacuated when the Union attacked in 1862. No one knew the deep loss she felt.

She supposed it was her own fault for not complaining. Carissa made sure everyone knew of her displeasures, where Laura remained silent in her grief. When the war came and she was forced to sell off some of her gowns, cloaks, shoes, and jewelry in order to help the family purchase much-needed food, she said nothing. She was proud to be able to help. But the fact that Carissa was treated like a princess and given gifts—while the others went without—irritated Laura. Carissa had become spoiled and opinionated over the years. If she thought everything would go back to the way it was before the war, Laura figured her to be mistaken. Leaders in Washington weren't sympathetic to the Southern states, and fears and rumor of punishments persisted.

Of course, they hadn't suffered as much as others had. Father had been wise and his provision and plans had helped the Marquardt family endure the worst of the hardships. Even now, they were faring far better than their friends.

"I do hope that your Mr. Lowe is doing well," Mother said, turning to Carissa. "Do you suppose he will be coming to call today?"

"I believe so. He did ask to do just that," Carissa replied.

"But Laura tells me that we're to be in attendance at your ladies' meeting."

"Oh, that's not necessary for you," Mother countered. She smiled at Carissa, then turned her attention back to her plate. "After all, you are close to becoming engaged, and I would not want to interfere with that."

"Mother, how can you encourage such a thing? She hardly knows Mr. Lowe," Laura interjected. "Not only that, he fought for the Confederacy. Besides," she said, turning to her father, "has he even asked for her hand?"

Carissa didn't wait for her father's reply. "A great many young men in Texas fought for the Confederacy. But as you keep saying, the war is over. We must put aside our differences."

"And you think to accomplish this new diplomacy by marrying a Union girl to a Confederate boy?" Laura asked.

"Laura! You needn't speak in such a manner to your father," Mother stated.

Carissa didn't let this stop her. "He's no boy, and I'm no girl. We are adults and quite capable of knowing our own hearts." Carissa picked up her fork and stabbed at a piece of melon. "Besides, I'm neither a Unionist nor a Confederate. I have no politics—it simply isn't fitting for a woman. Just ask Mother."

Laura knew her mother had clearly avoided concerning herself with such matters. Asking her would be akin to asking the cat. Even the black and Mexican servants had more of an opinion on the affairs of state.

"Girls, there is no need to become agitated," their father declared, replacing his empty coffee cup on its saucer. "Now, if you ladies will excuse me, I am already late for an appointment."

He got to his feet, leaned over to kiss their mother on the head, then threw a smile at the girls. "Be useful to your mother."

Laura nodded, but Carissa ignored him and appeared completely captivated by a basket of croissants. Esther, a former slave who had come to them from a plantation north of Austin, entered the room and began to clear away Father's dishes.

"Esther, please ask Cook to meet with me for a few minutes in the library." Mother got to her feet. "I must go over the menu and see that we have everything ready for the ladies."

"Yes'm." Esther's dark eyes met Laura's gaze. "Miss Laura, ya gonna want mo' tea?"

"No, thank you, Esther. I'm completely satisfied with this." Laura pushed her plate back a fraction of an inch.

"How 'bout mo' tea, Miss Carissa?"

"No. It's much too strong."

Esther nodded and returned to the kitchen. Carissa sighed and began to butter the croissant she'd chosen. "I hope that when I marry I can move far from here. This town is dreadful. I think I'd like to live in New Orleans. I hear it's positively wonderful there. The ladies never lack for the latest fashions and the houses are much grander." She put down the knife and bit into the bread.

"The grass always looks greener over in someone else's yard," Laura said. "Honestly, Carissa, I don't know why you worry about such things."

"A woman should concern herself with the future, Laura. Just because you're content to sit here as an old maid and care for our aged parents doesn't mean I am."

"Our parents are hardly aged."

Carissa put down the croissant. "They are in their fifties. That's old."

"They are both quite healthy," Laura corrected. "And as far as I can tell, do not require my care."

"So does that mean you will marry?" Carissa asked. "Have you a beau?"

Laura felt more than a little exasperation with her sibling. "You know very well that I do not. If God should have a mate for me, I am confident He will send Him along."

"Oh goodness, you are such a goose. God doesn't do things like that," Carissa said, shaking her head. "He's much too busy. God only handles important things."

"Such as knowing the number of hairs on our heads?" Laura asked with a questioning expression.

Carissa jerked her chin upward. "Of course He knows that. God knows everything. But there is an entire world out there for Him to watch over. Do you truly suppose He cares about whether or not you find a beau?"

Laura nodded. "I do. I believe God cares about all the details of our lives. Look at the Bible. There are many stories of God bringing people together for marriage."

"But those were important people," Carissa countered. "Goodness, Laura, one would think you were the Queen of Sheba the way you talk."

The clock in the hall chimed eight, and Carissa gently dabbed her mouth. "I simply must go. I have to make myself ready in case Malcolm arrives early." She got to her feet. "And if you are seriously thinking about getting a beau, sister, I would suggest you start dressing in brighter colors. That brown doesn't suit you at all."

Laura glanced down at her well-worn gown. The yellow lace trimming and gold buttons added very little in the way of decoration, but still Laura thought the gown suitable. Besides, she really didn't care what Carissa thought about her fashion sense.

⁓

Three hours later, Laura found herself enduring the final discussions of the church ladies her mother had invited over. Mother had surprised her by suggesting that as women married to Unionists, they should reach out to embrace their sisters of the Confederacy. Her mother never dabbled in politics, but apparently someone had put the notion in her mind.

"The sooner we are all of one accord again, the sooner life will return to normal," Mother stated. The women nodded in silent agreement.

"We've all lost loved ones, and even though this war was their fault," Mrs. Brighton announced, "I am the forgiving sort. I do believe, however, that we should perhaps limit our involvement to those whose husbands have taken the ironclad oath." The women around them nodded. Apparently grace only extended so far.

"Enough about that subject. I do believe Mrs. May has received word from a cousin in France that they are to receive a shipment of fabric for the store. I, for one, am very excited about this," Mother told the group as the conversation became less serious. "I wonder if we might consider a formal occasion—perhaps a ball or other party—where we can bring everyone together. Nothing does a lady's heart quite so much good as a ball."

"I think that idea is perfect," Mrs. Cole replied. She nibbled at a piece of pastry and sighed. "A wedding party would be even better. You know how it uplifts the spirit to share in the blessing of a new couple's nuptials."

The other dozen or so women murmured their agreement. Laura tried to smile when their gazes fell upon her. Mother quickly turned their attention elsewhere, however. "My Carissa may well be announcing an engagement any day. In fact, her beau came to call just before our meeting. A wedding in the near future would be quite possible."

"But you wouldn't want to rush it too much. People are given to talk," Mrs. Brighton said, leaning forward. "A lengthy engagement is always appropriate."

"Pshaw!" Laura's mother declared. "We have just survived a war. I believe etiquette can be imposed upon in such a case. Besides, my Carissa has never been one for waiting. I believe I could have her married by summer's end."

"It would help if the beau in mind would propose first, don't you think?" Laura asked.

Her mother threw her a glare, then continued. "I feel confident that a proposal is coming soon. My Carissa has said as much."

Laura sighed. The conversation was draining her of her last bits of energy. The heat was so intense she felt positively soaked from perspiring, and the humidity only served to add to her discomfort. She longed for a nice tepid bath or a swim.

Seeing that most of the women were engaged with their refreshments, Laura rose. "If you'll please excuse me." She offered no other explanation for her departure and simply walked from the room.

Making her way outside, she prayed there might be a refreshing breeze and was rewarded with a wisp of wind. She dabbed her neck with a handkerchief and prayed for the temperatures to cool. Walking the length of the yard, Laura spied her sister and Malcolm Lowe standing near the carriage house. When her sister threw her arms around Malcolm and allowed him to embrace and kiss her, Laura very nearly called out in protest. Instead, she fell back and waited to see what might happen next.

When the kiss seemed to go on for an unseemly amount of time, Laura made her way to the couple. "Excuse me, but such a display is hardly proper."

Carissa pulled away and laughed. "Of course it's proper. Malcolm just proposed and I have accepted. We are to be married."

Laura forced a smile as she gazed at her soon-to-be brother-in-law. "I congratulate you both; however, you are not yet married. Mother would have a fit of apoplexy if she were to see you."

"Mother will be delighted for me. You should be, too." Carissa smiled like the cat who'd found a bowl of cream. "You shall be my maid of honor, and we shall both have new gowns. Won't that be wonderful?"

"Yes. Well, be that as it may," Laura said, trying her best to refrain from rebuking, "it might serve you better to go and make your announcement. Mother would probably be pleased to have such a thing declared in the company of her dear friends."

"Oh, let's," Carissa said, pulling on Malcolm's arm. "We haven't spoken to Papa, but I'm certain he will approve."

The twenty-nine-year-old former Confederate lieutenant shook his head. "You go on ahead. I have to be back to my duties. I am hopeful about a position with the flour mill. I see them this afternoon."

"Oh, if you must," Carissa said, looking sad.

Laura took hold of her sister's arm. "We mustn't delay him. Jobs are important, now more than ever. If you are to be a well-kept bride, Malcolm must be able to provide. Good day to you, Malcolm."

❧

Malcolm walked in the opposite direction and made his way to the street. He picked up his step as the road descended from the bluff. His mount was being shod; while being afoot was not his desire, the smithy had no other horses to lend out.

He thought of what he'd just done and smiled. Proposing to Carissa Marquardt would serve his purpose well. In fact, it would serve many purposes. He was anxious to settle down and at least put on the pretense of being a decent citizen. He wouldn't—and couldn't—sign the ironclad oath, but by uniting himself to the Union-supporting Marquardt family, he would be allowed in a ring of society that he might never have known. He figured the citizens would be more forgiving, as well. Attaching his name to that of the Marquardts was nearly as good as having worn blue in the war.

"And with any luck at all, their wealth will serve my higher goal," he said to himself.

Skirting the busier streets, Malcolm approached a shellcrete blockhouse, pleased to see that the door was open, awaiting his arrival. He stepped inside and pulled off his hat. He drew out a handkerchief from his coat pocket and wiped his neck and forehead before proceeding into the front room, where seven men were gathered.

"Gentlemen," he said with a slight nod. "I'm glad you could make it today."

One of the men, someone Malcolm knew only through his former sergeant, rose. "I have to be leaving soon, so if you don't mind, I'd like to get right to it."

"I think that is wise," Malcolm agreed. "We don't want to attract attention to ourselves. We very much appreciate your willingness to aid us in our endeavors against the Union."

"It is my great pleasure," the man said. "I believe my newspaper will be more than happy to publish no end of stories that defame the Union and their thieving men who masquerade as honorable soldiers. Now tell me what you'd like us to do."

Malcolm smiled. "If you will take your seat, I will expand on our ideas."

"See? Didn't I tell you wonderful news was coming soon?" Agatha Marquardt declared at her daughter's announcement.

Laura remained at the door of the room, not wanting to become trapped among the women once again.

"I'm so happy I just might start to cry," Carissa said, hugging their mother.

"Oh, my dear, we are so happy for you," Mrs. Brighton began. "But your mother tells us that your young man was a soldier for the Confederacy. Has he repented of that action?"

Carissa nodded in firm assurance. "Oh, he is so very sorry for the past. He only joined up because his papa, God rest his soul, had pleaded with him to do so. He couldn't very well deny the man his dying wish."

"Of course not," Mrs. Tennyson interjected. "There were many such cases, I've heard Mr. Tennyson say. Bless those poor boys who went to war with nothing more than a heart to honor their fathers and mothers." She shook her head and gave a *tsk-*ing sound.

"Who are his people, dear?" another of the ladies asked.

Carissa looked quite sorrowful. "Oh, it's a tragic tale. He was an only child. His sweet mother nearly died giving him life. They were originally from South Carolina, but moved to Texas when Malcolm was very young. Unfortunately, his mother died shortly thereafter, and his father raised him all alone. Then just as the war was starting, his beloved father died and left him alone in the world. He has no other kin."

"Tragic indeed!" Mrs. Tennyson replied and the others nodded in unison.

Laura knew there was no way to prove or disprove this story, but she wondered about its truthfulness nevertheless. Malcolm always seemed far too secretive to suit her. Carissa was, in many ways, still a child. She would turn nineteen come November, but Laura wasn't sure maturity would follow. After all, it hadn't exactly embraced Carissa the first eighteen years. It was this immaturity that left Laura to fret for her sister. In many ways she was naïve and far too trusting. When things went bad for her, Carissa always found someone else to blame.

With a sigh, Laura shook her head. She longed to talk some sense into her sister's head, but Carissa thought Laura was jealous of her relationship with Malcolm. And perhaps she was right. As the eldest, Laura did find it rather offending that her sister should marry first. After all, Laura had always been quite popular with the young men in Corpus Christi. She had attended many a party where men spoke of love to her. Then the war had taken them away—never to return.

So many of the boys were gone now. And those who had survived . . . well . . . they had changed. They weren't the carefree young men who had marched off to fight the Yankees so long ago. Worse still, they weren't yet forgiving of those families who hadn't supported the cause. Families like the Marquardts.

Laura stepped into the hallway, her gaze still fixed on the scene in the parlor. She felt as if she were watching a tragedy—perhaps one of Shakespeare's tales of corruption, deception, and woe. She couldn't shake the feeling that this was a mistake. Worse still, she knew that if she voiced her concerns . . . no one would care.

June passed into July, the warmth and humidity rival-ing the tropics. Brandon was glad that he would soon be rid of the responsibility to wear a uniform. The layers of clothing required by the army made the heat nearly impossible to endure.

"So you'll soon be a free man," Major Justin Armstrong declared, looking over the report Brandon had just placed on his desk.

"Very soon," Brandon replied. "I was just thinking how I won't be sorry to shed this uniform and return to Indiana."

"So you've decided to go back home?"

Brandon cocked his head to one side and pretended to con-template the question. "Well . . . in truth, I haven't completely decided what I'm doing." His thoughts rested on the image of Laura Marquardt that had haunted his dreams of late. "I have to say that my time in the army has given me a new perspective on life in general. As you know, I greatly enjoy working with horses, and my father's horse breeding farm has produced some of the best Thoroughbreds around. And I did attend college with a mind to perhaps teach."

"You could teach or raise horses here in Texas," Justin countered. "This is a vast state with a great deal of cheap land. In the years to come the railroad will connect across this state and property values will increase dramatically. Why not at least invest in some land here to sell for a profit later?"

"It's a thought, I suppose. But I'm not fond of this heat. We knew warm days in Indiana, but weeks of temperatures hovering near a hundred degrees were not the norm for us. Down here folks just seem to take it in stride. It's given me a better understanding of why so many businesses practice the Mexican tradition of the *siesta* in the heat of the afternoon."

"Not all of Texas is this hot. Up north there are some lush green spreads, and to the east there are wondrous forests. If you venture west you would find the air considerably drier—though I daresay the temperatures would most likely remain high in the summer months. Still, all in all, this is a great state for raising animals. I've been doing some study on it. Cattle thrive here, and horses would no doubt do just as well."

"What about the Indian trouble? I hear up north the people are dealing with attacks from the Kiowa and Comanche. And out west it's the Apache, as well."

"Yes, but now that the army is returning to the western posts, the Indian wars will soon be a thing of the past. Those savage renegades will be moved onto reservations, where they can be watched and kept under control. I wouldn't let fear of Indians keep me from investing in property here in Texas. In fact, I haven't. I purchased a large parcel of land for my family and plan to bring them out sometime next year. If not sooner."

"That's quite a commitment," Brandon said.

"Susannah is all for this. She believes the boys will benefit by getting away from the city. Our daughter might not like it, but she's only two and can't raise too much fuss over the move." He grinned. "I would love having a neighbor like you close at hand. You really should think about it. I know there are some properties available near mine that are yet unspoken for."

"I'll think about it." Brandon thought again of Laura Marquardt and decided to pose a question. "What do you know about Stanley Marquardt and his family?"

Justin leaned back and thought for a moment. "Strong Union supporter with a wife and two or three daughters."

"Two," Brandon said without thinking. Seeing Justin's brow rise slightly, he shrugged. "I attended that party you were too busy for a couple weeks back."

"Ah yes, I remember. Why do you ask?"

"No reason, really." Brandon didn't want to hear the comments when he explained that his real interest was Laura Marquardt and not her father. "I suppose I just wondered what sort of business Marquardt was in. I didn't really have a chance to talk to him much."

Justin nodded. "I don't know what all he has on his plate, but I do know he has fought long and hard for a deeper channel in the harbor. I learned that much from the general. Apparently Marquardt has a hand in engineering the improvements, although I'm certain it wouldn't be a single-handed effort."

"No doubt it would require a lot of money and a great many hands to aid in the matter," Brandon said. "But given all that I've heard, it would greatly help the commerce of the town."

"Exactly." The major looked as if he were about to say something more, but just then a man appeared at the door.

"Sir, beggin' the major's pardon, but this just came from General Russell."

Justin motioned the sergeant to bring the missive forward. He took the letter and read the contents quickly. "It would seem a good thing that you're here, Brandon. General Russell wants to hear your report and see both of us in his office immediately." He cast the letter aside and got to his feet. "I suppose we'd better head right over."

Brandon got to his feet while Justin began buttoning his double-breasted coat. He couldn't help but wonder what Russell needed from them both. It would be the second time in a matter of weeks that Charles had requested his presence.

Taking up Brandon's report, Justin grabbed his hat and motioned to the door. "Let's not keep the man waiting."

They walked in quick step to the Ironclad House and found the corporal busy instructing two privates.

"Attention!" the corporal commanded, and all three drew themselves into the expected rigid stance.

Brandon let Justin take the lead since he was the senior officer. In no time at all they were seated in front of an angry-looking Russell, wondering what could possibly have happened to cause such a scowling countenance.

"Thank you for your prompt response. We have need of your services, gentlemen. As I already mentioned to Captain Reid, an ongoing investigation has brought certain former Confederates to our attention and we need to devise a way to ferret these animals out of hiding."

"Perhaps you could start at the beginning and explain what this investigation is about," the major suggested.

Russell nodded. "This involves the murders of several Union soldiers last May. We know this savage attack was conducted by former Confederates. Yesterday two men from the Twenty-eighth were found dead in a ditch south of town. We fear additional attacks are to come, and we need to capture these men before they have a chance to kill again."

"What do we have to go on?" Brandon asked.

"Not a great deal, but one name keeps coming up. Malcolm Lowe."

It was the same man Brandon had been urged to befriend at the Marquardt party. He'd hoped to meet the man, but learned shortly after arriving that Lowe had been detained elsewhere. Now it seemed the man was once again causing problems.

"I can't believe that you are pushing for this wedding to take place so soon," Laura said, looking at her mother in disbelief. "They've only just become engaged."

"Yes, but they are well suited," her mother countered. "A wedding in September would do a great deal to lift everyone's spirits."

Carissa looked at Laura and shook her head. "You're just jealous. You fear if I marry first, no one will step forward to ask for your hand. But honestly, Laura, this is the frontier. There are far more men than women. Papa has said so on many occasions, and prior to the war you knew that to be true. I'm sure that someone will marry you."

Laura would have laughed at her sister's comment had the subject not been so serious. "I am not jealous. I am concerned about your reputation and about your safety. You don't know Malcolm all that well."

"I know him well enough to know that I love him," Carissa said, kneeling at their mother's feet. She looked up at their mother with adoration. "Just like you knew you loved Papa when you agreed to marry him."

Their mother nodded. "I knew my heart well."

"As do I." Carissa cast a sly glance up to where Laura watched the scene.

Laura took a seat beside Mother on the cream and green striped settee. "Mother, I merely suggest that September is too soon. Tongues will wag and questions of her innocence will be discussed. You surely don't want people thinking Carissa needs to marry quickly."

"Pshaw. I discussed this with members of the Ladies' Church Society. They were all in agreement. A wedding and reception— even a dance—would do the whole community good."

A look of smug satisfaction crossed Carissa's face, but Laura wasn't yet defeated. "So your thoughts on the matter are merely to promote a party atmosphere to raise spirits?"

Their mother looked rather surprised at the question. "Of course not. I simply see no reason to delay the union of two people who are obviously in love. Where is your sense of romance, Laura?"

"It probably fades with each passing year that she remains unmarried," Carissa said in an almost, but not quite, sympathetic tone.

"This isn't about my situation," Laura countered.

"Exactly," Carissa agreed. "This is about me. I think it is my duty to uplift those around me. The war is behind us, but not so the sorrows. My wedding will be like a declaration of hope and future joy. We will cast off the old and take up the new."

"Oh yes!" Mother agreed. "It will be glorious. We will have a grand party right here. We will decorate the lawns and set up tables outdoors. We will invite everyone to attend and serve a wonderful wedding breakfast and later host a dance. It will be a grand celebration."

Carissa clapped her hands in delight. "Oh, I am so happy. I shall speak immediately to Malcolm and set a date." She got to her feet and smiled at Laura. "And you and I must arrange our gowns. Since few have money for new creations, we should have no trouble in hiring a seamstress." She kissed their mother on the cheek, then glided from the room.

Laura looked at Mother and reached out to gently take hold of her hand. "Mother, you do realize that in a time when so many are struggling and suffering, we might be criticized for such an elaborate wedding."

"Let them criticize," she answered. "A woman only marries like this once. I would do the same for you . . . and will should you find a husband." Mother pulled her hand away and fussed with the lace on the collar of Laura's chemisette. "I don't want you to spoil this for Carissa. She has suffered enough from the war. We will make it up to her by giving her a wedding fit for a princess. Even your father agrees. He has already sent word to his brother in Chicago."

Laura knew that her uncle had safeguarded the family's fortune through the war years, as well as provided regular stipends for support. Now that the war was over, it would only be a matter of time before all of their assets were returned to Texas.

"There, now the lace lies properly," her mother said with a look of satisfaction.

"I hope you won't regret this," Laura said, standing. "I do only wish for the very best where Carissa is concerned."

"As do we all." Her mother pulled out her fan. "Goodness, but the heat is most unbearable. Do ask Esther to bring me a cool glass of lemonade."

Laura nodded and headed for the arched doorway. She paused for a moment, wishing she could make her mother see reason. "It would perhaps make me feel better if Malcolm had already secured a job and was able to purchase a home for them."

Her mother's face lit up. "Oh, that's part of the best news. Your father arranged a position for Malcolm, and as a wedding gift we are buying them a small, but sufficient, house."

Laura felt as though she'd been slapped. She tried not to react, however. Nodding, she considered the statement for a moment. "I'm glad that Father feels he is able to do so much for them."

"Malcolm will become the son your father always wanted," Mother said, smiling and working the fan with great fervor. "You will soon see, Laura. This is a wonderful thing for our family."

Brandon felt a sense of restlessness as another day concluded. He undressed and readied himself for bed, but all the while his mind was flooded with thoughts of what General Russell had told him.

Charles needed an insider—someone who could seek the proof they needed to identify those responsible for the rising violence. Some Southern supporters would kill in the name of the Confederacy for as long as they could get away with it. The Twenty-eighth Regiment was particularly vulnerable because they were black—and also because they wore blue.

Brandon thought long and hard about the general's proposal. He had hoped to be free of the army and all that it stood for in a matter of days, but following this order would change all of that. The plan was to still muster him out as far as the public was concerned, but in truth he would delay his complete resignation until after the Lowe situation was concluded. He would continue to answer to General Russell and Major Armstrong, but for all intents and purposes he would be a civilian. Brandon wasn't convinced that he'd made the right decision in accepting this role, but for the time it seemed the best thing to do. The army was even providing a small cottage in which he could stay and a horse to use as long as he had need.

Picking up his Bible, Brandon settled into his bed and opened the well-read book. His father had given him this gift on the day of Brandon's baptism. He'd been ten years old and had told his father that it was time he accepted Jesus as his Savior. He had said it so matter-of-factly that he might have been discussing the need for a haircut, but Brandon knew it was the most important decision of his life.

Having a pastor for a father, Brandon had no memory of a life without God at the center of it. He had been taught to memorize Scripture, pray faithfully, and take compassion on the less fortunate. Brandon had also seen firsthand the blessings and woes of being a man of God. He wasn't deluded. But what he had known were parents who were faithful to their beliefs, and that had given him a great deal of strength.

He started to read, but soon his thoughts strayed to Laura Marquardt. He could still picture her face and its delicate lines. She was far more serious than her playful sister, but he liked that about her. She didn't display the nonsensical theatrics that he'd witnessed in Carissa Marquardt. Perhaps that was due to her seniority in years—although they couldn't be many—or maybe Laura was by nature more thoughtful.

Glancing down at the open Bible, Brandon's gaze fell to the last chapter of Proverbs. The tenth verse caught his eye. *Who can find a virtuous woman? for her price is far above rubies.* He thought again of Laura and read on.

The heart of her husband doth safely trust in her, so that he shall have no need of spoil. She will do him good and not evil all the days of her life.

He could see those verses applying to a woman such as Laura. He could sense her strength and passion for life. She displayed a streak of fearlessness but was also quite reserved and obedient. During their encounter on the street she had tried to explain herself, but she had done so with modesty and decorum. He couldn't find fault in anything she'd said.

Then at the party, he had watched her interact with the guests. She was congenial and sincere to everyone.

He shook his head and glanced heavenward. "Is she your will for me?"

His father had taught him this type of questioning as a young-ster. *"When you are presented with decisions and choices, as you are certain to be,"* his father had said, *"you should always stop and ask the Lord if this is His will for your life."*

Brandon had heeded his father's advice, and it had served him well to seek God's will before his own. Of course, sometimes the answers weren't exactly clear.

He looked back at the verses and released a long breath. He needed God's direction now more than ever. The days ahead would not be easy. He had a job to do and needed to be cautious, as the interest he had in Laura Marquardt overlapped with the duties he had to find evidence against Malcolm Lowe.

At the conclusion of Sunday services on July twenty-third, Carissa and Malcolm's engagement was formally announced. The atmosphere immediately turned to one of revelry and joy as the congregation congratulated the happy couple. Laura tried to brush aside her feelings of unease, but her sister's immaturity worried her. Carissa couldn't cook or keep house, and there wouldn't be money for servants. Unless, of course, Mother and Father stepped in to aid the situation.

And of course, they very well might do just that. After all, they had purchased the little house on the far south side of the town. Laura tried not to be jealous. But she couldn't deny a sense of disappointment. She always figured she'd marry first—have children first. She supposed it was a silly thought . . . and perhaps prideful, too. Maybe that's why this was happening. Perhaps God was trying to teach her to deal with her pride.

Stepping outside, Laura decided to wait for her family on

the church lawn. It was at least a little cooler here than it had been inside. She was glad she'd chosen to wear her striped silk summer gown. The dress was lighter in weight than most she owned, and instead of being designed to wear with multiple layers of petticoats, the hem had been reinforced with stiffened muslin. This allowed Laura to limit her undergarments and still maintain a proper and fashionable silhouette.

"You look quite lovely today, Miss Marquardt."

She turned to find Captain Reid resplendent in his army uniform. She smiled at his compliment. "Why, thank you, sir." She looked around at the people who had gathered in little groups to visit. "I had no idea you were in attendance."

"I often share services with my men, but since I will muster out this week, I thought it would serve me well to explore my options amongst the civilians."

Goodness, but he's handsome, Laura thought. She immediately felt her cheeks grow hot and hoped most sincerely that Brandon Reid was unable to read her thoughts. Unfortunately, the slight twitch at the corner of his lips did nothing to reassure her, and Laura quickly ducked her head.

After an awkward moment of silence, Brandon spoke. "So your sister is to be married."

Laura forced herself to look up. Brandon towered over her five-foot-six-inch frame. She felt small and fragile beside this broad-shouldered soldier. "Ah . . . yes. I fear I do not share the same enthusiasm as my family, but I do pray for Carissa's happiness."

"Why do you not share the same enthusiasm, if I might ask?"

Carissa and Malcolm were receiving well-wishers as they exited the church. Laura caught sight of her sister's joyful expression and felt guilty. "I shouldn't have said that. I do apologize."

"Should you not have said it because it wasn't true?"

Laura looked back to Brandon and shook her head. "No, those are my feelings. However, I shouldn't have spoken about them publicly. I love my sister dearly. I only want her happiness, and if this marriage will bring that . . . well . . . I'm content."

"But you don't believe it will."

The statement was given matter-of-factly. Laura could see that Captain Reid was giving her his undivided attention, so this wasn't simply small talk. He truly seemed to care.

"They haven't known each other long," Laura admitted. "I believe marriage should be based on something more than sentiment."

"I quite agree. I have often cautioned my men on the dangers of such relationships. Sentiment and emotion are easily extinguished in the face of hardship and trial."

"Exactly," she said, nodding. "That was my point. Carissa is so naïve and vulnerable. She isn't ready to be a wife; she knows very little of how to care for a house and even less about men."

Brandon chuckled at this, and Laura felt a delicious shiver run down her spine. "You speak as one who knows," he said, his voice low.

Laura shrugged. "I've paid close attention to my father and his associates. My mother taught me early on that there was a wealth of information to be learned by simply watching and listening to others. I have found that to serve me well."

"But did your sister not receive the same training?" he asked, his brow raised ever so slightly.

"To some extent. My mother tried to train Carissa, but she's something of a . . . free spirit."

"Ah. Well perhaps during the long months of her engagement, you can help to tutor her."

"I'm afraid there's not going to be a long engagement. My mother and sister believe that a wedding—particularly a wedding between a Unionist's daughter and a former Confederate soldier—will do much to reunite the hearts and minds of the people of Corpus Christi."

"And how will this be?"

She shook her head. "I cannot possibly imagine. Mother has never been one for political matters, and while I understand her weariness of the war and all that it did to family and friendships, I believe her rather ignorant of the true hearts and minds of those who lost this war. The anger felt by so many of the local families will not be abated while dancing at a wedding party."

"That is true enough."

Laura saw her father and mother coming toward them. She immediately put on a smile. "Mother, see who I found."

Her father extended his hand. "Captain Reid. Did you enjoy the service?"

Brandon shook hands and smiled. "I did indeed. I find it a wonderful way to start the week."

"I simply despise the stuffiness of the church in the summer," Mother said, fanning herself. She was dressed much too richly in her layers of finery. Laura had mentioned this at home in regard to the temperature, but Mother had ignored her.

"Captain Reid, would you care to join us for dinner?" Father asked. "We're planning a nice meal on the lawn. It should prove to be much cooler than dining inside."

Brandon looked at Laura. She smiled and gave a nod. "It really is quite pleasant," she told him. "Father arranged to have a lovely canopy put up under the trees."

"I am most grateful for the invitation and would be happy to attend."

Mother tapped Father's arm. "Do save further conversation for home. I am quite overcome by this heat."

"Of course." Father took hold of her arm. "Do you have a mount, Captain?"

"I do. Shall I follow your carriage to the house? Or would you prefer that I come at a later time?"

"No, by all means accompany us. The food will be ready and waiting. I'm certain the ladies will wish to change their clothes. Perhaps you and I might rid ourselves of our coats, as well. After all, it will be a most informal luncheon."

"I think that would suit me quite well."

Laura felt a rush of pleasure at the thought of spending the afternoon with the captain. When they arrived home, Laura hurried to change to a casual pink and white gingham dress. She had always liked this gown, especially for its detachable sleeves. She also liked the way the basque waist and snug bodice showed off her slender frame. Laura glanced quickly in the mirror to check her hair. Perhaps something wonderful would come about from their misunderstanding in the alleyway. Wouldn't that be a wondrous story to tell their children?

"Your father and I met when he thought I was being hostile

toward his troops." She giggled and made her way downstairs as Carissa was making her way up.

"What's so funny?" she asked. Then with an inspecting glance she threw Laura a questioning look. "You are dressed rather fine for Sunday luncheon. Could it be due to our visitor?"

Laura laughed. "It might be, but I would hardly call this gown fine. It's four years old and wearing fast."

"Even so, you are quite pretty, sister dear." Carissa leaned over and kissed Laura's cheek. "I'm glad Malcolm isn't here. Otherwise he might be tempted to rescind his proposal and pursue you instead."

"Hardly. Malcolm only has eyes for you," Laura assured her, although she wasn't at all convinced that was true. "Will he join us later?"

"If he can," Carissa said, her tone betraying her disappointment.

"Let us hope so. Perhaps we can get up a game of croquet."

"I am sorry . . . for the way I've acted."

Surprised by her sister's sudden declaration, Laura turned. "What are you talking about?"

Carissa gave a sigh. "I have been rather insensitive toward you, and it wasn't kind. You are my dearest friend in all the world, and I do not want anything to come between us—especially my marriage."

"Silly goose," Laura replied, seeing the sincerity in her sister's expression, "nothing will ever separate us. We are sisters, and as such we cannot ever be parted."

She left Carissa and hurried down the steps. Perhaps her little sister was finally growing up. Laura smiled at the thought and rejoined Captain Reid and her father.

"The attack in 1862 caused many of the undecided families to clearly choose allegiance with the Confederacy," her father was stating. Both men had discarded their jackets and now looked much more relaxed in the shade of a chittamwood tree. The small white flowers of the tree had nearly run their course, but their fragrance lingered in the air and they occasionally drifted down like snowflakes.

The men turned to greet her, pausing only a moment to nod in acknowledgment. Laura didn't mind that they went quickly back to their discussion; she rather enjoyed listening.

"Of course, there were those who remained completely loyal to the Union. I was certainly not the only one who felt that secession was wrong."

Brandon nodded. "I've heard there was a stronghold of Unionists in Corpus Christi."

"It's true," Father said. "But there were also a great many who hated us. I lost many a good friend over this war."

"Yet you continued to support the Union," Brandon offered almost casually.

"It's true," Laura's father replied. "I felt strongly that America should remain united. I felt that differences should be worked through on a state-by-state basis, with the good of the whole in mind. I have never truly favored slavery, although I cannot admit to fighting against it, per se. It seemed . . . well, it seemed a necessary evil. Even now, I know of friends who have lost the ability to continue farming without the help of slave labor."

"Perhaps then they should never have begun in the first place," Brandon countered.

Laura didn't know what her father's reaction would be, but

she thought it a good place to jump in. "I suppose that the lure of profit was too strong. However, I am glad to see that we have done away with the institution of slavery. I'm certain that people will find ways to adapt. Perhaps their profits will suffer if they pay for their labor, but then again, perhaps they won't."

"Not if they pass along the cost to the consumer," Father replied. "And they will. They will have no choice. The price of cotton has already risen dramatically both from shortages and anticipated labor costs. I doubt the Northern textile mills will be quite so enthusiastic about the emancipation of slaves when they see what it will do to their production costs."

"Be that as it may," Brandon said, "slavery should have no place among civilized, God-fearing people. I do not believe God ever intended us to enslave one another."

"I suppose I could be wrong, but the Bible does speak of slavery," Malcolm Lowe declared as he joined the trio.

"I see you were able to join us after all," Laura said, giving him a nod.

"Yes, well it's hard to pass up an afternoon with the woman you love." He grinned. "I do apologize for interrupting your conversation."

"That's quite all right," Brandon said. "You are correct in saying that the Bible speaks of slavery. However, I would point out that those were different times and even different kinds of slavery." Brandon met Malcolm's hard expression, then smiled. "I'm Captain Brandon Reid, by the way. Congratulations on your engagement."

Laura took Brandon's cue to change the topic as she spied her mother and sister arriving. "Why don't we sit? Malcolm, you can tell us about your plans for the new house. I understand from Carissa that you have ideas for adding on."

"I do indeed," he said.

"Oh, you were able to come," Carissa said, moving quickly to take her place at Malcolm's side.

He patted her arm as though she were his favorite pet. "Of course, my dear. I long only to be in your presence."

Laura thought his words sounded forced and untrue. She couldn't help but wonder at this man her family hardly knew. What was it about him that made her feel so uneasy?

They made their way under the canopy to the table where Esther was placing a large bowl. The mélange of fruit looked cool and inviting, as did the platter of sliced cheeses and vegetables.

"I'll bring da fish shortly," Esther told Laura's mother.

Mother nodded and awaited her husband's assistance before sitting. Brandon helped Laura with her chair, while Malcolm took Carissa to sit on the opposite side of the table beside him. To Laura's delight, that left Brandon at her side.

Father offered a brief prayer of thanks before instructing everyone to eat. Laura handed a basket of cornbread squares and biscuits to Brandon.

"You will find these to be some of the best in the city," she told him.

Brandon took one of each. "I'm betting it's better than army food."

Malcolm gave a harsh laugh. "At least you Yanks had food to eat. Our boys often went hungry."

"If you don't mind, Malcolm, could we please not speak of

the war?" Mother asked. "I would much rather focus on the pleasant topic of your marriage to Carissa."

Carissa nodded with great enthusiasm at this. "Oh yes, let's talk about the wedding. I want to go shopping tomorrow and see what new fabrics are available."

The conversation continued with Mother and Carissa mostly chattering about wedding gown fashions and the guest list. It seemed to Laura that Carissa would invite the entire town with exception of the black troops.

"And what of you, Captain Reid?" Father asked after taking a long sip of lemonade. "Will you make the army your life's work?"

"No. In fact, I muster out this week," he replied.

Father considered this for a moment as he chewed. "Then will you head back north?"

"Not immediately. I'm not certain that I will return. I would like to check into some possibilities here in Texas."

"What kind of possibilities?" Malcolm inquired.

"Cattle and horses, mainly. I was raised on a horse breeding farm in Indiana. It is something that I've thought to go back to. My father is a minister, and the horse breeding was merely a side venture that proved to be quite lucrative. He could use me to run the business."

Her father nodded. "Our Laura is quite the horsewoman. She is a superb judge of horseflesh. Why, those two matched bays you saw pulling our carriage were chosen by her prior to the war."

Brandon turned to Laura. "They were exceptional, I must say. How is it that you developed such an eye for horses?"

Laura felt flush under his praise and scrutiny. "I have loved horses since I was old enough to know what they were. I suppose that I have watched and listened as others had detailed their strengths and flaws."

"She's also read every book Papa could buy on the topic," Carissa said with a giggle. "I used to tease her about reading so much that her eyes would fall out."

"Guilty as charged," Laura said, looking to Brandon. "I'm afraid that with the war going on and products and money being extremely limited, books were good friends. I probably reread my father's entire library."

"I, too, find great pleasure in reading," Brandon said.

"Never had any time for such things myself." Malcolm's voice was edged with anger. "But I suppose that's the difference between workin' folks and the well-to-do."

"My family was hardly well-to-do," Brandon said, meeting Malcolm's sneer. "The life of a pastor's family is one of sacrifice both in time and monetary ease. The horse breeding was a good benefit, but also a lot of work."

"Did you have slaves?" Carissa asked innocently.

"Not exactly," Brandon replied. "We had some who had escaped their situations."

"You took in runaways?" Malcolm asked. "That would have been against the law."

Brandon considered this for a moment. "My father believed we served a higher calling and that God's law superseded man's. We did not go south to help slaves escape, but rather once they had crossed the Ohio River, we offered them a place to stay and work. They would regain their strength with us and then move on. It was one of the most rewarding ministries I've ever known."

"That was no ministry," Malcolm spat. "You harbored fugitives."

"We also buried the dead," Brandon said, narrowing his gaze. "Many of the folks who made it to us weren't strong enough to continue. They had been severely abused by their masters. Oftentimes they had been starved or beaten. By the time they made it to us, their bodies had simply given out."

"How sad," Laura whispered, shaking her head.

"Gentlemen," Mother said, picking up the bowl of fruit, "that is enough serious talk for one meal. Let us speak of something more lighthearted and merry."

Malcolm muttered something unintelligible, but Brandon was quick to heed the request. "I would like to invite you all to attend a party that is being given in my honor the day after tomorrow. It's being hosted by my commanding officer. It will be a most amusing evening I'm assured, with music and food and perhaps even dancing. I know the men would be delighted to see it attended by three such lovely ladies."

"Oh yes, Papa. May we go?" Carissa begged. She looked to Malcolm. "You would come as my escort, wouldn't you?"

"I'm afraid not, my dear," Malcolm said, his gaze never leaving Brandon. "As a former Confederate—a man unable to sign the ironclad oath, I'm certain the captain's friends would refuse my attendance."

"Nonsense," Brandon replied. "It's my party. I am entitled to invite whom I will. I would be honored to have you there, Mr. Lowe."

"I think it sounds like a wonderful entertainment." Mother looked to Father. "What say you, my dear?"

Father nodded. "I believe we could tolerate such a diversion quite easily, Mrs. Marquardt." Laura saw her mother smile adoringly at her husband, and longed to share the same affection in her own marriage.

If I'm to ever marry. Somehow her heart wasn't convinced that this would ever be possible for her.

"And what of you, Miss Marquardt?" Brandon asked, pulling Laura from her thoughts.

"I would be honored. I believe it will be a most enjoyable evening."

"I am glad to hear you say so." He turned back to her father. "What say I come here and then I can escort you to the place?"

Father nodded. "That sounds good to me."

Carissa clapped her hands. "I'm so excited to have a party to look forward to. I do hope there will be dancing. Malcolm and I have never had a chance to dance together."

"And we won't have one now, either." Malcolm's voice was terse. "As I said, I won't be attending."

Laura met his fixed gaze and smiled. "We shall have to endure the evening without you then." She could see he wasn't at all pleased with her words, but the man was smart enough to keep his mouth closed from further protest.

"I shall arrive for you at six." Brandon looked at Laura. "Now I can look forward to this party. Before, it held little interest."

Laura couldn't help but wonder if he was implying that her presence made it worth his interest or if he was simply grateful to have civilian friends present. Either way, she couldn't deny that the way he looked at her caused her stomach to do somersaults.

6

Brandon pushed aside his feelings of apprehension as he approached the Marquardt house that Tuesday night. He had spent the day reviewing what little information the army had regarding the murder of six soldiers the previous May. The soldiers had been killed while they slept—a most heinous attack to be sure.

There was clear evidence that the murders had been committed as an act of revenge by Confederate soldiers. Not that there had been any note declaring it such, but the letters *CSA* had been carved into the chest of each of the dead men. The only potential witness wasn't even all that sure of what he'd seen. It had occurred in the wee hours of the morning, and the light was minimal at best. The man reported seeing two or three men running from the location of the murders and stated that one of the men bore a resemblance to Malcolm Lowe. Not only that, but a leather knife sheath had been found with the initials *ML* carved into the side. The evidence could have been planted, of course. Someone could have a vendetta against Lowe, hoping to see him wrongly accused and convicted. But Brandon seriously doubted that was the case.

He dismounted and tied his gelding to a post before making his way to the Marquardts' door. He gave a brief but heavy knock and waited for someone to greet him. In a few moments the door was opened by the same elderly butler he'd first met weeks ago.

"Captain Reid," Mr. Gaston announced as they made their way into the front sitting room.

Laura stood as he entered and said, "Captain, it's good to see you again."

"And you, Miss Marquardt." He gave Laura a slight bow, then turned to Carissa and greeted her much the same way before his gaze went back to rest on Laura's alluring features. *What a color*, he thought as he studied her eyes. *Like pale maple with glints of gold.*

She cleared her throat. "I am sorry to tell you that our parents cannot attend this evening's festivities. Mother is feeling unwell, and Father has no desire to go without her."

Brandon forced himself to pull his focus from her eyes and concentrate on her announcement. "I am sorry to hear of your Mother's illness. I pray it is nothing serious."

Laura nodded and looked to Carissa. "Thank you. If you are still of a mind to have company, Carissa and I will be happy to join you."

Brandon wanted to tell her just how pleasurable an evening in her company sounded to him, but he held his tongue. No sense in scaring her off by acting the rogue. "I will most gladly escort you. And might I say you both look lovely."

Carissa all but danced around the room. She gave a twirl to accentuate the cut of her powder-blue gown. The silk and lace shimmered in the lamplight as she moved. "Thank you, Captain. It has been ever so long since we attended a real party."

"Well, I cannot account for whether or not this party will meet your standards, but the wives of several officers have been hard at work. I believe it will be satisfactory."

Carissa laughed. "They could be racing dogs on the beach, and I would find it far more thrilling than any experience I've had of late."

He laughed at this. "Very well. Then I suggest we call for your carriage and be off."

"You will ride with us, won't you?" Laura asked. "I mean, there is no sense in you riding your horse and having us go separately in the carriage. Give your mount a rest. You can trust our groom to see to him."

"That would be very nice," Brandon replied. "I cannot find fault with that idea."

"Wonderful. I'll go instruct him now."

Laura stepped out and when she returned after several minutes, she held a fan in one gloved hand and a small reticule in the other. "The carriage will be brought around momentarily. Would you care for some refreshment before we go, Captain?"

"Please call me Brandon. I will no longer be a captain after tomorrow."

"I daresay you will go on being thought of in that manner for years to come. However, it would hardly be appropriate for us to presume a familiarity with you."

"Oh, pshaw!" Carissa declared. "He has asked us to call

him by his Christian name, and I for one intend to do so. You can have your social formalities if you like, Laura, but I would rather avoid them."

"Sometimes social formalities keep us safe," Laura countered.

Brandon could see that she wasn't happy with her sister's flippant attitude and he certainly didn't want to see a family feud break out. "Either way, ladies, do use whatever name makes you most comfortable."

They stepped outside, and Brandon noted that the warmth of summer had faded somewhat with the setting sun. The twilight left a golden hue on the western horizon, while the skies over the Gulf were a darkening shade of blue. Brandon remembered this time of evening in Indiana with fondness. There was a sense of comfort and ease that came with the night—especially after a day of hard work.

"You seem to be deep in thought."

Brandon looked at Laura and smiled. "I suppose I am. I was just remembering my home."

"Do you miss it a great deal?" she asked.

"I do. It's been a long time since I've been home. Battles and war do not exactly concern themselves with one's nostalgia and longing."

"Were you . . . well . . . in a great many battles?" Laura's hesitation was apparent. Perhaps she thought her question too personal.

"We were in quite a few," he replied. "Too many, if you ask me. Nevertheless, we did our duty."

"Oh, please let us not speak of the war tonight," Carissa interjected. "I want to have fun and to enjoy myself without remembering all that has gone on. Please."

Brandon jumped in before Laura could chide her outburst. "I believe you are quite right, Miss Marquardt. It would be to our benefit to put aside such gloomy topics."

"You should call me Carissa, and I will of course call you Brandon," she said, batting her lashes. "I think we will be great friends."

Brandon noted that Laura stiffened at her sister's statement. He wondered if she was uncomfortable with the attention Carissa showed him. That thought made him smile.

Upon arriving at the party, however, Carissa soon forgot about Brandon and her sister. She moved through the gathering speaking to first one person and then another with ease.

"It would seem your sister is already familiar with most of the people here," Brandon commented.

Laura frowned and snapped her fan into place. "Her actions are quite inappropriate at times."

"Perhaps it's her youth."

"I have thought as much myself," Laura admitted, "but at times I fear no amount of time will mature her."

"It matured you."

She gave him a most serious expression. "I was never that immature . . . even as a child. Mother said I was always serious."

He could easily imagine her as a studious and obedient little girl. He leaned down to whisper in her ear. "Perhaps you've just never had the right person to show you how to enjoy life."

Before he could hear her response, they were interrupted. "Ah, here's the man of the hour," Justin Armstrong said as he came to greet Brandon and Laura. "And leave it to you to have the prettiest gal of all on your arm."

Brandon glanced to Laura. "Miss Marquardt, may I introduce Major Justin Armstrong, my commanding officer."

"Major Armstrong, I believe I have heard my father speak of you. It is an honor to meet you."

"And I am pleased to meet you, Miss Marquardt. Your father is Stanley Marquardt, I presume."

"Yes. He has long been a Union supporter, although it has not always benefited him."

Armstrong chuckled. "Well, I believe he will find it a benefit to him now. Many of the men who refused to bear arms against the Union are finding it so."

"I understand that this is the house where the men come to take the loyalty oath," Laura said.

"It is indeed," Brandon interjected. "General Charles Russell stands just over there. We are friends from a long way back. His wife and daughters are good friends with my folks."

"I have met the general on several occasions," Laura said. "He seems a good and fair man."

"He is," Armstrong confirmed. He motioned to her delicate fan. "That's a lovely piece. Do you know where I might purchase something similar for my wife?"

She seemed to consider this for a moment. "This fan was brought to me by way of Mexico. You might be able to find another if you were to search some of the shops where such goods are sold. I can direct you to a few of them if you are unfamiliar."

"That would be good. My wife is fond of fans, and the hand painting on that one is beautiful. Is it true that you can learn to speak an entire language with a fan?"

Brandon would have laughed at his commanding officer's

comments regarding ladies' fans, but he presumed the major was just trying to make conversation.

"It is true, Major." Laura placed the open fan to cover her left ear. "This requests, 'Do not betray our secret.'" She opened and closed the fan several times. "This suggests that you are being cruel and I am quite vexed with you." She smiled. "But of course, I am not."

"For that I am glad," the major replied.

Just then Laura dropped the fan and let it dangle on her wrist. "This says, 'We will be friends.' And that is my wish, Major."

He laughed. "Not only beautiful, but charming, as well. I would be happy to be your friend, Miss Marquardt. But for now, I have other duties. I hope you will enjoy yourself this evening."

"Thank you, Major. I believe I will."

Brandon waited until Justin had moved off to discuss something with another of the officers before turning to Laura. "You are quite impressive with your secret language and all."

"Well, of course it only works if the gentleman in question also speaks the language. Or should I say, reads the language. My mother says that a couple can conduct an entire courtship without words if they both know the secrets of the fan."

He laughed and took hold of her arm. "You will have to teach me then."

"Are you planning a courtship, Captain?" she asked innocently.

He raised a brow. "Are you proposing one?"

She blushed as he had expected and looked lost for words. Taking her fan in hand, she opened it fully and held it in her right hand.

"And what does that mean?" he asked, unable to resist.

She smiled in a coy fashion. "It means, 'You are too willing.' "

He roared with laughter, causing several people—including Carissa—to take note. Brandon couldn't help himself and offered no explanation. He liked this young woman. Liked her spunk and wit. Perhaps it was time he learned more about fans.

⁓

Laura listened with interest as the general shared Brandon's accomplishments. Apparently Brandon Reid was a strong leader. She was impressed with his heroic measures, as well. It seemed he had risked his life on multiple occasions to rescue fallen comrades.

Once the speeches were completed, a little band assembled and the room was cleared for dancing. Laura watched her sister move from partner to partner, flirting openly as she went. Carissa seemed to have no awareness of her actions. Laura didn't want to put an end to her sister's good time, but gracious, the girl had just announced her engagement!

"Might I have a word with you?" Laura asked as the music concluded and Carissa came to a stop not but two feet away.

"I suppose if you must," her sister replied. "I have promised the next dance, however."

Laura took Carissa by the arm and led her to the corner of the room. "You are making quite a spectacle of yourself. Would Malcolm approve of your actions?"

"I've done nothing wrong," she protested. "I'm not yet a married woman. Besides, I'm only being nice to the officers. They are far from home and they miss their wives and sweethearts. I'm simply trying to cheer their spirits."

"Well, perhaps you should do less cheering," Laura suggested.

Brandon joined them just then and gave Laura a sweeping bow. "I wonder if I might have the next dance?"

She'd been surprised that he hadn't asked before then. There had already been half a dozen dances, and while Laura hadn't wanted for a partner, she couldn't help but wonder why Brandon had not attempted to be one of them.

She let her fan rest on her right cheek and smiled. "This means yes."

He laughed and took hold of her arm. "Come along, then. They are playing a waltz."

Pulling her into his arms, Brandon carefully maneuvered her around the other couples. The house was not designed for large crowds of dancers, leaving the pairs in close proximity.

"Are you having a good time?" he asked. "I saw that the general's entire staff had gathered in your corner."

She shook her head. "They were there to see Carissa, I assure you."

"Hardly. You outshine your sister like the sun to the moon."

"Are you toying with my affections, Captain?" She asked the question quite casually but found she longed to know his true feelings on the matter.

"Madam, I would never stoop to such behavior. I assure you, I am quite honorable."

She wondered at his statement. Honorable? About what? Was he testing her feelings? If so, to what purpose? A million questions flooded her mind, but few answers came to light.

When the music concluded, Brandon surprised her by

suggesting they leave. "I promised that I would have you home by nine. It's already half past eight."

Laura nodded, although she felt a tremendous sense of disappointment. "I would imagine we will struggle to disentangle Carissa. She is having a great deal of fun being the center of everyone's attention."

But it proved easier than she had thought. Brandon merely stepped in and took Carissa by the arm. With apologies to her companions, he explained that he was honor bound to have the young ladies home by nine. They were halfway to the carriage before Carissa found her tongue.

"I don't see why we need to leave now," she declared. "This is, after all, a party for you, Brandon. Surely you don't want to disappoint your guests."

"They are the general's guests and will go on having a wonderful time even in my absence."

Carissa gave a bit of a pout as Brandon handed her into the carriage. "It hardly seems fair. This is the first party I've attended in ages."

"Be glad that the captain invited us at all," Laura said, joining Carissa on the leather seat.

"I am that," Carissa told Brandon as he took the seat opposite them. "I do thank you for the invitation. I haven't had that much fun in a long, long while."

"Well, you are most welcome. Soon, however, I would imagine you will have your own celebrations. Perhaps an engagement party?"

"Oh yes! I am already speaking to mother about the plans. I do hope you will attend."

"I hope I will as well," he said to Carissa, though his eyes were on Laura.

Laura couldn't help but wonder at his behavior. She had enjoyed the attentions of several potential suitors prior to the war, but Brandon was a man full grown where the others had simply been boys. At least they'd acted that way.

He appears comfortable with me, she reasoned in silence. From time to time she would cast a quick glance at the man, but shadows concealed his expression. *Of course, Brandon is from Indiana. He may plan to return there once his duties are completed and his discharge is given. What if I'm merely a diversion until that time?* She let slip a sigh.

"Are you all right, Miss Marquardt?"

His soft voice seemed to fill the carriage, and Laura felt that same delicious shiver go up her spine. "I am quite well, thank you. And thank you for such a wonderful evening. I enjoyed it very much."

I do wish Carissa could have joined us." Laura's mother fingered a piece of Chantilly lace. "I believe she would want this lace for her veil."

Laura nodded. "Perhaps Mr. May can set aside the piece for her to inspect tomorrow?" she asked, looking to the portly store owner.

"I most certainly can," he said without further prompting. "I will keep it in the back, and when Miss Carissa is feeling better you can bring her by."

Mother released the piece. "Thank you so much. That would be very kind of you. I would hate for such an exquisite piece to get away from us."

"It came from France, by way of New Orleans." He carefully wrapped the piece for storage. "I'm told it takes countless hours to make."

"To be certain," Mother replied. "Now, what about satins, Mr. May. Have you any white satin?"

Laura watched and listened as her mother inspected one piece of material after another. She held up a beautiful piece of iridescent cloth. The pale pearly pink was some of the nicest Laura had seen since before the war.

"This would make a beautiful gown for you, Laura. It would go well with your complexion."

"I agree it's lovely, Mother. However, it is certain to be expensive. Remember what I said before: We do not want to alienate those who are less fortunate by flaunting our wealth."

"Nonsense. This is a wedding. I will not have my daughters looking shabby. Just because others did not have the foresight to secure their valuables and assets as your father has done, is no reason we must pretend to be as ill prepared." She turned to Mr. May. "We will take the bolt. Have it delivered to Mrs. Demarist. She is to design and sew the gown."

"Very good," Mr. May declared in a voice that clearly showed his excitement over such a sale.

They visited another three stores before finally exhausting their choices. As they were about to leave Mercer's Mercantile, the owner hurried to stop them.

"Mrs. Marquardt, I have news that you will want to know." He leaned close so that if anyone was trying to overhear, they would be thwarted. "My brother is bringing up a shipment from Matamoros."

Although Laura knew her mother was exhausted, Agatha Marquardt was not about to be left out of this news. "Do tell. Will there be flour?"

"I am told," he said in a barely audible voice, "that he will bring at least six barrels of flour."

"I will happily pledge to take as much as can be spared," Mother replied. "At a minimum I shall want to secure half a barrel."

Mr. Mercer nodded. "I thought as much. There will also be good cane sugar, salt, and coffee, as well. Real coffee," he added as if she might question him.

"Save us some of each," Mother instructed. "As much as you dare. I do not wish to be greedy, but I have a good number of people to feed."

"I will have it brought to you upon its arrival." The man hurried off to help another customer.

Laura couldn't help but smile. "It will be wonderful to have flour again. The supplies have been so difficult to get with any regularity."

"I often think back to the days before the war when we were more than a little wasteful," Mother said with a heavy sigh. "I have come to greatly appreciate the comforts of good food, warm fires, and plenty of soap."

Laura noted that her mother looked rather tired, so she suggested, "I believe it would do us both good to sit for a time and enjoy something cool to drink. Perhaps have some cakes." She knew her mother's penchant for sweets and played upon it now.

"That would be most welcome," Mother replied. "I do find such shopping to be a bit exhausting. When I think of having to return tomorrow with Carissa . . . well, it's quite overwhelming."

"Then let me bring her tomorrow," Laura offered as they made their way to a small restaurant. "I can show her the items you thought appropriate."

Mother nodded. "Thank you. That would be wonderful. I cannot tell you how much this wears on my nerves."

They entered the small establishment and were immediately seated by the front window. Laura liked this, for it afforded her a front-row view to watch the townsfolk pass by. Every day since the conclusion of the war, it seemed that Corpus Christi was regaining some of its former glory. New people were moving in while a few of the older, established families were returning to reclaim their homes.

They placed an order for iced tea, chilled shrimp, and iced cakes. The latter seemed to revive Laura's mother almost immediately as she began to nibble on the sweet treat.

"Agatha?" a veiled woman in black mourning clothes questioned.

Laura turned toward the voice and was able to make out the features of the gaunt and troubled Margaret Meuly. She smiled at the woman, but she didn't receive one in return.

"I thought that was you, but these days I can't be certain of even my own name."

"I never expected to see you here, Margaret," Laura's mother said. "Won't you sit?"

She took the seat beside Laura's mother. "I cannot stay. My daughter is seeing to the bill." She wrung her hands. "I am quite distraught." She lowered her voice and glanced around the room for a moment. "The colored troops ransacked my house."

"What!" Mother looked at Laura in disbelief. "What are you saying?"

"They came and destroyed my home. Never mind that we faithfully supported the Union. They were drunk, and they carried off most everything that wasn't nailed down. They took my beloved rosewood piano."

"No," Mother gasped. "How can this be?"

The woman leaned in closer and narrowed her eyes. "You have not yet heard the worst of it. They broke into the family vault behind the house. They . . . they . . ." Her voice broke and a sob escaped. "They destroyed Baby's coffin. They spilled the bones on the ground."

Laura's hand went to her mouth while Mother looked as if she actually might swoon. Laura took up her fan and waved it furiously to calm her mother. "Mrs. Meuly, surely you should tell General Russell about this."

"I did," the woman said, straightening. "He said nothing could be done. I believe the white officers are afraid of the blacks. If you ask me, I think the Colored Troops are out of control and the white officers can no longer keep order."

"This is most distressing news," Mother said, shaking her head. "I cannot believe such a violation would go unpunished. To desecrate the grave . . ." Her words faded as she looked to Laura.

"Is there anything we can do, Mrs. Meuly?" Laura asked.

"No. If my Conrad hadn't succumbed to yellow fever, he would have never allowed this to happen."

Laura had heard that Mr. Meuly had died earlier in the month while in Brownsville. For that reason alone, Laura was startled that Mrs. Meuly was even allowing herself to be seen in public, but the times had wreaked havoc with traditions. Especially the customs of mourning.

"We are so sorry, my dear," Mother finally replied, patting the woman's black-gloved hand. "Do let us know if there is anything we can do to assist you. These are most troubling days. I suppose it shall take a long time to see order reestablished and for life to return to as it once was."

"This used to be such a wonderful city." Mrs. Meuly shook her head. "I must go now."

"Please accept our condolences once again on Conrad's passing." Mother leaned forward to give the woman's cheek a kiss through the veil. "If you need anything, do let us know. You are always welcome to come and stay with us."

"You are a good friend, Agatha," the woman said, turning to her daughter. "But I will be well looked after."

"I cannot understand why the men in charge of this city fail to keep order," Mother said as they watched Mrs. Meuly and her daughter depart.

"I wonder if it might help were we to speak to Captain Reid," Laura said thoughtfully. "He seems an admirable man, and he is good friends with General Russell. Perhaps he could convince the general to do something more for Mrs. Meuly."

"That's a wonderful idea," Mother replied. "I do like Captain Reid, and he seems more than a little sweet on you. Has he given you any indication that he might come to call?"

Laura thought of his comments at the party, but shook her head. "I find him to be attentive, but he hasn't really shared his thoughts on such matters."

"Well, I have faith he will. In fact, your father has been approached by several other would-be suitors, but they were not acceptable."

Laura looked up in surprise. She had been about to eat a shrimp, but instead put the fork down. "What suitors?"

Her mother shrugged. "Mostly older war veterans returning to start their lives anew. Certainly no one who had come to call before the war."

"Most of them are dead," Laura admitted. She remembered sadly reading the casualty lists with her mother and sister and commenting on all the families who had lost someone dear.

"Your father is looking out for your best interests, I will say that. He knows that you are of a particular nature, and it will be his job to find a man who will be well matched with your temperament."

Laura knew her father to be a fair man. He cared a great deal about her happiness, and she was certain he wouldn't force her into a marriage of convenience. Across the street several men came into view and Laura was surprised to see her future brother-in-law among them. The men darted down the alley so quickly, almost as if they were being pursued, that Laura had no chance to point him out to Mother.

What in the world was Malcolm doing there in the middle of the day? Laura took a sip of tea. Wasn't he supposed to be working at the flour mill . . . or at least training at such a job?

"Mother, did Carissa ever say if Malcolm likes his job at the mill?"

"No, she doesn't talk about anything but the wedding. And can you blame her? There is so much to arrange. Goodness, but it makes me question my sense in pushing for a quick wedding."

"Well, you know my thoughts on that," Laura declared. "It isn't too late to reset the date."

"Oh, it would be a scandal to change dates now—bad luck, too." Mother shook her head. "No, we will work together and make this the wedding of the year. No matter how bad things have gotten in Texas, we will show our spirit and put on a good face."

When they finally headed home, Laura handled the small carriage. She loved the feel of driving the horses. There was a certain thrill at possessing so much power in her hands. Upon their arrival, Laura was more than a little pleased to find Brandon's mount hitched outside the house.

"Oh, I daresay Captain Reid is here," Laura murmured. "Perhaps I can speak to him about Mrs. Meuly."

Mother led the way to the front sitting room, and that was where they found Brandon and Laura's father enjoying a cup of coffee.

"Ladies, we were just discussing you," Father announced as he and Brandon got to their feet.

"Captain Reid, it is an honor to see you again." Mother beamed him a smile. "Will you be able to visit for a while?"

"I'm no longer a captain, ma'am, but rather a simple civilian." He smiled. "I would be honored if you were to call me Brandon." He gave a slight bow and straightened. "As for your question, that will depend upon Miss Marquardt."

Laura looked around the room, and not seeing her sister, put her gloved hand to her chest. "Me?"

"You indeed," Brandon said.

"Why would I have anything to say over whether you stayed to visit?" She looked to her father, who was now smiling. "Have I missed the joke?"

"Not at all," Brandon said with a chuckle. "I've merely come to speak with your father about a most important matter. I have asked if I might call on you—court you."

Laura felt her heart beat wildly. She suddenly felt dry-mouthed and unable to speak. She couldn't look away from Brandon's piercing gaze.

"Well goodness, Mr. Marquardt. Do not keep us in suspense. What did you say?" Mother asked.

"I told him I would happily allow him to court Laura. He is a decorated war hero and he's convinced me of his intentions to treat our daughter in an admirable manner. However, I told him the final approval would have to come from Laura herself. I will not have a suitor imposed upon my daughter."

At this everyone turned in unison to Laura. She saw the question in each person's eyes and might have laughed had it not been such an important moment. "I would . . . would be glad to receive the captain."

"Brandon," he said firmly.

"Brandon." She murmured the name as if trying it on for size.

"Then let us celebrate," Father declared. "Call for Esther to serve us under the canopy."

Mother nodded and hurried from the room, while Father turned to Laura. "I have no doubt you will conduct your courtship in an honorable manner." He kissed her forehead. "I will see you both outside."

Once he was gone, Laura was very conscious that she was alone with Brandon. She gazed at him, still not quite believing what had just happened.

"You look as though you've just seen a ghost," Brandon said with a grin. "Have I troubled you?"

"You know you have not," she answered quickly. "I am surprised, however. I thought you might have . . . well . . . spoken to me about such a matter first. You had no way of knowing if I would agree to such a thing."

"Didn't I?" he asked, sounding amused.

Laura felt her face grow hot. Goodness, but this man could fluster her in a way no other had. He seemed to know what she was thinking before she could even rationalize it for herself.

Brandon reached out and took hold of her hands. "Don't be embarrassed. I love that you wear your feelings so obviously. I find it most refreshing." He leaned over and kissed the back of her gloved hands before offering her a devilish smile. "I'm also quite captivated by your beauty, Miss Marquardt."

"Laura," she whispered. "If I am to call you Brandon, you must call me Laura."

He nodded. "I would very much like that . . . Laura."

Carissa sat up in bed at Laura's announcement later that night. "Oh, this is wonderful news. I had hoped you might find a beau and now you have. And Brandon is so very dashing." She clapped her hands together. "And he is to be my brother!"

Laura shook her head. "You're putting the cart before the horse, Carissa. He has only asked to court me—not to marry me."

"Oh, pshaw. He's merely following protocol. I wouldn't expect anything less from a gentleman. Besides, no one asks to court a woman unless he's serious." Carissa sat back against a mound of pillows and sighed. "It would be wonderful if we were to have double wedding. I would love sharing that day with you. Oh, wouldn't it be grand?"

Laura continued pulling pins from her hair and ignored her sister's prattling. Carissa was always given to daydreams. It was a part of her girlish spirit. Taking up her brush, Laura began combing through her long, thick hair. It fell below her waist and had never been cut. Over the years, she had sometimes wished her hair had been lighter—more golden like Carissa's, but now she was completely content with her warm brown tones.

"I'll bet Mother was beside herself with joy," Carissa declared. "She has often said that she feared the war would leave us both spinsters and deprive her of grandchildren. Now she will have everything that she desires."

"As I said, you are getting well ahead of yourself." Laura put aside the brush and stood to undress. "Are you feeling better? Would you be up to visiting Mr. May's shop tomorrow? He has some beautiful lace put aside for you. Mother thinks it would make a lovely veil."

"I should be just fine," Carissa said, patting her stomach. "The cramping has improved. I should be perfectly well on the morrow."

Laura nodded. "Then I shall drive you myself. Mother was nearly beside herself from the stress of the day. It didn't help that Mrs. Meuly shared her awful news. Her house was devastated by some of the colored troops."

"No! How awful. But why would they do such a thing?"

"It seems there has been much looting and pillaging. When I mentioned it to Brandon, he was more than a little distressed to hear of it. Apparently the army is seeking to find the culprits and stop such madness, but they are limited by how much time they can spend on such matters."

"Still, that is completely uncalled for. The Meulys were Unionists. They shouldn't meet with harm by the troops."

"I agree. My hope is that Brandon can figure out some way to help. It's a sorry day when widows and orphans have to fear their very protectors."

"Stand still, you ninny, or Mrs. Demarist will stick a pin in you," Laura rebuked. Her sister's wedding dress fitting was turning into something of a circus.

"I want to see how it looks," Carissa complained, straining to see her reflection in the cheval mirror.

"Wait until she's done pinning the hem and then you can."

Laura knew her sister's impatience was starting to get on the older woman's nerves. Mrs. Demarist, a determined perfectionist, moved with painstakingly slow attention to detail. Often she would stop and eye the hem of the gown, then redo a section until she had it just right.

"You are going to make a beautiful bride," Laura said, smiling at Carissa.

"I can hardly believe the wedding is only a month away. Less than that, in fact. Today is the tenth and we will marry on the ninth of September." Carissa gave a little sigh. "I'm so happy."

Laura thought perhaps by mentioning the day's date, Carissa might remember it was in fact Laura's twenty-second birthday. But there was no forthcoming comment. The girl was clearly consumed by thoughts of her upcoming nuptials. During the war, it was easy to understand forgetting such personal celebrations, but Laura had been surprised when no one had even mentioned her birthday at breakfast. She was trying not to be angry about it; after all, it wasn't like she expected presents or a lavish party.

Mrs. Demarist finally had the hem pinned in place and stood back, eyeing her creation. "The bodice is a little loose, but I can easily adjust that," she commented. Pulling up a little pad of paper that hung from her chatelaine, she jotted a note to herself.

Carissa was now in front of the mirror trying to eye her wedding dress from all sides. "It's everything I had hoped for. I look like a princess." She giggled and gave a turn and watched herself in the mirror. "I can scarcely wait another month."

"But you must," Laura said. "And you should be waiting longer than that. Getting married so quickly will only cause the gossips to talk about you."

"I don't mind that. At least they're thinking about me," Carissa declared.

Laura shook her head. "Let's get you out of the dress so that Mrs. Demarist can get back to work."

The fitting had already taken three hours, and Laura was more than a little anxious to get back home. Brandon had arranged to call on her that afternoon, and she still wanted time to freshen up and change into something more appealing.

She glanced down at her simple gown of dark blue. The

skirt had been cut down a bit to draw it in and lessen the fullness. The style seemed to be changing from hoops and crinolines to bustles and stiffened hems, and those with the means were busy having gowns altered whenever possible. Mrs. Demarist's talent for remaking a gown was quite well-known, and Laura had her to thank for the perfectly fitted walking dress.

Once the girls returned home, Laura quickly made her way upstairs and had Carlita fill the small copper bathing tub with tepid water. Laura would have liked to have stayed in the water for a long soak if the fitting had not taken so long. Instead, she hurriedly bathed and allowed Carlita to help her dress.

"This gown is good for you," Carlita said, easing the sprigged cotton dress over Laura's head. "It make you look so beautiful." She smoothed the folds of material into place, and then did up the buttons in back.

"Thank you for suggesting it," Laura replied, "and for your compliment. I'm quite a nervous wreck today. I suppose that given the fact that I'm about to embark on a new adventure with Captain—I mean Mr. Reid, it is to be expected. Nevertheless, I really want to enjoy myself. Instead, I feel like a hundred butterflies are flittering about in my stomach."

Carlita giggled. "My sister would say she have cats fighting inside. But you no look nervous at all." She finished with the buttons and Laura turned.

"What shall we do with my hair?"

The little Mexican maid considered this question for a moment, then said, "I get a hot iron, and we make beautiful curls. We pin them to fall down your back." When Carlita hurried from the room, Laura took a moment to really study herself in the mirror.

Despite her birthday having been forgotten, Laura had to admit she looked happy. "Perhaps because I am," she told her reflection.

She took a seat at the vanity and picked up her fan. The day was miserably warm, and they were in desperate need of rain. What few storms they'd had that summer had been brief and had done little to resolve the drought they were suffering.

"Here we are," Carlita declared, holding up the iron in one hand.

It was only then that it dawned on Laura that they would need to lay a fire if they were to use the iron.

"Oh bother," she said, looking to Carlita. "Let's forget about it. I have no desire to suffer a heatstroke, but if we start a fire, I most certainly will."

Carlita frowned. "I did not think." She shrugged and put the iron aside. "I will make for you a special style." She picked up the brush and immediately set to work.

Laura had no idea what Carlita had in mind, but once the little maid stepped back, Laura gasped in pleasure. "It's perfect. Thank you!"

She touched her hand to the small braided coil atop her head. From this a wave of hair bounded down from the center to the middle of her back. "It looks very German," she told Carlita. "They often use braiding to decorate their hair."

The chiming of the clock let Laura know it was time for Brandon's arrival. She got to her feet and snapped shut her fan. She had just opened her bedroom door when she heard voices coming from somewhere downstairs. It was Brandon speaking with the butler.

"He's already here!" Her heart skipped a beat as it picked up its pace. This was to be their first official outing, and Laura could only pray that it would be as wonderful as she had already imagined it.

Brandon was seated in the front parlor to await Laura's arrival. He had borrowed a small phaeton with the idea of taking a leisurely drive with her. With the top down, the couple would be visible for all to see and hopefully there would be no need for an accompanying chaperone. Of course, the vehicle was often considered quite dangerous and rather risky due to its large wheels and ability for speed, but Brandon felt confident he could handle the spirited team.

Laura entered the room with a radiant smile. She was wearing a white dress with touches of green and pink, where the patterns of leaves and flowers were clustered. She looked so small and delicate that when she extended her gloved hand, Brandon worried about gripping her too hard as he claimed her fingers.

"Miss Marquardt, you do look most beautiful."

She blushed. "Thank you. You are most kind."

Brandon released her hand. "I thought a drive might be fun. Do you suppose your parents would object? I have already put the hood back on the phaeton, and we will be quite visible."

"I do not believe they would refuse us. My mother and sister are making calls, but my father is in his office. Why don't we ask him to make certain?"

Brandon nodded. "I would be glad to do so."

He allowed Laura to lead the way. Mr. Marquardt sat behind a large oak desk, poring over several charts that appeared to be of the Corpus Christi Bay.

"Mr. Reid. How good to see you again."

"I have come to inquire if you have any objection to my taking Miss Marquardt on a summer drive. I have borrowed a phaeton and am quite capable with the team. I have already positioned the top down to make us visible to anyone."

Mr. Marquardt smiled. "You have my approval for such an adventure."

Brandon turned to Laura. "If you are ready, m'lady, your carriage awaits."

Laura laughed, and Brandon grinned in response. There wasn't much about her that he didn't find appealing.

"Do be back in time for supper," Mr. Marquardt called after them. "Mrs. Marquardt is planning quite an affair, and I'm to extend an invitation to you, Mr. Reid. It's a special occasion."

Brandon saw Laura's face light up, and her father continued. "This is something of an engagement dinner. The happy couple will be present as well as several other couples. We would be honored if you would agree to stay, Mr. Reid." Laura's expression changed and she quickly ducked her head.

Concerned, Brandon nevertheless gave Mr. Marquardt an answer. "I would never pass up the opportunity for a delicious meal with such a beautiful young lady." He would have to ask her later what the problem was.

"Wonderful. I'll let Agatha know, and she can add your name to the list."

With that, Stanley Marquardt directed his attention to the work before him and Brandon took hold of Laura's elbow. "The day is quite lovely. I thought we might drive near the water and enjoy the breeze off the Gulf."

Laura seemed pleased with his suggestion. Outside, he stopped beside the phaeton. "It's awfully high and I do apologize, but if you will allow me to help you, I believe we will master it easily." She nodded and took his lead without question. In a flash she was seated and he had joined her.

The carriage was designed to seat two close to each other. Brandon folded his large frame into the small area and found his broad shoulders all but pinned Laura in place. He tried to adjust, but it didn't help all that much.

"You needn't worry," she told him. "I am perfectly fine."

He picked up the reins and started the horses. "I should have borrowed a different conveyance."

"No," she assured him, snapping open her parasol, "it is fine."

They drove in silence for several minutes. Brandon wanted to ask her about her change of emotions, but he didn't know how to broach the subject. Laura appeared happy just to watch the world go by, so he decided to enjoy the quiet. She was unlike most women he'd known, who felt the need to keep a constant conversation going.

By the time they reached a wonderful Gulf view road, however, Brandon felt almost a sense of urgency to speak. "You . . . That is, I am glad you could accept my invitation today. In fact, you are probably quite busy with the engagement party. You looked rather upset when your father extended an invitation to me. I won't attend if you would prefer I not."

Laura looked at him oddly. "I have no objection to your being present." She looked away. "I'm sorry if I gave you reason to think otherwise."

Brandon found a place where he could park the team. There was a lovely view of the water from there, and the rhythmic crashing of the waves on shore was most relaxing.

"Would you care to tell me what upset you then?" he asked.

She shrugged. "It's prideful and silly. I'm ashamed to even mention it."

"Don't be." She looked at him, and he was surprised to find tears in her eyes. "What is it, Laura?"

"I thought perhaps . . . the special occasion was for me. It's my birthday." She shook her head and forced a smile. "I told you it was silly."

"Not at all. I think it entirely appropriate that you would expect a celebration. A birthday is a very important occasion."

"Well, they always have been in our family," Laura admitted. "At least until this one. Still, I understand Mother's enthusiasm to see Carissa's engagement properly celebrated." She paused and seemed to fight for words. "It's . . . just . . . well, no one has even acknowledged that it is my birthday." A single tear slipped down her cheek. "Oh, I feel so foolish. Please forgive me. I'm ruining our first outing."

Brandon handed her a folded white handkerchief. "There is no need for forgiveness, and you are not ruining anything."

Laura shifted the parasol to her right hand and took the handkerchief with her left. She dabbed her eyes and handed him back the cloth. "Thank you."

"I assure you," he promised, "that I will not forget your

birthday. What say we go have some refreshments to celebrate your day?"

"Oh, that isn't necessary. I truly didn't mean to make such a fuss." She seemed a little less burdened. "Besides, I think this lovely drive is a wonderful way to spend the day. I am quite content."

"As you wish." He released the brake and snapped the reins lightly. "Let us see what trouble we can get into." With that, she laughed and Brandon couldn't help but add, "And Laura, happy birthday."

❧

Laura didn't know when she'd ever enjoyed a day more. As Brandon drove the team slowly back toward home, she couldn't help but feel her spirits revived from the earlier disappointment about her birthday.

"Thank you for not thinking me a complete ninny for my tears earlier," she told him as they neared the house. "I'm not generally given to such fits of emotion."

"There is no need for an apology."

"I enjoyed hearing about your horse farm in Indiana," Laura continued. "I love horses and have always enjoyed helping my father select new purchases. Even when I was as young as fourteen, I would insist he take me with him when considering new mounts or teams."

"Perhaps you will have a future in such things."

Laura tilted her head. "Who can say at this point?"

"Would you enjoy that?" he asked.

"I would enjoy anything the Lord called me to do," she

replied. "Of late I have thought that might take me in another direction, however."

He brought the horses to a stop in front of the Marquardt house. "And what direction might that be?"

"I feel it would be beneficial to teach the former slaves to read." She waited to see if he would be shocked by this, but when he only continued to think on her statement, Laura went on. "I have helped several of our Mexican servants learn to read. I had Mexican nannies when we were little; I learned to speak Spanish and in turn taught them to read and speak English. Now I see all of these former slaves who are desperate to find work and fit into our society. They cannot read for themselves so they cannot sign contracts or further their education. I believe, like my father, that freedom is only the first step in many for the blacks. We owe it to them to educate them . . . in hopes of their being able to make it on their own. Don't you agree?"

She waited nervously for Brandon to speak.

"I don't know how it would be received among the blacks, but I think it admirable that you wish to help them." He looked at her with great intensity. "You have a beautiful heart, Laura. I admire that greatly."

She smiled at his praise. "Thank you for saying so, but it is only because of Him who holds my heart."

Brandon nodded. "I admire that most of all."

Two weeks later, Brandon reported to Major Armstrong. It felt strange to wear his civilian clothes in the office of his former commander. As he watched Armstrong unbutton his coat and discard it across the back of his chair, however, Brandon smiled.

"You're out of uniform, Major."

Justin looked at him and scowled. "They're lucky I'm wearing trousers in this heat. I long for cooler weather."

"Or at least drier weather would be nice. Then the heat wouldn't feel so bad." Brandon handed his friend a two-page report. "I have managed to get quite close to the Marquardt family. Malcolm Lowe is engaged to the younger daughter, Carissa Marquardt, and I have asked to call on Carissa's sister, Laura."

Justin grinned. "Leave it to you to sacrifice in such a manner."

Brandon felt a moment of hesitation, but then continued. "I genuinely find her company appealing."

"So you didn't have to sacrifice," Justin said, laughing.

The way Justin laughed and commented made Brandon feel uncomfortable. He'd already worried that Laura would learn of his investigation of Malcolm Lowe and presume that Brandon had only come calling in order to learn about her sister's beau. Now it seemed Justin felt the same way.

"The two matters are completely separate issues," Brandon assured him.

Justin sobered. "I know you to be an honorable man, Brandon. I'm sorry if my jest offended." He took a seat and eyed Brandon quite seriously. "I hope you'll forgive me for making light of this situation."

"It's just that I'm already concerned that when the truth is exposed, Laura will think I only asked to call on her in order to spy. I assure you that was not my intention. I find that although our acquaintance has been brief . . . I truly care for Laura Marquardt."

"So you love her?" Justin asked in surprise.

Brandon nodded. "I believe I do."

Justin laughed and took up the papers. "Good. Perhaps that will encourage you to remain in Texas rather than leave for the cold and distant north."

Brandon smiled. "Perhaps."

"So is this all you have?" Justin asked, looking at the written report Brandon had furnished.

"Yes. I have observed Mr. Lowe meeting with several former Confederate soldiers, as well as a man who is known to run the Confederate supporting newspaper, *The Ranchero*. I haven't been able to learn what they are planning, but it would seem they support some type of conspiracy."

"Conspiracies seem to abound with these Southerners. Look at what is spilling out from the investigation of the president's assassination. It seems every day we learn of new participants. John Wilkes Booth was only one of many who wanted to see Lincoln dead."

"Hatred is a strong unifier, and from what I can tell with Mr. Lowe and his friends, their hatred is what compels them to move forward from defeat. Lowe is not shy about sharing his views, although he does appear to temper his comments when around his fiancée's parents. When he's with his friends he has no such control—at least that's what I've observed those times I've been able to get close enough to overhear."

"It will be that hatred that causes them to make mistakes, and when they do, you must be there to thwart their plans. Pity we can't get them to discuss and confess to the murders from last May. That alone would put an end once and for all to whatever they are planning."

"It would be useful if we could find someone who could participate in their meetings—someone who might be allowed in as a conspirator. Do we have any Texans who spied on the South for us? A man who wasn't well-known to anyone as a Northern supporter?"

"It would be worth checking into," Justin agreed. "If I can find such a man, however, can you arrange to get him involved with Lowe?"

"I'm sure we can figure something out." Brandon tried to imagine how this might all come together. "For now, I will continue to learn what I can. If you can find someone to help us, someone we can trust, I believe the rest will fall in order. It seems to me that

Lowe and his friends are desperate for support. To have former Confederates come to them for companionship would be natural. Where it goes from there will be up to Lowe and his friends."

"I agree." Justin leaned back in his chair. "I've had word from Susannah. She's quite excited about moving out here. I still think it would be mighty fine if you were to buy some land near mine."

"And where exactly is your ranch to be located?"

Justin pulled out a map and unrolled it. Placing a couple of books on one end of the map, he held the other end down with his left hand. Pointing to a place just west of Dallas, he looked up and grinned. "Right here. I happen to know that there is an available homestead about two miles from mine. I know you haven't seen it, but I can vouch for it. There's a creek that runs through it, watering holes for livestock, and a stretch of trees. Otherwise it's good grazing land."

"What about a house?"

"Well, that leaves something to be desired. The folks didn't get around to really proving up due to the war. I'm telling you, though, the property is prime. You'd be a fool to let it get away. Homesteading is the way to go, and you could no doubt prove it up soon enough and build a nice house for you and your gal."

Brandon looked at the map a moment longer. "I'll think on it. I'm still not convinced about remaining in Texas. My folks are expecting me to return to Indiana."

"They won't be the first parents to suffer disappointment," Justin countered. "Besides, you just might interest them in moving to Texas. We could use another good preacher. General Russell says nobody can preach hellfire and damnation like your pa."

Laughing, Brandon got to his feet. "He's got that right. I'll pray on it, Justin. Rest assured that I'm open to whatever direction God wants to take me. I just need to know for sure that it's God's leading and not my own."

Brandon left his friend's office and headed toward the boardinghouse where he'd taken up residence. He wasn't but a few yards down the street, however, when he came face-to-face with two of his former men.

"Cap'n," the first man said, coming to attention.

"Not any longer," Brandon countered. "How are you, Simon . . . Claypas?"

The two men smiled. "We be fine, Cap'n," Claypas answered. "We was wishin' you were still with us."

"Sometimes I wish that, as well." A thought came to him as he remembered Laura's desire to teach reading to the blacks. "I have a question for you two, if you don't mind."

"No, suh," Claypas said.

"I have a friend who is interested in starting a school for former slaves. She wants to teach reading and writing. Would former slaves be willing to be taught by a white woman?"

The two men exchanged a glance before Claypas replied. "Womenfolk and children might. I reckon it would figure on the cost. Colored folks ain't gonna have extra money to learn to read and write."

"Matters, too, on how far away they'd have to go to get to this schoolin'," Simon threw in. "But I'm thinkin' folks would go to jest about any lengths to educate themselves."

Brandon nodded. "Education is going to be essential in helping former slaves get ahead. Without the ability to read and write, they will be forced to take on the menial jobs they had while in bondage. I hope you'll remember that."

"You ain't sayin' nothing we don't know, Cap'n," Claypas said. "Problem is, most white folks don't feel the same way."

"Shore don't," Simon agreed.

Brandon knew what they said was true. "Perhaps my friend can help things change." He knew they needed to get on with their patrol. "I'd best let you get back to your duties. It's good to see you again, men."

"Good seein' you, too, Cap'n." Simon replied and Claypas nodded in agreement.

Brandon watched the two men move off down the street. They were good men. He'd known them to be quick learners. Even so, what would the future hold for them? Where would they be accepted and given a fair chance? Like Claypas said, most white people wanted no part in associating with the blacks for anything other than free labor.

Heaving a sigh, Brandon moved out. *In so many ways*, he thought, *this war will go on for a great many years to come.*

Once their mother departed the breakfast table, Laura and Carissa were left alone. Laura figured it was a perfect opportunity to speak to Carissa about Malcolm. The memory of his appearing to sneak around and slip down the alleyway still haunted her.

Laura reached for a piece of melon. "Is Malcolm enjoying his work at the flour mill?"

Carissa looked up in surprise. "Goodness, how would I know?"

"Don't you ever discuss his work?"

"Never. I have no reason to. In fact, nothing is further from my mind." Carissa spread butter on a biscuit. "Planning this wedding is taking all of my time."

"Still, it is important for a wife to understand her husband's livelihood to a certain degree. I just thought perhaps you knew if he was enjoying his work."

"He seems happy enough," Carissa replied and took a bite of the biscuit.

Laura shrugged and sliced into the melon. "I saw him in town a while back when Mother and I were shopping. There were several men with him and they seemed to be . . . well . . . rather focused on something."

"No doubt they were," Carissa said, still not at all interested. "Laura, do you think I should wear my hair in curls for the wedding?"

"I suppose you could." Laura immediately went back to her questions regarding Malcolm. "So it doesn't concern you that when Malcolm should have been working at the mill, he was in fact elsewhere?"

Carissa put the biscuit down and shook her head. "I swear you should have been born a boy. You worry about the silliest things. Men will be men and do whatever interests them. I have no desire to put myself in the middle of that. Malcolm has friends and dealings that do not interest or involve me. You would do better to put such thoughts aside and be . . . well, be more feminine."

"I hardly see this as an issue of femininity," Laura countered in offense. "I just thought you'd want to know that your husband-to-be appeared to be up to no good."

"Oh, pshaw. How would you know what he was up to—

whether good or bad? You simply saw him in town with his friends. There's no harm to that. Perhaps you are jealous."

"Jealous?"

Carissa gave her a sympathetic gaze. "Yes. I know this is hard on you. I know you expected to marry first. Even so, you have Captain Reid now. If you will conduct yourself properly, you might soon receive your own proposal. Then you won't have to be jealous of my plans."

"I don't have any plans for proposals at this time," Laura said, shaking her head. "You misjudge me."

Carissa pushed back her plate. "I don't think so. I think you are just out of sorts, sister. From what I understand, there have already been many suitors who have called to pay you court and now there's Brandon. You needn't fear being a spinster for long."

Laura rolled her eyes. "This is impossible. I'm not concerned about being a spinster. I'm concerned for your welfare. If your fiancé is up to no good, you should know that."

"I'm only a woman and can hardly judge whether his actions are good or bad. Now, let's put this unpleasant topic behind us. I want to talk about the wedding." She smiled and got to her feet. "Come. I think we should have Carlita work with our hair and see what style would best suit."

"I haven't yet finished my breakfast," Laura said, feeling a great sense of frustration. "You go ahead. I know that's all you care about."

Carissa gave a pout. "It isn't all that I care about. But this is my wedding. I've dreamed of it my entire life. You could at least pretend to be happy for me."

Her words brought immediate guilt to Laura's heart. Abandoning her food, Laura went to Carissa and took hold of her hands. "I am happy for you. I'm also quite worried. You and Malcolm haven't known each other very long. I simply want you to be certain that this is the plan God has for you."

Carissa's expression lightened. "I say my prayers same as you, so it must be God's will." She gave Laura's hands a squeeze. "Now, please come with me and tell me what style will look best with my veil. I think curls will be the most charming."

Malcolm Lowe inspected the barrels with great interest. Black powder from Mexico hadn't been easy to secure, but it was slowly trickling in. His men had been able to smuggle a few barrels in over the last couple of weeks, but he knew they would need a great deal more if they were to accomplish all that they wanted.

"How soon can we get another load?"

One of the men standing nearby shrugged. "Anything can be had for enough money."

Malcolm nodded. "Then we shall have to work to raise funds." He looked at another man. "Do you have any ideas?"

"There are several families in and around the area who supported the Union. They've managed to reclaim their wealth after hiding it in the North or elsewhere. I say we form a plan to steal and sell what we can get."

Malcolm considered this for a moment. "If we work it right, we can have the blacks do it for us. There are a number of the black soldiers who are happy to help for a few coins. I think we could arrange for their assistance, and in turn, all of the blame would fall upon them if they were to be caught."

"We can move the stuff to New Orleans, where it would be easier to sell," another man chimed in. "My uncle could help us with that."

"It might even be possible to trade the goods in Mexico," Malcolm suggested. "Either way, it's probably our best chance."

"So when do you think we'll have enough gunpowder set aside?" someone asked.

Malcolm looked at the ledger he'd been keeping. "If I have my way about it, we'll collect enough to do the job by Thanksgiving. And how better to celebrate that ridiculous Northern-imposed holiday? Lincoln might be dead, but I weary at the way his mistakes keep burdening us." Several of the men grunted in agreement. "Southern folks don't need a Yankee holiday to celebrate being thankful."

Putting the ledger aside, Malcolm smiled. "Still, we will overcome. As you know, I'm to be married in a couple of weeks. The Marquardts have proven to be very useful in providing information, and now that my fiancée's sister is being called upon by a former Union captain, I believe I shall have even greater chances to gather information. Sometimes the most innocent comment over dinner can be helpful.

"What's most important, however, is that we not waiver from our plans. We must press forward, and we must do what we can to teach the Yankees a lesson they won't soon forget."

"I'm all for that," one of the men said. "It's about time they pay for what they did to us."

Malcolm smiled. "As far as I'm concerned, that very thought is worth any amount of sacrifice or bloodshed."

The morning of September ninth dawned with a gentle sea breeze and cooler temperatures. Laura felt relieved—despite her trepidation over Carissa's marriage, at least the day wouldn't be completely unbearable. Of late the temperatures had hovered near or over one hundred degrees with equally high humidity. This would be a welcome break.

As she sent prayers of thanksgiving for the weather, Laura couldn't deny the sense of foreboding that overcame her. She decided to make one last attempt to persuade Carissa to reconsider.

"You know, if you have any concerns about marrying Malcolm, you could still decide to postpone the ceremony."

Carissa looked at her in complete puzzlement. "You are such a ninny, Laura. Of course I'm going through with this. Goodness, but by now the church will be nearly full."

"That doesn't mean you have to go through with the wedding," Laura said as Carissa toyed with her veil.

"I am going to marry Malcolm," Carissa stated matter-of-factly. "I love him."

Her sister's certainty did nothing to calm Laura's concerned heart. "Please let me know if you need anything." Laura stood back, then drew out the folds of Carissa's bishop sleeves. "You hardly know how to care for yourself, much less an entire household."

"Oh, don't be such a mother hen," Carissa replied, seeming almost dazzled by her own appearance in the mirror. "I can take perfectly good care of myself and of Malcolm. Now, where are my gloves?" She looked for a moment atop the vanity, then looked to her bed. "I know they were here just a moment ago."

Laura would have laughed at the frantic search that ensued had it not been such a poignant reminder of what she was sure would be Carissa's life as a wife. Once the gloves were located on the opposite side of the room, Laura breathed a sigh.

"Are you ladies ready?" their father called through the bedroom door.

Carissa hurried to admit him and Laura took that moment to glance at her own reflection in the mirror. The iridescent pink gown had a rounded but modest neckline, and the bishop sleeves were capped with lace at the shoulder. The waistline came together in a V of delicate ruching that made Laura look quite slender. From there, the simple skirt belled out and fell gently to the floor. Their mother had wanted the gown to have flounces of lace and additional ruching in the skirt, but Laura had insisted the bodice was creative enough and that the focus was, after all, to be on Carissa.

"My, don't you both look lovely," their father said.

Carissa grasped his elbow. "I'm so excited. I can't believe this day has finally come."

"Nor can I. My little girls are all grown up." His smile was rather sad. "I remember when we used to go to the beach to fly kites and search for shells."

"Oh, so do I," Carissa said, nodding. "I will always have the best memories of my girlhood days. Won't you, Laura?"

Laura nodded, still unable to shake a feeling of sorrow. "I'm sure one day you will fly kites with your own children."

"Of course," Carissa replied. "Now help me pull the veil over my face, and let's get to the church. I don't want to keep Malcolm waiting."

Laura did her sister's bidding. "You two go ahead. I'll be right there."

As they departed, she went quickly to her dresser, where delicate white crocheted gloves awaited. "I will not begrudge her this day or interfere in it anymore," she said aloud to no one.

She drew a deep breath and made her way to the carriage, where Carissa was already nervously waiting for Laura to join her. Their father handed her up, and once Laura was seated, the driver put the horses in motion.

Very little was said on the way to the church, but Laura could see that Carissa was more than a bit nervous. She wondered if it was just normal bridal jitters or if her sister was finally feeling a little apprehensive about what she was doing. Perhaps Carissa was only pushing for the early wedding to please their mother. But then Laura thought better of this. Carissa wasn't generally given to pleasing anyone but herself.

When they finally arrived, Laura couldn't help but lean over and whisper, "This is forever; make sure you know what you're doing."

She couldn't see Carissa's expression well through the Chantilly lace, but a slight nod of her sister's head told Laura that she had heard and understood. Laura shrugged and gathered her skirts to climb the church steps. If Carissa wanted to marry a man she hardly knew, she would have to bear the consequences.

The church was packed to capacity, and although the ceremony was brief, Laura couldn't deny she'd never seen Carissa happier. After a brief kiss the happy couple turned to be presented to the congregation. As the guests moved forward to congratulate the bride and groom, Mother stood to one side weeping softly while Father tried his best to comfort her. Laura frowned. Could it be that their mother also worried about Carissa's welfare?

"You are quite beautiful, despite the frown."

Laura looked up to find Brandon Reid in a wonderfully tailored blue suit. The rich cut of the cloth hugged his broad shoulders, and Laura found herself longing to touch him.

"Thank you, I think." She tried to collect her thoughts.

"What seems to be the problem?" he asked. Following her gaze, he studied the bride and groom.

"I fear my sister is far too immature to know the full weight of responsibility she's just taken on. She says it is because I'm jealous, but I honestly feel otherwise."

"Jealous that she's marrying Malcolm Lowe?" he asked, teasing.

Laura shook her head and smiled. "No, jealous that she's marrying before I am. She thinks I'm worried that this wedding will somehow solidify my spinster status."

He laughed out loud, causing several people to look their way.

Laura couldn't help but grin as she looked up at him. "You're causing a scene. Now everyone will think we are sporting fun of the happy couple."

"Nonsense. They'll most likely worry that you've said something risqué."

Laura shook her head and changed the subject. "You will attend the wedding festivities at our home, won't you?"

"I wouldn't miss it. You'll be there." He took hold of her arm and led her toward the back of the church. "Have I mentioned that you are quite beautiful?"

"I believe you did say something about that," she said.

"Oh, Laura, don't you look pretty," Mrs. Tennyson declared. "Why, you look just like an angel."

"I wholeheartedly agree," Brandon commented before Laura could reply. "I was just admiring her myself."

Mrs. Tennyson looked at Brandon and smiled. "Perhaps there will be another wedding soon?"

Laura wanted to crawl into a hole. The woman was putting Brandon most uncomfortably on the spot. To her surprise, however, he handled it with great finesse.

"Perhaps. One can never tell where Cupid's arrow will land."

Mrs. Tennyson laughed and nodded. "That is true. Will we see you at the reception, Captain Reid? I had feared rain, but it looks to be a clear day—perfect for celebrating."

"I will most assuredly be there," he replied. "Wild horses couldn't keep me away."

She nodded knowingly and looked back at Laura with a smile. "You have him quite charmed, my dear. Quite charmed." With that she hurried away, and Laura let out a sigh of relief.

"She's right, you know," Brandon whispered in her ear.

Laura shivered with delight at the warmth of his breath against her skin. "Whatever do you mean?" Laura wished to hear him tell her again that she was beautiful.

"She said it looked like rain earlier," he replied with a wink. "But now I believe we are in for a most . . . beautiful . . . rewarding day."

Laura carried Brandon's words with her throughout the morning and into the afternoon. By the time the cool of the evening was upon them and torches were being lit in the yard in preparation for the dance, Laura found herself longing to slip away with this tall, handsome man. Was she in love? She couldn't help but wonder. Whenever she caught sight of Brandon, her heart picked up its pace and her breathing quickened. Not only that, but her stomach felt as though it were being flipped over and over. Either she was in love or she was ill. Still, it seemed silly to imagine herself in love so quickly. Hadn't she chided Carissa for that very same thing?

"I suppose romance makes ninnies of us all," Laura murmured to herself.

Slipping into the house for a change of shoes, Laura began to realize just how important Brandon had become to her. They'd only known each other for just over two months, but she was already impressed by his intelligence and kindness. Brandon embodied so much of what she'd prayed to find in a husband. He was good-natured, honorable, and well informed. He loved God and cared deeply about all humanity despite the color of their skin. Not only that, but Brandon never seemed to mind Laura's endless questions about his childhood and home. Even when she'd asked if he'd ever been serious about a young lady up north, Brandon had answered without hesitation.

"There was one young woman," he'd said, appearing to lose himself momentarily in thought. "She was beautiful with golden hair and blue eyes. She was as pretty as a doll and just as delicate." Laura had felt a moment of discomfort as he continued. "I thought for sure I would spend the rest of my life with her. I think our parents thought so, too."

Laura cleared her throat uncomfortably to ask, "What happened?"

Brandon shrugged and smiled. "She wasn't inclined to wait for me."

"Until after the war?" Laura was almost afraid to know the answer.

He shook his head. "No, for the fifteen or so years we needed to grow up. I was only seven at the time and she was five. At sixteen, she ran off with a riverboat captain while I was away at school."

Laura then had realized the silliness of her jealous heart. However, she had simply replied with all seriousness, "Her loss."

Now, with a more comfortable pair of dancing shoes secured on her feet, Laura made her way back downstairs and through the house. Passing by an open window, she heard her brother-in-law speak.

"So did they deliver everything we asked for?"

"That last shipment was a good one," a man declared.

"He's right. There's enough powder there to blow the Yankees to kingdom come," another added.

Laura knew it was foolish to linger, but she couldn't help but await her brother-in-law's reply.

"We will move ahead then. Perhaps if the supplies continue to come regularly, we can even arrange to complete our plans earlier than we'd originally thought . . . say the early part of November. But just remember, secrecy is of the utmost importance. We don't want anyone snooping around, trying to figure out what we're about."

What are you about? Laura wondered, leaning back against the wall lest anyone see her from the window. She backed away and returned to her upstairs bedroom. She didn't want anyone to observe her exiting the house; the last thing she wanted was to arouse Malcolm's suspicions. It was clear he was plotting against the Northerners, but at this point she didn't have any proof. It would be her word against his.

For several minutes she paced her room, wondering whom she should speak to. If she told her father, he might make a scene. The last thing Laura wanted to do was ruin her sister's wedding celebration. Then again, maybe no one would believe her.

She thought of Brandon. "I could tell him," she whispered. "He would believe me." Sitting on the edge of her bed, Laura considered what she might say to him. He would likely feel it necessary to report this to his former superiors. And what would happen to her sister then, if they decided to investigate her husband?

"But I can't just remain silent," she continued. "Something needs to be done. If I say nothing and people are killed, their blood will be on my hands."

A ruckus sounded from outside her open bedroom window,

sounds of shouting and angry replies. She peered out and watched as her sister's reception turned into a free-for-all. Men were swinging at each other as if the war had started anew on the Marquardt lawn.

Laura strained to see in the glow of the torchlight. It was nearly dark, but she could make out several angry former Confederate soldiers surrounding a tall man who stood in their midst.

Closer inspection revealed that the victim was none other than Brandon. Laura gasped and put her hand to her mouth. Whatever had happened to cause Brandon to fight? She watched in fascination as Brandon easily put down two men who attacked him at the same time. For such a tall man, he was surprisingly agile.

When the others saw how easily he'd landed the first two on their backs, they seemed to calm a bit. Laura saw her father move in to break up the fight. She could hear him speaking but couldn't make out what he was saying. Laura felt confident that whatever had happened to stir this situation into violence must have been quite important.

❧

Brandon watched the disgruntled men walk away, knowing that he'd just made new enemies. All he had said was that the former Confederates needed to accept their defeat and look to building a new future. He'd thought it a reasonable statement, but he knew in their eyes it was anything but.

He glanced around, hoping that Laura hadn't witnessed the altercation. He wasn't proud of the fact that he'd been put in the middle of it. He'd tried hard for her sake to ignore the snide comments given by those who clearly still believed themselves to be at war.

"That looked interesting," Laura said, joining him from out of nowhere.

"I was just standing here hoping you hadn't seen my indiscretion," Brandon admitted.

She smiled and took hold of his arm. "I'm certain, for whatever your reasons, those men deserved your . . . attention. Now, I don't know about you, but I would very much like to dance."

He pushed aside his concern with a huge sense of relief. She didn't care that he'd just fought two men on her sister's wedding day. He smiled. "With whom do you plan to dance?"

She looked at him with an expression of innocence. "Hmm, I suppose that could be a problem. After all, no one has yet asked me." Her eyes widened. "Do you think someone might?"

He tried to maintain a serious, reflective look, but it was nearly impossible. "I hope not."

"What? Truly?" she asked, putting aside her pretense.

Nodding, Brandon led her toward where the others were already waltzing. "Because," he said, "I intend to claim all of your dances."

And he very nearly did. The night passed much too quickly as far as Brandon was concerned. But, as seemed to befall all good things, the bad had to emerge once again. He had no sooner stepped away from the others when an angry declaration was shouted from behind him.

"I wasn't finished with you, Reid," a man declared, giving Brandon a push.

Catching himself, Brandon swung around, ready for a fight. He eyed the man for a moment. "This isn't the time or place, Johnny Reb."

"You Yankees don't get to call all of the battles," the man said, then rushed Brandon with flailing fists.

Laura could hardly believe that the men were fighting again. This time she'd seen the attack and knew that Brandon had little to do with it. She hurried to her father's side and explained.

"You must put a stop to this," she told him. "Malcolm's friends are not fighting fair. I saw them just attack Brandon."

"Stay here," he said. "I'll return shortly." He hurried into the house, and Laura turned her attention back to the fight. The men had fought their way out of the lighted circle where the torches were, and now she couldn't see how Brandon was faring. When the sound of a shotgun blast ripped through the air, she couldn't suppress a scream.

The entire world seemed to stop in that moment, but it was her father's actions that had brought the fight to a stop.

"Gentlemen, this is completely uncalled for. My daughter's wedding is no place to start another war. I believe we have concluded our celebration, and I would appreciate it if you would leave now."

Laura caught her breath in surprise. It was the height of rudeness for a host to make such a declaration.

"He's a Yankee," one man called, then followed his accusation with a string of curses. "He ain't got enough sense to know when it's time to go back to his own people."

"We're all one people now," Stanley Marquardt declared. "We're Americans. This war put us at odds for too long as it is. If you will condemn him, will you also condemn me? Will you condemn James Sonderson and his family, as well as the others who stood in support of our country?"

"They stood in support of freein' the darkies," another man said, spitting on the ground as if the words had left a bad taste in his mouth. "The Yankees ruined my folks' rice plantation. You ain't gonna see me offering up much sympathy for a Yankee in the South. I figure he gets what he deserves."

"Which in my house and at my affairs is respect." Father turned to Malcolm. "I thought you assured me this wouldn't be a problem."

Malcolm shrugged. "It wouldn't have escalated if Captain Reid hadn't been so touchy."

"Nevertheless, your comrades have stepped outside the bounds of decent society and they must go."

Looking to his friends, Malcolm nodded. "You heard my father-in-law, boys."

One by one the guests began to leave. Carissa was beside herself, but Malcolm turned to calm her. "Don't fret, darlin'," he said as Laura came to her sister's side. "The boys were just havin' a little fun."

"Strange fun, if you ask me," Laura muttered. She took hold of her sister's arm. "Are you all right?"

Malcolm pulled Carissa toward him. "She's my responsibility now, and she's just fine."

Laura met his possessive expression and wanted to say something flippant. How she managed to hold her tongue, she'd never know. But instead of causing a scene, she released her hold and walked away. Only time would tell if her feelings of concern were rational.

Brandon was making his way to where the groom was readying his mount when Laura finally caught up to him. She could see he looked no worse for the wear. "Are you all right?" she asked.

"I'm fine. I am sorry about that. It truly wasn't my intention to fight." He smiled at her. "I hope your sister won't hold it against me."

"Carissa will soon forget all about it," Laura said, not entirely sure that was true. "I just wanted to assure myself that you were unharmed."

"I'm fine."

The Marquardts' groom brought Brandon's horse. Brandon thanked the man and mounted quickly. Smiling down at her, he asked, "Will I see you in church tomorrow?"

"Yes. I'm sure to be there."

"Would you allow me to sit with you and your family?"

To ask such a thing was to make a definite public statement that they were a couple. Laura wanted to clap her hands and squeal with delight. There was still enough little girl inside her that she was sorely tempted to throw caution to the wind and do exactly that. Instead, she nodded most solemnly.

"I . . . would be honored."

He grinned, seeming to understand her emotions. "Until tomorrow then."

She waited until he had made his way from their drive and down the street a bit before heading back to the house. Laura wandered to the back, where their regular servants, along with a dozen specially hired laborers, worked to clean up the remnants of the party. Some of the well-wishers were gathered to one side of the yard speaking with her parents, while others were bidding Malcolm and Carissa farewell as they climbed into a borrowed buggy.

Laura began gathering several china plates to assist in the cleanup. She longed to soak in the tub and spied Carlita near the back door. Taking the dishes, she went to the maid. "Would you please take these and then sneak away to prepare me a bath?"

Carlita smiled. "*Sí*. I already have water heating. You wish for me to put in the lavender or the rose salts?"

Just the thought of such luxury caused Laura to sigh. "The rose, I think. Thank you. I'll be along shortly."

Carlita nodded and hurried into the house with the plates. No doubt Mother would need the maid's attention as soon as all of their guests had departed. By that time, Laura would be in the tub with dreams of having danced all evening with Brandon.

She went again to the main table and began gathering some of the empty platters. The food had been exquisite, with a variety of shrimp and other seafood, as well as a lovely selection of fruits, vegetables, and cakes. Most of the plates held nothing more than crumbs, but here and there a few pieces were left behind as evidence of all that they'd enjoyed.

126

"What are you doing?"

Laura looked up to find her mother watching from the end of the reception table. "I'm just helping to clear the dishes."

"That's why we hired servants," her mother said, sounding almost offended. "Put those down at once. Someone might see you."

Placing the dishes on the table, Laura looked at her mother in the glow of torchlight. "Really, Mother, I was only attempting to ease the burden. Do you never feel compelled to assist?"

"That's utter nonsense. You have been brought up to be a lady—to have servants to do the menial tasks. There's no need for us to work. Your father is quite capable of hiring it done."

Laura knew there was no sense in arguing with her mother. "Very well. I shall retire then. Good night." She came to her mother and kissed her cheek. "Carlita is already drawing my bath."

"Good night." She started to go, then turned back. "Oh, and Laura, send Carlita to my room when she's completed your bath."

"I will, Mother."

Slipping upstairs, Laura thought again of the conversation she'd overheard earlier in the evening. The fight had caused her to completely forget until that moment. She frowned, wishing she'd remembered to tell Brandon about it. Whatever Malcolm was up to, it wasn't going to bode well for Brandon's Yankee friends. Perhaps not even for Brandon himself, now that he'd clearly made enemies of Malcolm's comrades.

"I can tell him in the morning," she reasoned. That should be soon enough.

༄

To her surprise and disappointment, Brandon was nowhere to be found the next day. He didn't show up at church, and he sent no word to the house to explain. Laura tried not to fret, but she found his absence most unusual. He had been quite faithful to attend services each Sunday. What might have kept him from coming, especially since he had planned to sit with her family?

After dinner Mother made her way upstairs to nap, while Laura's father went into his study to read. Laura paced the rooms of their home, wishing she could put her mind at ease. She couldn't help but worry that perhaps some of Malcolm's friends had waylaid Brandon the night before. After all, some of them had left well before he had. They could have set a trap for him.

She tried to read a book for a time, then went to the piano and played several sonatas before giving that up, as well. Her mind simply wasn't able to think on anything but Brandon's welfare.

"I rather liked that last song," her father told her as he joined her in the music room. "Would you mind playing it again?"

"Of course not, Father." She picked up the music for Beethoven's *"Quasi Una Fantasia"* and began to play. Her piano teacher had told her that most people referred to the song by its unofficial title, "Moonlight Sonata," and that it had been written for one of Beethoven's loves. She found the haunting melody captured her mood nicely.

Upon concluding, her father smiled. "Thank you. It soothes the soul, does it not?"

Laura nodded. "I find it to be so."

"You have seemed rather lost today," he said, offering her a compassionate gaze. "I suppose you miss your sister. I know I do. I was thinking how quiet the house is without her. I thought it in poor taste that they did not appear in church today."

"Carissa follows her own rules of etiquette. No doubt she presumed folks would understand. Anyway, she does have a way of bringing excitement to the day and I agree, the house is silent without her," Laura admitted. She sighed, thinking of what she'd overheard Malcolm say. Should she say something to her father? Would he be able to do anything, or would he simply put the matter aside and forbid her to tell anyone else?

"Your young man seems quite devoted and you seem happy with his attention."

Her father's comment caused Laura to smile. "I like him very much, Father. He is quite . . . honorable and attentive."

Father leaned back in his chair. "I have found him to be so myself. He has been forthcoming with his views and his upbringing. Did he tell you that his family was active with the Underground Railroad?"

Laura nodded and came to her father's side. She pulled a chair close and sat very nearly directly in front of him. "Yes. He told me so many stories of their work. I found it all very exciting."

"It was risky, certainly," her father replied. "Perhaps not entirely prudent."

"Why do you say that?"

"Well, the legalities for one thing. It could have cost them their livelihood—even their lives."

"But you yourself said that slavery was wrong, Father. They were merely trying to offer help to those slaves who had managed to escape."

"I agree, slavery was an abomination and I am glad to see its demise, although I'm still not convinced that an instantaneous freeing was the answer. It might have served the slaves better had there been a mandate for education first."

"I'm glad you said that." Laura tried to choose her words carefully. "I've been thinking about what I'd like to do with my life, Father. I want to start a school for the former slaves and their children. I want to teach them to read and write so that they can better themselves."

Her father's shocked expression was not at all what she had expected. "You what?"

Laura held up her hand as if to ward off his concerns. "You have often stated that the former slaves need to be educated. I merely want to assist in that. You know very well I've helped Carlita and some of the others to better their English and to read and write it, as well. I would like to do it for the former slaves, in an organized fashion. And I would like to do it . . . for free."

"Laura, your heart is most tender and I respect your concerns, but for a single white woman of your youth and beauty to take on such an endeavor would surely be disastrous. The damage to your reputation alone would be a severe penalty to pay."

"But don't you see, Father?" She leaned forward to take hold of his hand. "I don't care about such things. My reputation has already suffered because I'm a Unionist in a Southern state. Many of my childhood friends no longer speak to me, and even more of them have left Corpus Christi altogether. You must agree that there are those in our community who hold us in great contempt."

"I do agree, but to allow you to take on such a task would

surely cause problems that none of us wish to bear. I cannot allow you to put yourself in harm's way."

Laura frowned and dropped his hand. Getting to her feet, she shook her head. "So we are to simply notice the problem, but do nothing about it?"

"Rest assured, daughter, there will be those who come forward to help. Your heart is good and your motives pure. I greatly admire that about you. You are selfless and loving, but you lack understanding about the consequences. Please understand: I only want to see you safe."

She thought to debate the subject further, but her father stood and walked from the room. Before she could think of what she wanted to say, he was gone. Laura stared after him, not at all sure what she would do now. Without her father's support it would be very hard to move ahead with her desires.

Brandon pulled his spyglass from the saddlebag and studied the horizon carefully. He had found a small ridge on which to position his horse for the best view, but even so, he didn't want to be obvious and was mindful to stay in the shadows of the brush and few trees.

Two men were riding south, just as he'd expected. The night before he'd overheard only the tiniest snippet of information when Malcolm Lowe had instructed the men to leave at first light for Mexico. Apparently there was something they needed in the way of supplies, and Lowe wanted them to go immediately. Brandon figured this might well be the break he needed to finally learn what Lowe and his men were up to.

He put away the spyglass and maneuvered the horse back to the road. The tracks were clear and easy to follow, and so long as the road stayed fairly quiet and untraveled, Brandon figured trailing the men would be easy.

Laura's image flooded his thoughts. With the growing affection he had for her, it would only be a matter of time before he would have to make some decisions. He had never asked her about the possibility of leaving Texas. Would she oppose the idea or readily accept it? She seemed to like her Southern life well enough, but she'd also appeared eager to hear his stories of Indiana.

"Perhaps she'd welcome a change." The horse continued plodding along at the even pace Brandon had set, but bobbed his head slightly as if the statement were offered to him.

Brandon thought back on his life prior to the war. He had attended the university in hopes of becoming a teacher or perhaps a preacher like his father. He loved books and learning, but being cooped up inside all day was not to his liking at all. He missed the outdoors and his work on the farm. He found himself longing for open fields and clear skies. The longer he'd attended school, the more it had seemed evident that he couldn't live a life that required him to be at a desk or even a pulpit.

He'd returned home at the age of twenty for the wedding of one of his two sisters. Both were older and eventually married brothers from Kentucky. They had met when the men had come to Indiana to purchase horses, and their romances had quickly blossomed. Brandon could still remember the moment when he'd arrived from the city and stepped out into the pasture and breathed in the clean air of the country. He knew then and there that he would not return to school, despite the fact that he had only another year to attend.

His father, though disappointed, had understood; similar feelings resonated inside of him and he accepted that his son was no different. It had been the reason Brandon's father had taken up horse breeding. His church work was of the utmost importance, but he had wanted to maintain a connection with the land.

Brandon could still hear what his father had said that day. *"You must heed God's call, no matter where that leads. Remember, God calls some men to build railroads and others to work in countinghouses. No matter what He has in store for you, Brandon, you would do well to follow it quickly. Delays only have a way of turning into difficult lessons."*

The choice was easy enough to make, but then the difficulties of the world began to creep in. The issue of slavery turned quite ugly, and Brandon's abolitionist parents were determined to help where they could. When they told Brandon of their desire to hide runaways, he had eagerly agreed to help, as had his sisters and their husbands. Brandon could still remember the first time they'd all met together to arrange their plans. He'd been surprised at the fervent support offered by the Kentucky brothers. They were level-headed, hardworking men, who weren't afraid to sweat and toil for their living. They despised slavery, and to participate in helping folks out of bondage and into a new life was something they both fully supported.

Brandon had been eager for their plans to work, but when the first runaways showed up at his father's farm, he had been shocked. Most were underfed and sickly. In many cases, there were signs of severe beatings and lashings that had left hideous scars.

"Why do they run away if they know they will be beaten or chained?" his sister had once asked during a visit.

Their father had countered with a question of his own. "If you were forced to live a life of poverty and imprisonment would you not attempt to flee it? Even if fleeing meant the possibility of your own death?"

Brandon had been deeply moved by that statement. Would he not risk everything he had to live in freedom? When the war started, he knew there was no other choice but to join up and lend a hand. It wasn't until he learned of the colored troops, however, that he knew this would be the proper place for an abolitionist.

He'd never been sorry for his choices. The men he'd served under and over had been cut from a different kind of cloth. He admired the blacks, as well as the white officers who trained them. There were of course problems and issues that reared up between them, but throughout the war, Brandon had been proud to serve with the men of the Twenty-eighth.

His horse gave a whinny, bringing Brandon's attention back to the road. They were approaching a small town. It wasn't much to speak of, but there would be water and food, and apparently the gelding was ready for both. He gave the horse a quick pat.

"I agree, boy. We'll take a rest. It's not like they can get all that far without us catching up."

He pulled the horse to a halt in front of a well-worn building. The sign out front proclaimed *Frijoles and Tortillas—All You Can Eat, Twenty-Five Cents*. That would serve him well enough, but he needed to care for the horse first. A young boy came running up to him as Brandon dismounted.

"You give me money and I will water your horse," the boy announced.

"Will you allow him to graze, as well?" Brandon asked, looking around for any sign of the two men he'd been following.

"Sí, he can have grain and hay. My papa will feed him for money."

The dark-eyed boy looked up with great hope in his expression. "My papa is inside. This is his store."

"Then let's go strike a bargain with him. My horse and I are both hungry."

The boy nodded enthusiastically. Brandon tied off the horse and turned back to the child. "Say, were there two other men who came here, as well? Maybe an hour or so ago?"

Again the child nodded. "They did not pay for their horses. They just wanted beer and food. They were here only very short time."

Brandon smiled. "No doubt they had to be somewhere important." He cast a quick glance down the road before turning back to the boy. "Come along. Take me to meet your papa."

I followed them all the way to Brownsville, but then they caught wind of me," Brandon told Justin Armstrong days later. "After that, I couldn't seem to pick up their trail. I'm sure they were headed to Mexico, but where and for what reasons . . . I can't say."

"Well, you gave it your best," the major declared. He leaned back in his desk chair and folded his hands. "What about Lowe?"

"He's been quite elusive. He's spending time in seclusion with his bride, as far as I can figure. I've tried to make sure someone watches the house around the clock, but according to the men, no one is coming or going from the place."

"I suppose that's to be expected," Justin said with a hint of a smile. "I understand Miss Marquardt, or should I say Mrs. Lowe, is quite beautiful."

"She is that, but honestly, she's also rather childish," Brandon replied. "Her sister, Laura, is much more suited to marriage."

"So have you asked her yet?"

Brandon was unable to hide his surprise, which only caused Justin to laugh. "It's obvious," the major continued, "that you're besotted with her. You two make a handsome couple! And given the ratio of women and men in this state, I wouldn't think you'd want to pass up an opportunity to marry a beautiful woman. Especially one you find so companionable."

"I have to admit, I've come to care deeply for her," Brandon said, almost relieved to talk to someone about the relationship. "We've not known each other for long, but I have considered proposing."

"So what is keeping you from doing so?"

Brandon considered the question for a moment. "Well, her sister just married, for one thing. For another, my interest with the Marquardt family started because of you and the general. I'm supposed to find answers and reveal the actions of Malcolm Lowe in order to see him hang for murder. Paying court to Laura has made my task much easier, but I don't want her to think it was my only reason for spending time with her."

"So why not explain it to her?"

"Tell her what I'm up to?" Brandon questioned, shaking his head. "I'm not sure that would be wise. She believes strongly in the Union, but I doubt such beliefs would extend to seeing her brother-in-law face murder charges. For all her sister's immaturity, Laura is completely devoted to her."

"Well, perhaps you could just remind her that the business of keeping the peace brought you two together. You could even credit the general with giving you an excuse to show up at the Marquardt house. It would at least give her the understanding that it was business mingled with pleasure that brought about your calling on her."

"I suppose so. I just don't want her to think she was used."

"But aren't you using her?" Justin asked in a most serious manner.

Brandon heaved a sigh. "See . . . that's what I'm talking about. If you believe that to be the case, how can she think anything else? I didn't ask to court her in order to get closer to Lowe. I wanted to get closer to her. I never believed in love at first sight before meeting Laura."

"But now you do?" Justin asked with a smile. "It was the same for me with Susannah, so I won't blame you for falling for her."

"I just want to keep her safe. She was right in the middle of the ugly scene at her sister's wedding party, and I worried that she would be hurt. That's not healthy for me or the investigation."

Brandon got to his feet. "I need to think clearly, and yet I cannot help but think of Laura and what is best for her. Perhaps I'm not the best man for this job anymore."

Justin rose. "Nonsense. You are a good man, Brandon. You are fair and honorable in all that you do. You'll find a way to work this out. I know you will."

Shaking his head, Brandon let go another sigh. "I hope you're right."

He opened the door to find two black soldiers standing with a white woman between them. The older woman was clearly insulted at being detained by the men. When she spied Brandon, she began to hurl insults.

"Tell these . . . men . . . to let me go. They have no say over genteel Southern women. This is an outrage."

Justin joined Brandon in the outer room and looked to the saluting men for an explanation. The taller of the two men stepped forward.

"This here woman was throwin' rotten tomatoes at the men. She was callin' us names and threatening us.".

"You have no right to be here!" she all but yelled. "You are abominations unto the Lord. He will rise to avenge the South. He will show you your place."

"Madam, is it true that you assaulted my men?" Justin asked.

The gray-haired woman narrowed her eyes. "Nothin' much has changed, has it? The coloreds were our men first and now they're yours. Still workin' for one master or another as I see it."

"With the exception that they joined the army of their own free will," Justin countered.

"Bah! They joined to cheat their masters of the laborers needed to tend the fields. They don't hold any allegiance to you. Animals are incapable of such things."

Justin turned to Brandon. "I believe this will take some time."

"I'll bid you good-day," Brandon said, taking up his hat. He glanced at the woman, who was dressed head to toe in black, and nodded. "Madam."

She all but spat at him as she let loose a hiss. Brandon shook his head. "So much for gentility."

"But I have no desire to attend a gathering at the Beauregard house," Laura declared firmly.

Her mother wasn't being swayed, however. "It would be the height of rudeness to refuse. I need you to accompany me." Her mother took hold of the footman's arm and stepped from the carriage. She nodded to the driver. "You wait here for us. We will be at least an hour, maybe more."

Laura squared her shoulders and allowed the footman to help her from the carriage. "Mother, they are strong Southern supporters. They will know our stand, as well. Do you really think this wise?"

"If we are to mend the pain of the past, we must attend functions that are being held by Southern supporters. This is the only way to clear the air between us," Mother insisted. "Now, you know I have no use for politics, but Mrs. Beauregard used to host one of the finest Christmas parties in the city. We don't want her to think that we're uninterested simply because your father is a Union supporter."

Laura rolled her eyes, but her mother didn't see. Already the older woman was moving forward to greet an old friend. Laura followed dutifully.

"Sadie, I didn't know you would be attending," Mother declared. "I had heard you were unwell."

"Just a bit of the ague," Sadie Cole replied. She patted her ample waist. "It does do wonders for me, however. I always manage to lose a few pounds and then my gowns all fit loosely." She smiled. "And what of you, my dear Agatha? Have you been well? I feared the wedding and party would have completely taken your health."

"It tried to," she assured, "but I took to my bed for three full days and now am much improved."

Laura listened to the women prattle on about their health issues before finally making their way to the door of the two-story house. Mrs. Cole knocked and the ladies found the door immediately opened by a smartly dressed black man.

"We're here at the invitation of Mrs. Beauregard," Mrs. Cole announced.

"Yes'm. The ladies be in the garden room."

Laura had been in this house on many occasions and knew the garden room to be one of Mrs. Beauregard's crowning achievements. Inside the room more than twenty women were gathered amidst the huge bouquets and potted plants for which the hostess was well known. She had a wide variety of exotic vegetation that had been brought to her prior to the war. Much of it had come from the South Sea Islands and required constant tending.

"Why, Agatha, I wasn't at all certain you would be able to attend," Mrs. Beauregard said, stepping forward with two of her three daughters. Laura knew the Beauregard daughters to be a half dozen years her senior, but at one time, they had all shared social events and parties. Now married with children of their own, the ladies looked rather pale and weary.

"Mamie, I am so glad to be here," Mother said. "And just look at your beautiful gown. That color of lavender gray suits you so well."

Mrs. Beauregard smiled in a tolerant manner. "I prefer blue, but the war took that choice from me. We have all agreed to swear off the Yankee blue until . . . Well . . . most likely I will never wear blue again." She looked at Laura's mother and eyed her dress of dark navy with a raised brow. "You look very . . . nice. I've been so weary of black. We were fortunate to have suffered no immediate losses from the war, so we aren't wearing mourning ourselves, but so many do. My dear sister lost four sons. I truly doubt she will ever discard her mourning clothes."

"How sad. Is she still living in Mississippi?" Mother asked.

"Yes. She has the three girls and two younger boys still at home. Her husband suffered at the hands of the Yankee soldiers, but she hopes they will be able to make a new start. I've tried to encourage her to move here, but I don't believe she would ever leave the graves of her sons."

"How very sad." Mother gave a nod to Mrs. Beauregard's daughters. "Esmerelda and Lenore, it is good to see you, as well. Will your sister Winona be attending?"

"Oh goodness, no," Lenore replied before anyone else could. "She's in her confinement now."

Mother nodded. "And when is the baby due to arrive?"

"Not until Christmas, but she is already showing considerably and hasn't been at all healthy," Mrs. Beauregard answered in a matter-of-fact manner.

"We shall pray for her and the child," Laura's mother declared.

"Come and meet some of the other ladies. I know you will be surprised to find a few of the old families have returned to Corpus Christi. I was quite delighted." Mrs. Beauregard led Mother and Mrs. Cole away.

"We've heard you've been keeping company with a Yankee officer," Lenore said in an accusing tone. Esmerelda nodded and looked to Laura for explanation.

"Captain Brandon Reid asked for permission to court me," Laura admitted. "As a good many of our men, he is no longer a soldier."

"But he *is* a Yankee," Esmerelda said with great distaste.

"My father supported the Union," Laura told them, "as you both well know. He now supports the healing of our country by putting aside our differences. I feel the same way."

Lenore touched a hand to her blond curls. "There will be no healing this wound. It runs much too deep."

"There will be no healing," Laura replied, "if good people will not allow for it. Should we continue to pick at our wounds, they will never heal."

Esmerelda gave a *harrumph* and shook her head. "She's one of them, sister."

Laura looked at the two women and shrugged. "If by 'one of them' you mean that I support our people joining together in a common cause of goodwill and Christian charity, then yes; I'm one of them."

"You dare to suggest that we hold less than Christian charity in our hearts?" Esmerelda questioned.

"I have done no such thing." Laura silently prayed that her mother would find some excuse to leave the party immediately. "I merely stated that this was my heart. You and God alone know what lies in your own."

The two sisters were clearly insulted.

"If you'll excuse me," Laura said with a forced smile, "I simply must rejoin my mother."

She heard them whisper behind her back but decided it wasn't worth acknowledging. She had known Brandon and her father to say on more than one occasion that the war wasn't really and truly over. She sadly wondered if it ever would be. Could these once decent and loving people put aside their anger and bitter hatred? Both sides of the war had suffered from painful losses, mistakes, and hurtful words and deeds. What would it take to heal this country, Laura wondered. Was it possible that the riff would go right on separating the North and the South?

Worst of all, would it only be a short number of years before they found themselves once again in a war?

13

It was more than two weeks after the wedding before Laura saw her sister again. When Carissa showed up at the house, Laura thought her rather pale . . . perhaps even sick. Their mother had gone with Esther to visit Mrs. Cole and would likely not return for a few hours. Laura felt a deep sense of God's providence that Mother had allowed her to remain at home.

"You should have let us know of your plans to visit," Laura told her sister. "Mother has gone out for the afternoon."

"I am sorry. It was a last-minute decision. A neighbor was making a trip to this part of town and I asked for a ride." Carissa followed Laura into the music room.

"I was just practicing a few pieces. I'll send for refreshments if you're hungry."

"That would be nice." Carissa took a seat near the window and sighed. "I do love it here. Our place is so tiny."

"You are fortunate, however, to have a place of your own,"

Laura said. She rang for the galley maid and instructed her to set lunch for two. With that accomplished she turned back to find Carissa distracted by the crocheted doily that covered the arm of her chair.

"Are you all right?" Laura asked.

Carissa startled at this. "What do you mean?"

"You seem . . . well . . . as if something might be troubling you."

A forced laugh escaped her sister. "Goodness, but you do go on. I'm perfectly fine. I suppose I've changed now that I'm a married woman."

"It's only been two weeks," Laura countered. "You couldn't have changed that much."

"Married life is much different than that of being a maiden daughter," Carissa said with a sigh. "So how is Mother? I presume if she's out calling she has completely recovered from the wedding."

"Yes, she's been making calls and attending social events. I believe she's quite concerned about being excluded from the upcoming Christmas season." Laura smiled and took a seat in a tall walnut chair near Carissa. Laura studied her sister's face for a moment. She felt almost certain something was wrong, but knew she could never force Carissa to admit it. She thought for a moment of commenting about Malcolm's friends and the fight at the wedding, and then thought better of it.

"Have you begun to arrange the house as you like it?" Laura asked.

Carissa nodded. "Mother and Father were very generous, as I'm sure you know. They arranged for workers to assist us as

148

soon as I felt up to having them. I plan to order the front sitting room papered. I thought something with a white background would make the room seem brighter and perhaps larger."

"I'm sure it would. Mother said the house has three bedrooms. Are they very large?"

"Large enough," Carissa replied. "Two are upstairs and our bedroom is one of them. Malcolm has taken the downstairs bedroom for an office. He says there is much that he must be responsible for."

"As a flour mill worker?"

Carissa shrugged. "I have no idea. I really don't know what he does. He leaves in the morning and returns in the evening. Sometimes he comes home quite late." She smiled, as if fearful that she'd said too much. "So you must tell me all the gossip. What did people say about my wedding?"

"Miss Laura, the table is set for you and Miss Carissa," the maid announced.

Laura looked to her sister as she rose. "Come, we can talk while we enjoy some lunch. I'm quite famished."

The ladies made their way to the dining room and seated themselves to plates of cold chicken, fresh melon slices, and a bevy of other delights. Laura offered grace, then began to choose from a selection of cheeses.

"I know that the guests enjoyed your wedding very much," Laura said without meeting her sister's watchful eye. "Everyone thought your gown quite lovely. They thought it rivaled those imported from France."

"I'm so glad," Carissa said, cutting into a piece of chicken breast. "I felt beautiful. Mother's choice of that Chantilly lace made the perfect veil. I've packed it all away for my daughter to use one day."

"Your daughter?" Laura questioned. "You're already making plans for a daughter?"

"Well, I suppose we could have boys instead," Carissa said absentmindedly. She let her shawl slip from her shoulders. "It's rather warm today."

"Yes." Laura glanced up and noticed a dark bruise on her sister's arm. "You're hurt. What happened?"

Carissa seemed surprised. "What?"

Laura pointed to her arm. "You have bruises."

"Oh," Carissa replied casually. "I suppose I got it moving the furniture around. As I told you, I've been busy arranging." She refocused on her plate and ate for several minutes without saying another word.

Laura too fell silent. Carissa hardly seemed herself. Sipping her lemonade, Laura wondered what was really going on with her sister.

A knock echoed through the otherwise quiet house. Laura could hear the butler's muffled talk. She prayed none of her mother's friends had come to call. She wanted this time with Carissa—not a gathering of gossips.

"Miss Laura, Mr. Reid has asked to see you. Are you in?" Mr. Gaston announced.

"Oh yes," Laura replied. She hadn't seen Brandon since the wedding and was beginning to worry about him. "Have him join us here."

When he strode into the room, however, her fears were all dispelled. "It's good to see you," she said, getting to her feet.

"Please remain seated. I didn't mean to interrupt your luncheon." He nodded toward Carissa, then returned his gaze to Laura. "I can return at a better time."

"Nonsense. Join us, please. I'll have another place set."

"No, I've just eaten. I would be happy to sit and share your company, however."

His smile warmed her, and Laura nodded her approval. "I think that would be wonderful . . . don't you, Carissa?"

"Of course, Captain Reid. It is perfectly acceptable for you to be here even if our mother and father are out. Since I am a married woman, no one would frown upon Laura receiving you."

Brandon chuckled. "Well, we wouldn't want to shock society."

Laura reclaimed her chair as Brandon assisted her. Once she was secure, he took his place between them.

"I thought perhaps you'd fallen ill," Laura said, trying not to sound overly concerned. "You didn't come to church as you had said you would."

"I know, and I do apologize. Something came up at the last minute."

"Well, this is the first time I've seen either of you since the day of the wedding," Laura replied. "It's definitely the best thing to happen all week."

He chuckled. "So have you ladies been enjoying the lovely weather? I thought we were most fortunate to have cooler temperatures."

"Yes, but today has been quite warm," Laura stated. "Though not unpleasantly so." She cut a piece of melon. "Do tell us what you have been doing, Mr. Reid. Are you making plans to return to Indiana?"

"I have considered it." He smiled in a teasing fashion, adding, "But I find myself rather intrigued by Texas. Corpus Christi in particular."

"I don't suppose my sister has anything to do with that," Carissa said, giving him a coy glance.

"She might," he replied with a wink. "I've also had the good fortune to spend some time learning about ranching and horse breeding in Texas. It would seem that there are a great many parcels of land available for purchase. My good friend Major Armstrong is trying to convince me to purchase one near him. I believe the ranch he has chosen is near Dallas."

Laura nodded. "I have heard it's quite beautiful there."

"But you've not seen it for yourself?" he asked.

Shaking her head, Laura picked up her glass. "I was born in eastern Texas, but other than that, I've not seen much beyond Corpus Christi. Not that I wouldn't like to. In fact, I think I would very much enjoy traveling. Things have changed so much here." She paused and sipped the cool liquid. "Do you suppose it will ever return to as it was before?"

"Would you want it to?" Brandon asked casually.

Laura studied his expression for a moment. "No, I wouldn't . . . but perhaps I should have asked, do you suppose things will ever get better? People are so angry. You know that as well as anyone, after serving in the army. But I continue to be amazed at the anger and ugliness spewed by women I once considered the epitome of gentility and civil society."

Brandon nodded. "Maybe it's because we have some expectation that men will act that way, but when the ladies take on that role, it comes across as more shocking and distasteful."

"I think the women feel betrayed," Carissa said, surprising Laura.

She looked at her sister. "Why do you say that?"

Carissa shrugged. "Well, they figured that their men were capable of keeping them safe. They thought life would go on in the same manner as it always had, but then it was taken from them. The only life they'd known was gone. Food and supplies were cut off, and people suffered and died."

Surprised by her sister's sudden depth of thought, Laura pressed her to continue. "I suppose Malcolm speaks against the Union constantly?"

"He seldom says anything. He is troubled by nightmares sometimes." She seemed to lose herself momentarily in thought. "He saw so much death."

"As did the soldiers on both sides of the war," Brandon countered. "However, I think you make a valid point. Betrayal is a difficult thing to endure. I think that's part of the anger the North holds against the South. They feel betrayed by the Southerners who so quickly cast off their American ties to form their own nation."

Carissa looked at him oddly but said nothing. Laura couldn't help but wonder at her sister's sudden silence. "Well, this has certainly made our conversation gloomy."

"Then let us consider something more positive," Brandon said with a smile. "My original purpose in coming here was to invite you and your family to a musical performance tonight. I realize this is very late notice, but I only got back to town yesterday."

"You were out of town?" Laura said, shaking her head. "I don't recall your mentioning a trip."

"I was on army business," Brandon said, shrugging it off. "It came up without warning and I didn't have a chance to let you know I'd be gone. However, upon returning I learned of this musical diversion. We have a group of soldiers who are quite talented. They have entertained before, and I have to say they are as good as any musicians I've ever heard back East."

"That does sound like a wonderful distraction," Laura declared.

"The invitation is for you and your parents." He looked to Carissa. "And you and Mr. Lowe are welcome to join us, as well."

"We already have plans," Carissa said. She got up rather abruptly from the table and Brandon too rose. She waved him back down. "I need to go. I was supposed to meet my ride back in town by one. I'm afoot so I must allow for the time."

"Nonsense," Laura said. "Wait until Mother returns, and we will drive you home ourselves."

Carissa shook her head and grabbed her shawl. "No. I need to go now." She came and embraced Laura. "I'm sorry."

Laura stared after her sister's retreating form. "I'm worried for her."

"Why are you worried?" Brandon asked.

Laura considered the situation for a moment. She trusted Brandon and needed to share with him the things she'd overheard. "I think her husband is up to something . . . dangerous. In fact, I believe he means to commit murder."

Brandon's eyes widened. "Murder?"

She nodded. "I overheard him the night of the wedding party. He was talking to his friends—I don't know for sure which ones, but there were several gathered—and they were talking about powder. Someone said something about having enough to blow the Yankees to kingdom come. Malcolm replied that with the way things were going, they might be able to move their plans up to the early part of November. I really don't know much else."

Brandon frowned. "That's enough, don't you think? Why didn't you tell me that night?"

"I wanted to, but one thing led to another and then there was the fight. I figured to let you know at church the next morning. When you didn't show up, I presumed I could tell you the next time you came to visit, and I suppose I have done just that. I'm very worried, Brandon."

"And well you should be. Worried for your brother-in-law." He wondered how much he should say. "I know that the army has been concerned about a plot. I'll check in with my friends and let them know what you've said."

"A plot? With Malcolm involved in it?" Laura questioned. "I didn't realize the army was involved."

Brandon felt momentarily panicked. "Well . . . that is to say . . . your brother-in-law is very vocal in his feelings about the war and how things turned out. I wouldn't be surprised if the army hasn't been watching him since the war ended."

This seemed to satisfy her. "I do hope you'll be careful." Laura wrung her hands. "I think Malcolm is dangerous. I noticed Carissa had bruises on her arm. She told me it was from moving furniture, but I don't believe her."

"You think he hit her?"

"I do. The bruises looked like fingerprints." She met his eyes.

"Like he had grabbed her hard. Carissa was not at all herself. I really don't know what to think."

"Do you suppose she knows about Malcolm's exploits?"

"If she does, she isn't saying anything. Carissa has never been overly interested in anything but herself, so I doubt she is a part of this or even knows about Malcolm's conspiracies. I just asked her about his work, and she knows nothing of what he does."

Brandon felt horrible for what he was about to do. "Laura, this is most grave. A great many men could lose their lives if what you've overheard is carried out to completion."

"I know," she whispered. "That's why I felt it important to tell you. I don't know what else to do."

He nodded. "I have an idea, but it will mean a bit of a risk to you."

She raised a brow. "I'm not afraid of that. Tell me how I can help."

"Do you think you could get your sister to answer a few questions? Maybe assist the army in observing what Malcolm is up to?"

Her eyes widened, and Brandon feared he'd gone too far. This would all be for naught if she decided to warn Malcolm that the army was watching him.

"I'll help in any way I can," Laura stated. "So long as it doesn't endanger Carissa." She sighed. "Unfortunately, I think she's already in danger."

"Don't worry. I'll do whatever I can to keep her safe. If Malcolm is plotting against the army, then most of his plans will take place away from Carissa and her home."

"What do you need to know?" Laura asked. "Should I even

question Malcolm himself? Are there questions I could pose that would be useful?"

"No. I don't want you interacting with him unless it's absolutely necessary. If you should overhear him speaking with your father or others, that's fine. But it would be best for you if we did nothing to cause him to take notice."

"I agree." Laura pushed back her plate and bit her lower lip.

Brandon wanted only to reassure her that everything would be all right, but he couldn't. Her news only served to confirm his suspicions and worst fears. Plans to wreak havoc and destruction were in the works—enough so that Lowe felt they could move up their target date. He frowned. Early November was only weeks away. If they couldn't pin down the information and learn the truth, a great many people might die.

His frown only deepened as he glanced back to Laura's fearful expression. *And now I've involved the woman I love.* He shook his head. What price would this cost him?

14

ater that day, Laura sat curled up in the front parlor, reading. The draperies were open to let in the fading afternoon
light, and Laura settled comfortably on the newly covered settee
by the window.

She tried for the fifth time to begin the tedious narrative of
the final book in James Fenimore Cooper's LEATHERSTOCKING
TALES. Natty Bumppo was unable to hold her attention, however, and she finally gave up. Closing the book harder than she'd
meant to, Laura was surprised to hear a gasp from behind her.

Looking over her shoulder, Laura found Esther quietly dust-
ing some of the furniture. "'Scuse me," Esther said. "Ya startled
me—tha's all."

"I'm the one who's sorry," Laura said, getting to her feet.
"I'm afraid this book is utterly boring."

"Cain't 'magine a book bein' borin', iffn y'all pardon my
sayin' so."

"Well, normally I would agree with you, but Mr. Cooper has managed quite capably."

Esther's expression took on a faraway look. "I reckon iffn I could read, I'd be happy for to read Mr. Cooper. Be like touchin' the sky."

Laura cocked her head to one side as she considered the woman's words. "What do you mean . . . touching the sky?"

The black woman looked at her sheepishly. "I apologize for goin' on. Never did know when to keep my mouth shut."

"No, I'm curious." Laura could see that Esther was rather embarrassed. "Please tell me."

The black woman's face took on a distant look. "I always wanted to learn to read. I saw the white folks readin' . . . writin', too, and wished I could do the same. Since I was jes a girl I wanted to read. My ma used to say that wantin' what ya couldn't never have was like touchin' the sky. It'd be mighty nice, but weren't ever gonna happen. All ya could do was gwan dreamin' 'bout it."

Laura recognized the start of an opportunity and stepped toward Esther in a most conspiratorial manner. "I could teach you to read."

Esther's dark eyes widened. "I ain't got the brains for such learnin'."

"Of course you have. You just haven't been given a chance to use that brain for learning. If you give it a try, I think you'll find that reading will be easy for you." Laura wasn't sure that would be the case, but she firmly believed that heading into any project with a positive spirit gave a person a leg up on those with a negative one.

"How ya reckon we could do it?" Esther asked in a hush.

Laura smiled at her nervousness. "Well, we could meet in the morning before breakfast."

"I gots to start workin' at five."

"Then what if we met at four thirty? At first we will just meet for about twenty minutes. No sense overwhelming you."

"But ya'd have to be gettin' up so early."

Laura shrugged. "I can always go back to bed. In fact, if I meet you in the kitchen before Cook gets up, we could have our lesson there. I could just come down in my nightgown and robe and if anyone sees me, it will just look as if I came down for an early morning snack."

Esther put her hand to her heart. "Iffn you truly think I can read, I'd be proud to try."

A smile spread across Laura's face. "Then it's settled. We can start in the morning."

Laura didn't think about the fact that she might be up quite late until Brandon arrived to join them for supper. Her mother and father were delighted with the prospect of an evening's entertainment.

"We haven't had any quality musicians since the war began. So many of the men who played were called away," Mother explained as they finished their dessert.

"I can vouch for the musicians in this group. They once played for President Lincoln himself," Brandon explained.

Mother got to her feet, and the men rose, as well. "I will go freshen up a bit and perhaps you men can have a cigar before we depart."

"I do not smoke, ma'am," Brandon told her, "but I thank you for the invitation."

"If you'll excuse me," Laura's father said, "I will arrange for the carriage."

This left Brandon and Laura alone. Laura accepted Brandon's help up from the chair and smiled. "I believe you've made my parents very happy. My mother delights in social events, and my father delights in my mother. When you make her happy, he is not far behind."

Brandon laughed. "I could hear my father saying something similar. He always believed that the woman of the house commanded the emotions of the family."

Laura led him to the front sitting room, where she'd left her shawl. She had just retrieved it when Brandon drew close.

"I hope you'll pardon the whispers, but I wanted to tell you something in private."

She nodded and gave him a hint of a smile. "Do tell."

"I spoke with my friend Major Armstrong. He's the one who is helping General Russell with the investigation I mentioned earlier. He believes your information will be quite valuable. He wonders how you feel about aiding the army in this matter."

"I told you before that I would help in any way I can. I've never trusted Malcolm, and now I'm worried that he is hurting my sister. Carissa has always been quite naïve, and I fear this time she's gotten herself into more trouble than she can manage."

"As I mentioned earlier, this isn't without risk. If your brother-in-law is the ringleader that the army believes him to be, then this won't be the first time he's plotted murder."

Laura swallowed hard. "Truly?"

Brandon nodded in a solemn manner. "I'm afraid so."

"Sam will bring the carriage around momentarily," Laura's

father announced as he joined them. "It looks to be a pleasant evening. There isn't a cloud in the sky."

"I am certainly happy for the lower temperatures," Laura declared. "Goodness, but I don't know how you men manage in your coats and vests, not to mention long sleeves. Why, at least I can shorten mine."

"That is why you most often see me working without a coat," Father said with a wink. "I keep it close at hand, however, just in case your mother comes to check up on me."

Laura laughed. "Mother should understand. She was the one who mentioned that perhaps now that the war was over, we could consider trips north during the heat of the summer."

Father rolled his eyes. "Yes, she mentioned it most every day last summer. Had she not had your sister's wedding to contend with, I believe she would have insisted we travel north to check out properties."

Laura patted his arm. "Well, it wouldn't be such a very terrible thing now, would it? To have a little house up north where the summers are cool and easy? I believe that sounds quite pleasant."

"You're from Indiana, if I remember right," Laura's father said, looking to Brandon. "How do you fare in the summers?"

"They can be quite oppressive," Brandon replied. "You must remember: We are near the Ohio River, not that far north at all. We have our share of humidity and heat to be sure. However, we grow some of the finest crops you could ever want and certainly do not contend with the same degree of temperature and dampness that you do here in Corpus Christi. We also have some very lovely shade trees. . . ."

"Ah, there you all are," Mother said, unaware of what Brandon had been saying. She swept into the room and handed her shawl to Laura's father. Allowing him to assist her with it, she smiled. "I'm not sure I'll need this, but I feel a chill in the air."

"Indeed," Brandon said as he helped Laura with her own wrap. "The breeze off the water is cool. I would imagine you'll be thankful for your wraps by the time we return."

Mr. Gaston appeared at the door. "Your carriage is ready, sir."

Father grasped Mother's elbow and led her to the door. Brandon leaned close to Laura and asked, "Have I told you how lovely you are tonight?"

A wave of satisfaction washed over Laura. She'd picked this particular gown of pale pink Indian muslin just for him. The delicate pink was overlaid with a very fine weave of Irish lace on the bodice, while the skirt billowed from several stiffened muslin petticoats.

"You are quite generous with your compliments," she replied. "I only just received this gown a week ago. Mother had ordered it some time ago, but things were put on hold in order to have Carissa's wedding gown made. It's better suited to summer, but I couldn't resist wearing it tonight."

He gave her mischievous grin. "I'm glad you did. You look beautiful."

Laura lost herself for a moment in his gaze. He had the most beautiful sapphire-colored eyes, and his lips practically begged her touch. She found herself starting to reach out and then stopped herself short.

"You take my breath away," he whispered. "If you continue to look at me that way, we might never make it to the musical performance."

Laura's mouth dropped open, and he reached up with a finger to close it again. "Now, now. Your parents will wonder what in the world is amiss, and then what would you say?"

"I would tell them the truth," she said, regaining her composure. "I would simply explain that you were . . . breathless . . . and needed a moment to regain your composure."

He chuckled and pulled her forward. "Come along. We mustn't keep you parents waiting."

The following morning, Laura moaned as she forced herself to get up. Esther had come to wake her but had departed before Laura managed to push back the covers. She'd gotten to bed quite late, just as she'd feared, and four o'clock in the morning seemed impossibly early.

Nevertheless, a promise was a promise and she intended to see it through. Donning her robe, Laura fastened the ties and went to her vanity. Esther had left a single lighted candle on the table beside the door, and from this glow, Laura could see well enough to brush her long hair and braid it into a single plait. She suppressed a yawn.

The evening had been magical. The music had been superb, but Laura was even more in awe of the way she felt about Brandon Reid. She knew without a doubt that this was the man she hoped to marry. Never had she felt this way about any other man.

She all but floated down the back stairs and into the kitchen, where Esther was waiting at the table. Smiling, Laura nodded at the small black slate and chalk.

"I see you found them without trouble."

"They was in the pantry jes like you told Cook." Esther looked at the slate and chalk as if they were gifts of gold and silver. "Thank ya for lettin' me borrow 'em."

"They are yours to keep," Laura said. "They were some we used when still in the nursery. I found them upstairs in the attic."

She took a seat at the kitchen table beside Esther. "Now, we will begin with the alphabet."

Esther turned up the lamp a bit to brighten the room. "Pardon my sayin' so, Miss Laura, but mebbe it would be best iffn we begin with prayin'. I'm gonna need the good Lord's help iffn I'm gonna read."

"You are very right. We should begin all of our endeavors with prayer."

By the time Cook made her appearance twenty-five minutes later, Laura and Esther were more than ready to wrap things up. Laura longed only to climb back into bed and catch a few more winks of sleep, and Esther was clearly overwhelmed with the information she'd been given.

"Don't fret, Esther," Laura assured her. "This will come to you in time. We will go as slow or as fast as you need."

"Thank ya, Miss Laura."

Cook, a thick-waisted black woman, smiled a toothy grin. "You learn that real good, Esther, then you can read to me."

"You could learn to read for yourself, Cook," Laura interjected. "I could teach you just as well."

"Ain't gettin' up any earlier than I hafta," the older woman declared. "My bunions and rheumatism are already actin' up sumptin' fierce."

Laura patted the woman on the arm. "We could always

arrange to meet in your room by the stove. I would be happy to teach you to read."

Cook shook her heavy face. "I'll jes let Esther read to me. It'll do her good to practice."

"Very well," Laura replied, heading for the stairs. "But if you change your mind . . . let me know."

Laura slipped back into bed and felt that she had barely drifted to sleep when Carlita was throwing back the draperies and bidding her good morning.

"I want to sleep for a while," Laura told her and pulled the covers up over her head.

"Your mother said you must accompany her to your sister's," Carlita declared. "You are going shopping, remember?"

Laura had all but forgotten her mother's plans for the day. With a sigh she lowered the covers and yawned. "Better get me some strong tea and lots of cream."

Carlita laughed. "I go get it now. I bring your breakfast, too, and tell your mother that you get ready. When I come back I help you dress."

Knowing there was no recourse, Laura got up and made her way to the vanity for the second time that morning. The clock on her mantel revealed the hour to be nearly nine. She had slept a long while, although her body didn't seem to realize it.

She couldn't help but think about the things Brandon had said regarding Carissa's husband. Her sister loved Malcolm Lowe; how could Laura interfere with that? But how could she put the lives of hundreds of men in jeopardy?

"Carissa doesn't even know what she feels," Laura told herself as she unplaited her hair. She ran her fingers through the long wavy mane and wondered how in the world her sister would take the news when the truth was finally revealed.

Malcolm would be hanged if Brandon was correct about him being a murderer. Laura couldn't suppress a shudder. She feared for her sister—the bruises on Carissa's arm had likely come from Malcolm's hands. The very thought filled Laura with such anger that she began to wonder how she would behave the next time she found herself alone with Malcolm.

Carlita entered the room soundlessly. She deposited the breakfast tray on the vanity top and took up the hairbrush. While Laura poured cream into her tea, Carlita began to brush and style her hair.

"You no sleep well last night?"

"I slept, but . . . well . . . you mustn't say anything." Laura paused and looked toward the door, then decided to switch to Spanish. "I got up early this morning to give Esther a reading lesson."

"Ah," Carlita said, nodding. "I remember when you taught me English," she replied in her native tongue. "You are a wonderful teacher, Miss Laura."

"Thank you. I think it's important that people be able to read and write English. It is very difficult to conduct even the simplest business transaction without a proper command of the language. Reading is especially important, especially for the children. Now that the war is over, we must endeavor to do what we can to educate the former slaves."

Carlita carefully tucked a pin into Laura's hair and nodded. Laura nibbled on a piece of toast, then sipped at the steaming tea.

"You must hurry," Carlita said in English as she finished arranging Laura's hair. "Your mama says be ready to go by ten. She is anxious to see your sister."

"She feels Carissa's absence very keenly. . . . I'm sure Mother worries for her." Laura didn't bother to add her suspicions that there was good reason for her to do so.

Carlita smiled. "All mothers worry about their children."

Laura nodded and gave a quick look in the mirror. Carlita had fashioned Laura's hair in a simple but fetching manner atop her head. "It's lovely. Thank you."

Carlita hurried to the wardrobe and flung open the doors. "It is sunny out today, but not hot. What will you wear?"

"I suppose the blue walking dress," Laura said, hoping the temperature would remain cool. Her mother would want her dressed properly for their outing, but Laura had no desire to pass out from the heat should the day warm overly much.

By ten minutes before ten, Laura made her way to the front parlor, where she'd expected to find her mother waiting most impatiently. Instead, she was surprised to find her brother-in-law and mother in deep conversation.

"Your brother-in-law brings sad tidings," Mother declared.

"I'm afraid Carissa is feeling unwell. I have demanded she stay in bed and rest," Malcolm said as Laura entered the room.

Laura couldn't help but frown. "Perhaps we should go and tend to her, Mother."

Malcolm spun on his heel. "There is no need. She was already sleeping by the time I left."

Laura met his gaze and raised a brow in question. "Surely when she awakens she will need someone to assist her."

Malcolm shook his head. "I have everything well under control. I just wanted to stop by and let you know that she would be unable to join you today. Now if you'll excuse me, I must hurry or I'll be late for my next appointment."

Laura wanted to ask him about his job, but Malcolm was already halfway to the door. She followed him and when he opened the front door, Laura called out, "What type of sickness is my sister suffering?"

Malcolm stopped just outside the house. He looked at her with an expression that suggested annoyance. "Nothing more than a headache. I'm sure she'll feel better soon."

Laura narrowed her gaze. "I suppose she's been working too hard . . . moving furniture and such."

Malcolm looked at her as if she'd lost her mind. "Movin' furniture? Hardly. Carissa wouldn't have the ability to move those heavy pieces. Now if you'll excuse me, I must be on my way."

Laura watched him hurry to where he'd tied off his horse. Malcolm mounted and gave her a brief salute, then kicked the horse harder than needed. He had no way of knowing that by his own admission he had condemned himself. No doubt the bruises Carissa suffered were delivered by his hands. Laura could only pray that Carissa's headache, if indeed it was a simple headache, wasn't also brought on by Malcolm's actions.

Malcolm rolled a cigarette between his fingers and threw a furtive glance at the man seated directly across from him.

"What were you able to learn, Jed?"

The man glanced over his shoulder toward the open door of Lowe's home office. "You sure we're safe here?" He didn't wait for a reply but continued in a rapid drawl. "I reckon you know about all them fellas who was taken off Mustang Island two days back. The army figures they were up to no good. Fact is, those men were just huntin' jackrabbits. Well, one of the men is Ralph Masters' little brother Tommie. Now Ralph wants to bust him and his friends out. Said he was figuring to come see you about it."

"We haven't got time to be worryin' over such trivial matters and we can't risk being found out. We have a higher callin' to put our minds to. Tell Masters I said to forget about springin' Tommie and get back to findin' a way to get us more guns."

Jed nodded. "I told him you'd say that. He don't cotton to

his baby brother havin' to sit in jail, but I told him weren't no skin off his nose. Them Yankees will let those boys go soon as they make a show at holdin' 'em."

"That's my thought, as well." Malcolm lit his cigarette. "What about the powder coming up from Mexico?"

The man leaned back and shrugged. "Ain't right sure. The fellas that was supposed to bring it in fell on hard times with the law in Brownsville."

Malcolm lowered his cigarette and blew out a thick puff of smoke. "We don't have time for this kind of nonsense. Where is the wagon?"

"I was told it's in a barn on the other side of the border. I'm guessin' it's probably with the Sanchez family."

"We haven't got time for guesswork. Ride down there tonight and bring that wagon back. Take Bill and Sam with you if you can't manage it alone. Just do what you need to do and get back here with that gunpowder."

Jed got to his feet. "There's one more thing."

Malcolm eyed him a moment, then took a long drag on the cigarette. "Go on," he finally said.

"Well, word's come that the Yankees are plannin' to move the colored troops out of here by the first part of November."

"They've been rumoring such things for months."

"But this time we got more proof," Jed replied. "Sam's wife works at the Ironclad House, as you'll recall. She says it's come down all official-like. The Yankees are trying to make the folks in Corpus feel better, I guess."

Malcolm considered this news for a moment. "The Yankees don't care how we feel. They imposed black soldiers on us as a means of humiliation. I doubt Sherman or Grant care a lick about our feelings." He grew silent for a moment and reflected on their plans. "We'll just have to work harder and faster. We can't hope to restart the fightin' unless we make a good show of killin' most of the colored forces. Once the Yankees see how determined we are, then they'll skedaddle in fear."

"You reckon they'll let Texas go back to bein' its own country?" Jed asked.

Malcolm shrugged. "If they need persuadin', I'm sure we can do that." Just then he heard the front door open and jumped to his feet.

Carissa had gone out shopping earlier and wasn't due back until much later. Malcolm put a finger to his lips and Jed nodded.

"Malcolm?" Carissa called. "Malcolm, are you home?"

She entered the office and stopped short at the sight of Jed Lanz.

"What are you doing here?" Malcolm demanded.

"I might ask you the same thing. I saw your horse out front." Her expression immediately turned worried. "You didn't lose your job, did you?"

Malcolm glared. "Jed, I think we're done for the day. Go on and see to those things we talked about."

Jed nodded and gave a slight bow in Carissa's direction. "Ma'am."

Malcolm barely allowed for the front door to slam before turning to his wife. "You said you'd be gone most of the day. I don't appreciate you lying to me."

"I wasn't lying," she stated. "I wasn't feeling well, so I finished my shopping early."

Malcolm glanced at the clock. It was nearly two. He still needed to ride out to meet with a couple of the men at the shack outside of town. He got to his feet and began to stuff papers into a satchel.

"Why are you home?" Carissa asked in an innocent manner.

Malcolm paused. "My business is just that. My business."

She shrugged. "I just wondered, that's all. I would have come home sooner and fixed you some lunch . . . had I known you were here." She smiled sweetly.

She was really quite a beauty, Malcolm thought to himself. If there were more time, he might very well like to linger here with her. They were, after all, newlyweds.

"You didn't lose your job, did you?" Carissa asked again. There was a disapproving tone to her voice that irritated Malcolm more than he could explain.

He fixed her with a cold, hard stare. "What did I just say about my business being my own?"

Carissa narrowed her eyes. He could see that her stubborn determination was about to rear its ugly head. He held up his index finger. "Before you think to sass me, remember what happened the last time."

He could see the words had their desired effect. Carissa seemed to shrink before his very eyes. Malcolm glanced at the clock again and went back to shoving papers into the satchel. "I did not lose my job. We were well ahead on orders and they closed the mill early."

Carissa accepted the lie as easily as she had accepted his others. "I see. Well, I certainly hope they won't dock you in pay. After all, good work should be rewarded."

"I'm sure that's what they meant to do by giving us time off," Malcolm said, barely keeping his temper in check. "So if I were you, I wouldn't worry my pretty little head about whether there will be a smaller paycheck. Haven't I provided well for you?"

He hadn't, but it didn't hurt to suggest that he had. Even if her parents had purchased the house and most of its furnishings, Malcolm put food on the table. She couldn't fault him for that.

"I suppose you have."

Her simple statement irked Malcolm, but he didn't have time to deal with her. "I won't be back until late. Maybe you should take that time to practice cooking and knitting."

"That reminds me of two things," Carissa said quickly. "One is that I wondered when we might hire some help. Nothing too fancy—maybe a cook and a housekeeper."

"You're the cook and housekeeper," he said, losing his patience. "That's what God intended you to do, along with pleasing me. And what would please me just now is for you to stop complainin' about hired help."

"Well then, I wonder if we might set plans into motion for our first dinner party."

He looked at her and shook his head. "A minute ago you were worried about whether the mill was going to dock my pay, and now you want to spend money to hire servants and throw an elaborate party?"

"Not elaborate. Just something simple. It's expected, and if you want to stay in the good graces of society . . . well . . . it's just one of those things that must be done."

Malcolm frowned. He'd never known much about society. Having been raised solely by his father, Malcolm had avoided such matters. It was only by happenstance that he had found himself marrying Carissa Marquardt from one of Corpus Christi's finer families. The money and connections her family afforded him were too great to pass by. Why her parents had ever agreed to allow them to court and eventually marry was beyond him. He supposed it had to do with the fact that Carissa was a spoiled brat. Even now she was pouting.

"If we do not host a dinner to show everyone how happy we are," Carissa continued, "people will talk."

"Let them," he said, closing the latches on the satchel. "Our happiness is none of their business."

Carissa shook her head. "I realize you aren't from . . . the city, but in society this is the way things are done. To breech that etiquette will bring unwanted attention. If we avoid socializing for much longer, the pastor will feel it necessary to pay us a visit."

Malcolm scowled. "I won't be dictated to by your social circles." But in truth, he needed those irritating people in order to move about freely and gain information. He softened his expression. "But if you want a dinner party, then I will allow for it."

She smiled and rushed into his arms. "Thank you. I'll be very careful with the expenses. Perhaps Mother would even help me."

He kissed her hard, then put her away from him. "I need to go. I have things to tend to."

"But when will you return?"

"Carissa, we've gone over this before. I'm a man of business. You are my wife. You have no right to challenge my authority." He narrowed his eyes. "Now stop pestering me or . . ." He let the words trail off. She knew good and well that his temper could get the best of him.

She hugged her arms to her breasts. "You've changed. You aren't the same man who courted me."

He laughed in a harsh manner and pushed past her. "I've always been this man, Carissa. You just never bothered to notice. You were too busy batting your eyes and playing upon my manly nature." Pausing at the door, Malcolm turned and met his wife's disappointed expression.

"The sooner you come to understand, the better. I'm a man of opportunity. Now that the war is over, there are a great many opportunities that demand my attention. Stay out of my business, or suffer the consequences."

Laura picked at her dinner and noticed that her mother and father were equally lost in thought. The house wasn't the same without the vivacious Carissa to entertain them with her stories of whom she'd seen that day and what they were doing.

Pushing back the half-eaten meal, Laura sighed. "What news is there from town, Father?"

Her father looked up in surprise. "News? I could not say. I've been busy working to push through those plans for the dredging of the harbor channels."

It was a boring topic, but Laura thought it better than nothing at all. "And have the plans been approved?"

"No," her father replied. "There are still arguments about the best places to dig and the cost to do so. I continue to remind everyone from the mayor to the businessmen of this fair city that the sooner we have a more adequate shipping lane, the more money and commerce we can move in Corpus."

"Seems reasonable," Laura said.

"You would like to imagine it so," her father said in disgust, "but it is far from the truth. As a Southern state, we are being punished, despite there being a fair number of Union supporters here who remained loyal."

Laura at last found interest in his comments. "Punished in what way?"

"Funding and leadership, primarily. Texas wouldn't have even joined the Union had it not been due to a desperate need for money and protection. The former more than the latter as far as most Texan men are concerned.

"Now the government in Washington wants to force its authority on each of the rebellious states to drive home a point of subjugation. We haven't even been formally allowed to rejoin the Union. God alone knows when sound judgment will prevail in Washington."

"Goodness, Stanley, must we talk of such things?" Mother said, motioning for the maid to clear the table.

"Well, it seems we must," he replied. "The days to come are going to be grim if people do not learn to put aside their anger. It's not just a matter of Union and Confederate; it's arguments over Protestant and Catholic, black and white, Mexican and Indian. Not to mention that there is a push to populate this state with those who would just as soon return to the days of the Texas Republic. If we don't find a way to unite in our efforts and stand together as an American state, I fear we may well find ourselves fighting yet another war."

"Oh, surely not," Mother said. "So much destruction has already been done. So many of our gallant lads have died or suffered horrible wounds." She shuddered. "I simply cannot speak on this subject anymore." She started to rise and Laura's father went quickly to assist her. "I will bid you both good evening. I believe I will retire early to my rooms. I feel a headache coming on."

"Good night, Mother," Laura said.

Father kissed Mother on her cheek and whispered something Laura couldn't hear. She hoped her father would sit again so that she might speak to him about her brother-in-law. She wanted to see if he might share any of her concerns.

Settling back in his chair, Father peered down at his empty coffee cup.

"I can pour you another cup," Laura said, getting to her feet. "I was hoping you might spend a few more minutes in my company. I must admit that I miss the long talks we used to have during the war. You always made me feel so safe. . . ." She retrieved the silver pot. "So safe and at peace. I knew that while the world had gone mad outside our walls, inside things remained much the same."

Laura poured the coffee and returned the pot to the sideboard. "You have always had a gentle spirit, Father. I love that about you. You care about the people around you, no matter the color of their skin or the view of their politics. I suppose that's why I've always enjoyed our talks. You've helped me to think and evaluate the world in a way that so many of my friends could not."

"You've a quick mind, Laura. It's not often appreciated in a woman, but I find it quite valuable."

"Thank you, Father. Brandon Reid has said much the same."

Her father's expression turned serious. "You have spent a good deal of time in his company."

Laura nodded. "I have."

"Has he spoken to you of marriage?"

She was stunned at this bold question. "No. Has he spoken to you?"

Her father chuckled. "No, but it wouldn't surprise me if he did."

"I can tell his affections for me are growing. I see a certain look in his eyes—a gentleness in his mannerisms." Laura's thoughts drifted.

"Ah, then it is mutual love."

She turned to her father. "Why do you say that?"

"I see a certain look in *your* eyes. It isn't one that is easily concealed. My guess is that you have lost your heart to this young man."

She nodded, feeling rather sheepish. "I suppose I have."

"And if he were to ask for your hand . . . you would want me to give my blessing?"

She smiled. "I would."

"Have you considered that such a thing might take you from Texas?" her father asked in a gentle manner.

It was the one thing Laura didn't like to think about. She longed to see other parts of the country, even the world, but she had no desire to leave Texas permanently. "I suppose I haven't dwelled for long on that possibility. Since Brandon has said nothing of making our courtship permanent, I suppose I have avoided such thoughts."

"Still, it is something that must be considered. He's from Indiana, and his family still hails from that state. It seems likely he would want to return. Especially now that he has resigned from his position in the army."

Laura thought of the situation with Malcolm. "Do you think that Carissa is happy?" she asked without meaning to.

Her father grew thoughtful. "I suppose you are wondering if she's happy because she married a Texan rather than someone from another part of the country." Laura said nothing and he continued. "I would imagine she's happy for such a choice. Although Malcolm is from the western reaches of the state, I believe he intends to remain in Corpus Christi."

"What makes you suppose that?" Laura asked, trying to sound only slightly interested.

"Well, he has asked a great many of my friends—Union men—as to how he might show his support. He wants to put the war behind him and get involved in businesses that will benefit the state—even the country. I admire his desire to do so. He could be bitter like many of his former ranks, but Malcolm wants something more."

Laura frowned and lowered her head to give a slight cough. She didn't want her father to see her reaction. Malcolm wanted something more—of this she had no doubt. Unfortunately that something more involved murder and destruction.

"Now, if you'll excuse me," her father said, getting to his feet, "I have some reports to read before I retire."

"I understand," Laura replied. "I love you, Father. I hope you will always remember that, no matter whom I marry or where I go. You were the first man I loved, and you will always hold that special place in my heart." She stretched up on tiptoe and kissed his cheek.

16

Laura accompanied Esther to the poorest part of town and barely managed to hide her frown as Esther pointed to the shack that was her home. "My boys be in there awaitin'. I's mighty happy ya comed to teach 'em to read."

"Everyone should have that opportunity," Laura said, trying not to reveal her distress over the conditions of the neighborhood. All around her garbage and animals littered the streets, while children of varying color played amid the debris.

Esther pushed open the unpainted wood door to her home. Laura imagined it afforded only the tiniest amount of security. The wood was thin and construction was poorer than any Laura had known. Inside the single room was a crude table by the window and two equally rough stools. A single chair was positioned by a small bed on the other side of the room.

"Shem, Ham, you knows Miss Laura," Esther said, pointing to her two boys. "Shem, bring Miss Laura the chair."

Laura hadn't seen the boys since they'd accompanied their mother during the summer to help with the gardening. The seven- and six-year-olds looked up at her in wide-eyed amazement. No doubt they had never seen a white woman in their house before. Shem hurried to do his mother's bidding.

"Your mother tells me that you would like to learn to read and write," Laura said with a smile. "You two look smart, so I would imagine you will learn very fast. Just like your mama."

Shem, the older of the two, positioned the chair by the table. "Ya's gonna teach us for sure?" His voice held an awe that made Laura smile.

"Well, many schools have men for their schoolmasters, but I'm hoping you won't mind having a lady teacher. I love to read, and I think you will love it, as well." She took a seat and put her satchel on the table.

Ham scooted off an old wooden crate and came to where Laura stood. Light filtered in from the single opening where a window should have been. "You is pretty, Miss Laura." He reached up as if to touch her hand, then drew back as if remembering such a thing was forbidden.

Laura would have no part of it. She reached out her hand and waited until the boy placed his tiny brown fingers in her palm. She smiled and closed her fingers over his. "I thank you for the compliment. Come, let's get to work."

Esther seemed far more at ease here in her own home than in the Marquardt kitchen. Studying at her own table, despite its deplorable condition, seemed to help Esther focus on her work.

She smiled at her boys. "Y'all do ever'thin' Miss Laura say, and she teach ya to read."

Two days before, Esther had approached Laura regarding her boys. Laura was pleased; Esther had proven herself a capable student and Laura hoped that as Esther continued to learn she could in turn teach her children. But for now, Laura was delighted Esther trusted her to instruct her sons. It fed Laura's desire to go among the blacks and teach, though her mother and father would no doubt disapprove.

"George Davies say no black boy can learn to read. It against the law," Shem declared.

Laura looked to Esther. The older woman shook her head. "George Davies be a no-account white trash boy. He mean as an ol' cracker." She seemed to be embarrassed by her words and lowered her face. "Pardon, Miss Laura."

Laura had heard the term *cracker* before. It referenced the whip-cracking slave owners who often beat their slaves into submission. "That's quite all right, Esther." Laura opened her satchel and drew out two slate boards and chalk. "I brought these for you two to use. Your mama already has one, so now you can practice your letters, as well."

The boys looked in wide-eyed amazement as Laura handed over the gifts.

"What ya say?" Esther prompted.

"Thank ya, Miss Laura," the boys replied in unison.

"You are very welcome. I want you to forget all about the things that other people have said to you. You are smart boys—I can tell." She picked up a piece of chalk. "Now I want to show you how to make the letter *A*."

At the end of the hour, Laura packed up her things and got to her feet. "I'll come again next Saturday," she promised. "In the meantime, you boys keep practicing and don't forget what you learned today. Try to find things that you think start with an *A* or a *B*."

"Like apple?" the younger of the two boys asked.

"She done tol' us that," Shem chided.

"But he is right. Apple starts with *A*, and I'm proud of Ham for remembering that."

Esther headed for the door. "Ham, ya needs to find yar Sunday shirt so's I can mend it. Shem, ya peel dem 'taters. I's gonna walk Miss Laura back to her carriage."

The boys nodded and Laura threw them a smile. "I'll see you next week."

She stepped out of the clean but sparse house and into the sad little neighborhood. How she wished she could help the people there. The shantytown had been inhabited mostly by poor whites and Mexicans prior to the war. Now more and more blacks were moving into the neighborhood. Laura knew that even with this hint at independence there were high prices to pay. If she understood correctly, the colored people—especially the men—were required to have a white sponsor in order to live and work. She'd heard her father discuss this in brief with Brandon and decided she would have to ask one or both for more information.

"I's mighty grateful for what yar doin' for my boys," Esther said as they walked. "Ain't nobody since Miz Bryant what treated me so good."

"Mrs. Bryant was the woman you were working for here in Corpus Christi?" Laura asked.

Esther nodded. "She and Mr. Bryant had theyselves a right

fine plantation up around Austin way. They owned me and my Jonah since we was lil 'uns. They let us marry, and when I had babies Miz Bryant say we would always stay with 'em. Weren't a lot of white folk that good."

Laura looked at Esther. "How did you make your way to Corpus Christi?"

"Mr. Bryant, he died in the same epidemic what kilt my man and youngest boy. Miz Bryant sell the farm and freed the slaves, but she asked iffn me and the boys wanna come with her to Corpus Christi. We had nowhere else to go. Afore she die last April, she give me a little bit of money and tell me to go take care of my boys. It were hard, but I rented that little shack what ya saw and then did what I could to earn me some money. Then I come to work for yar family."

"I'm so glad you did." Laura truly meant it. She knew her father was a generous employer. His kindness to those he employed generally resulted in workers who went above and beyond the mere requirements of their tasks.

As they approached the safer reaches of town where Laura had left the buggy, she paused and looked at Esther. "I know life has not always treated you well, but you are doing a good thing for your boys and for yourself in learning to read. Your boys will find it much easier to get work if they have the ability to read and write. Perhaps they can even go on to college."

Esther shook her head. "Bein' able to read still ain't gonna make they skin white. Ain't no white man ever gonna respect 'em so long as they black. Change like that ain't gonna come in my lifetime, not less'n we can touch the sky."

Laura knew the sad truth of the woman's words. "Perhaps in

time, things will be different. We've already seen a great many changes, Esther. We must trust God to help us through."

"God, He be all I got," she said with a thoughtful smile. "He all I need. He faithful."

Laura nodded. "So faithful."

When Brandon arrived later that day, Laura was still thinking about Esther's comments. Was there really so little hope that things could change in her lifetime? When she and Brandon stepped outside before supper, Laura found herself wanting to know what he thought.

"I have a secret," she began.

Brandon looked at her with a raised brow. "A secret?"

She smiled. "I'm giving reading lessons to Esther and her sons."

"Esther is the one who helps in the kitchen, isn't she?"

Laura nodded. "She used to be a slave. She was one of the few fortunate enough to remain with her husband and children. But her husband died a couple of years back. She lost an infant, as well. She mentioned to me how much she wanted to learn to read, and so I agreed to meet with her each morning. Now we're meeting just once a week. Trying to do it every day was too daunting." Laura gauged his expression for disapproval but found none. She hurried to continue.

"I know your family was involved in helping slaves escape the South. Can you tell me more about it? How did you get involved?"

Brandon placed her hand in the crook of his arm and began

to stroll the grounds. He was silent a moment before replying. "My father is a minister, as you know. He also raises some of the most beautiful Thoroughbred horses you would ever want to own."

"I remember your mentioning that." Laura smiled.

"Yes. His business as a horseman often took him south. He had many connections in Tennessee and Georgia. While there, he often saw the abuses going on. He would tell my mother and me how there were men who treated their horses better than their workers. Men who would never consider laying a whip to the back of a Thoroughbred would beat a Negro slave to death." Brandon shook his head. "Some of his stories were appalling, and I will not repeat them."

"I would not want you to dwell on the ugliness. Tell me instead what you did to help the slaves."

"We worked with friends and managed to locate safe havens for those on the run. Sometimes my father would even hide runaways in his wagon. He was very nearly caught on more than one occasion, but God always seemed to shield the eyes of those slave hunters. My father said it was almost as if they became invisible." Brandon paused and gave a chuckle. "He used to love to tell about the time he was heading home after having delivered a string of horses to a very harsh man in Georgia. He arranged to bring two young slaves—a husband and wife—back to Indiana with him. Unfortunately the owner found out the couple was missing and set out searching for them before my father got all that far."

"What happened?" Laura asked, gripping his arm a little tighter.

"They caught up to my father, though the owner had no idea he was the one who had helped the runaways. The man figured the couple had used my father's presence as a diversion and had probably run off in the night. He ranted and raved about what he was going to do to those two when he found them. When the dog handlers caught up with him, the hounds went crazy, baying at the wagon. My father thought for sure that he would be found out."

"But he wasn't?"

"No. The owner chided the driver for not controlling the animals. He reminded his men that only the night before Negros had been crawling all over that wagon loading some of the goods my father had purchased or taken in trade. This was especially true of the young man my father had helped to escape. He had been helping to stack the load and so of course his scent was all over that wagon."

"How like God," Laura said in amazement.

Brandon nodded. "The two were hidden in with the crates and no one was the wiser. Father even encouraged the owner to check the load, feeling confident that he would refuse, which he did. When Father arrived across the river in Indiana, he began to sing hymns of thanksgiving. But it wasn't until he was safely on his own property that he began to relax."

"Where did the slaves go after that?"

The day was fading and Brandon turned to guide them back toward the house, where the lights had already been lit. "We had friends who lived about twenty miles to the north of us. We would send the runaways on to them and they in turn had someone else they could send them to after that. It wasn't easy, but it was the best we had to offer."

"Were you ever found out?"

Brandon shook his head. "There were many close calls, but it was by God's divine providence that we escaped mostly unnoticed. When I joined the army, I knew I wanted to work with some of those same men I'd helped to free."

"And do you have any regrets?"

He stopped and looked at her. "Only that we saved so few. So many perished before getting to us or shortly after. They were malnourished and sick from being on the run. Some had severe wounds from beatings." He shuddered and Laura put her hand on his cheek.

"You needn't dwell on it further. I'm proud to call you friend—to know what you did to help your fellowman. That's what I want to do, as well. I want to help the former slaves. The way I see it, the men in charge didn't want the blacks to be able to read and write for fear of the power it would give them. Knowledge is power . . . power that can change lives. I want to help bring that about."

Brandon raised her hand to his lips and kissed the back. "That's only one of the many things I adore about you."

She laughed, but the feel of his lips sent a delicious tingle down her spine. Laura felt weak-kneed and awkward.

"So . . . so you'll keep my secret?" she asked.

"One among many." Brandon looked up at the house and then back to Laura. "Have you had any further news on your brother-in-law?"

"None," Laura admitted. "I've scarcely seen my sister or Malcolm. I talked briefly to my father last evening, but he hadn't spoken to Malcolm, either. At least not recently. Father did mention a while back that Malcolm likes spending time with Father's Unionist friends. He said Malcolm desires to see the city return to normal, but I think Malcolm is all talk. He most likely wants to be with my father and his friends for other reasons."

"No doubt he's anxious to gather any helpful information for his cause," Brandon said, frowning. "Do you suppose your sister might be of help?"

"Carissa? She hates the affairs of men." Then Laura remembered something Carissa had told her a while back. "She did mention that Malcolm is using the first floor bedroom as an office. Carissa had no idea why he would need an office."

"Does he keep it locked?" Brandon asked.

"That would be my guess. Although I really don't know. I suppose I could go visit Carissa and see for myself."

"I don't like the idea of putting you in danger, but that would be useful information."

Laura nodded. "I'll see if I can convince Mother that we need to call on Carissa Monday. Would that be too soon?"

"It would be perfect. What time do you think you'll call?"

"I'll suggest that we should take Carissa to lunch. We'll send a note to her tonight."

"No, don't. It would be better if Malcolm doesn't suspect anything. Just show up to see her."

Laura knew it wouldn't be hard to convince her mother that they should call on Carissa. Just that morning her mother had been adamant that they needed to discuss the upcoming holidays.

"I imagine supper is ready," Laura said. She glanced toward the house and remembered something. "I wanted to ask you about your mother and father," she said, disappointed that they needed to go inside. "Perhaps you could tell me about them after we eat?"

"Perhaps," Brandon replied. "But I was rather hoping you would play for me tonight. I've enjoyed those times when you've offered us entertainment." He gave her arm a squeeze. "I find I enjoy very nearly anything, so long as you're involved."

Laura found herself flushing from his sweet comments. Without meaning to be so bold, she looked into his face. "I feel exactly the same where you are concerned. I find myself content to merely sit in your presence."

"Don't we sound like ever the boring old couple," Brandon said with a laugh.

"Comfortable," she replied. "Not boring and certainly not old. We're just comfortable with each other. That's something I've not experienced with a man before. Most of the boys who tried to court me were awkward and annoying. They either talked of themselves or tried constantly to steal a kiss."

Brandon roared with laughter at this. "I'd thought of doing just that, but I suppose now I shall have to refrain. I wouldn't want it said that I was awkward or annoying."

Laura felt her heart skip a beat. She would have loved nothing better than having Brandon steal a kiss. She tried to appear ever so casual as she entered the house. "I seriously doubt you are awkward at anything you set to do." She paused to throw him a smile, and her breath caught in her throat.

Brandon's eyes seemed to burn in the glow of the window lamps. He leaned close and whispered. "One day . . . perhaps we shall put that thought to the test."

Laura trembled as he took hold of her hand and drew her fingertips inches from his lips. "Hopefully that day will come sooner . . . than later."

Laura might have fainted dead away had her father not appeared in the hall. "There you two are. I thought I might have to send someone for you. Brandon, I think you'll be pleased with the fare tonight. We were lucky enough to be given a roast. Imagine that! It's been so long since I've had a decent piece of beef that I am thrilled at the prospect. I don't know when I've ever longed for anything quite so much."

Brandon looked at Laura and gave her a wink. "Neither do I."

Laura and her mother tried to visit her sister the next day and several days following, but Malcolm always met them at the door, claiming she was indisposed. Then notes began to arrive in her sister's handwriting, telling the family that she was suffering headaches or fatigue and that she didn't wish to have any company.

When this continued for nearly two weeks, Laura's fears began to escalate. Her mother, too, was greatly concerned—enough so that she'd asked Laura's father to seek out Malcolm at the flour mill to find out what was going on.

"The entire situation is far too secretive," Mother declared. "My son-in-law barely bids me good-day, then denies me the right to see our daughter."

Father had initially brushed aside her insistence. However, when Mother refused to let the matter drop, explaining that no one had seen anything of Carissa in half a month's time, Father finally agreed. Laura felt a sense of relief and dread mingled as one. What if Malcolm refused to tell her father what the problem was? What if he refused to allow them to see Carissa at all?

Stanley Marquardt arrived home around four thirty, and to Laura's surprise, Brandon was at his side. She hurried to greet the men, giving her father a quick peck on the cheek.

"Did you see Malcolm?"

"No." Her father looked to Brandon, who seemed just as disturbed.

"What's wrong?" Laura asked. She stepped closer to her father. "Mother had a headache and is resting, but you must tell me what's going on."

Father met her worried gaze. "No one at the flour mill even knew Malcolm. He's never held a position there."

Laura felt as if the air were suddenly sucked from the room. "What?" she gasped. "But where is he getting the money to support himself and Carissa?"

"Most likely he's gambling," her father replied. "I've been told more than once that he has a weakness for cards."

Laura looked at Brandon. They'd both had suspicions of Malcolm's underhanded dealings. His financial support was probably aided by those covert activities, as well.

"I'm very worried, Father. I think we should make plans to go over to their house late in the evening. They would have to be there then."

Her father considered this for a moment. "I might be able to arrange that later. For now, however, we have three men joining us for supper. I'm hoping you can make the necessary arrangements since your mother is incapacitated."

"Of course," Laura replied. "I'd be happy to." She looked to Brandon. "And will you be staying, as well?"

"Indeed. Two of the men are actually guests of mine in a way. I know one from the war."

Laura nodded. "I'm sure I will be happy to meet them both. When should we plan for supper, Father?"

"I believe six o'clock will give our guests plenty of time, don't you?" he asked Brandon.

"That should be fine. Will said they were going to check in at the hotel and then ride over. I would imagine they will be here most any time."

Laura glanced at the grandfather clock. "I'll speak to Cook right away." She left the two men and hurried to the kitchen.

The heavyset woman was humming as she stirred a pot at the stove. She glanced up and smiled when Laura entered the room.

"Ya looks happy, Miss Laura. I'm guessin' that Mr. Brandon be here."

Laura smiled. "He is and he's staying for supper. There will be two other guests besides him. Father wanted me to let you know so you could have the table set accordingly."

The older woman nodded. "I's gonna have us a mighty fine supper. Got dem cheesy grits Mr. Brandon like and a hot peach pie jes outta the oven. I fixed it jes hopin' it would bring him along to the house. Be nice and cooled off by the time they be ready for it." She paused for a moment and tapped her chin. "Believe I'll open up some tomato preserves an' slice up some of dat fresh rye bread Miz Clarence's girl brung over."

The Clarence family lived at the bottom of the bluff and they were always sharing wonderful recipes or delicacies from the kitchen. Laura looked to the counter where a large fish was laid out, ready to go into the oven. "It all sounds wonderful. Father said we should eat around six."

Cook nodded. "I see to it, Miss Laura. You can rest assured. I gots Effie help'n me today." Effie was Cook's fourteen-year-old granddaughter.

Laura started to go, then remembered her mother. "Could you please send Effie upstairs to see if Mother needs anything? I'd go myself, but I'm afraid she'd detain me." She turned, but stopped again. "Oh, and please have Effie tell Mother that father has business associates attending dinner, as well."

"I send her a'right." She headed for the back door and called out for her granddaughter.

With that, Laura made her way back to her father and Brandon, who were greeting two newly arrived guests. She heard one of the men call Brandon *Captain*, and knew this must be his friend from the war.

The men caught sight of her and paused in their conversation. Laura's father motioned her to join them. "Gentlemen, this is my daughter Laura."

"Ma'am," the two men said in unison, giving a slight bow.

Laura smiled. "Gentlemen."

Brandon furthered the introductions. "This is William Barnett and his friend Tyler Atherton. Barnett and I met each other during the war."

"Well, any friend of Mr. Reid's is certainly welcome here. Can I offer you gentlemen something to drink? Supper will be ready shortly, but I could have Cook prepare some coffee or tea."

"No, thank you," William Barnett replied. "We don't want to cause any inconvenience."

"It wouldn't be any trouble," Laura assured him.

Barnett shook his head. "We're fine."

Laura looked to Mr. Atherton, who nodded in agreement. "Just fine, ma'am."

Brandon turned to Laura. "Will and Tyler have come from the Dallas area to purchase some breeding stock for their ranches up north. Your father has agreed to write them letters of introduction on my behalf since I've known Will for many years."

"In fact," her father said, "I will see to that just now. Laura, why don't you entertain our guests?" He smiled at the men. "My daughter is an accomplished pianist and singer."

"Indeed she is," Brandon agreed.

"I'm sure we would enjoy such entertainment," Tyler Atherton said, smiling.

Laura felt her cheeks flush a bit, but nevertheless led the way to the music room. She was disappointed that she couldn't learn more from her father about Malcolm and Carissa. Hearing that Malcolm didn't have a job at the flour mill meant Malcolm had lied to them—lied about a simple job. Carissa was certain he worked at the mill; how would she react when she learned the truth?

More than ever, Laura felt the urgent need to see Carissa and know if she was well.

Laura frowned and pulled out the piano bench. She picked up several pieces of sheet music and positioned them in a pleasing order. Brandon came to her side as the other men took their seats.

"Shall I turn the pages for you?"

She looked up and nodded. "Thank you."

Laura began to play a popular tune that had come out during the war. The men listened in appreciation, keeping time by tapping their feet. She picked up the pace a bit and thought the melody quite gay. So much better than the sad songs of war and lost love.

After that she played several classical pieces that she'd long ago memorized, and by the time she was ready to return to the sheet music, her father had joined them. Seeing it was nearly six, Laura got to her feet. Just then Effie popped into the room and gave a deep curtsy.

"Supper be ready, Mr. Marquardt."

"Thank you, Effie." He motioned for Laura to come to his side. He took hold of his daughter almost possessively. "If you'll follow me, gentlemen."

Over supper they discussed life in Texas both before the war and during it. Laura learned that Mr. Barnett was a married man with children, while Mr. Atherton was working to reestablish his family's ranch.

"We struggled—not so much from the war, but rather the Comanche," Tyler explained while helping himself to a basket of bread.

"We often hear of the Comanche and Kiowa problems up north," Laura's father said.

"And when you combine the war and the torn allegiances," Tyler continued, "it's been a very dark time indeed. It was as if Texas had its own separate war of aggression."

"And do I understand correctly that you both served in the war, but on opposite sides?" Father asked.

Mr. Barnett nodded. "My father was a strong Union supporter."

"And what of you, Mr. Barnett?" Laura asked.

The man shrugged. "I was a strong supporter of my father." He smiled, but it didn't quite reach his eyes. "I never wanted war and would probably have gone on happily running the family ranch had he not insisted my brother and I join him to defend the Union. They gave their lives and I took a bullet, so the price was high."

Laura heard the sadness in his voice. "We saw many families at odds with one another. I pray now we will find a spirit of unity—that God can somehow knit us back together."

"That is my prayer, as well," Mr. Barnett admitted.

"What are your thoughts, Mr. Atherton?" Brandon asked. "Are you ready to put the war behind you, or do you desire, like some, to continue the fight?"

Atherton frowned. "I want to forget it ever took place. I saw a lot of death and suffering. I don't reckon I want to see that go on. I don't like other people tellin' our state what they can and can't do, but I reckon I wouldn't go to war over it again."

The conversation turned again with talk about the year's ranching in the north. Barnett was anxious to acquire a good bull or two for breeding. He hoped to continue building his herd.

"Now that the war is over, the rest of the country is desperate for Texas beef," he said, looking at Tyler.

The man nodded. "He's right. We've already been contacted by several investors looking to get our cattle to the yards in Kansas City and Chicago."

"During the war you couldn't give the cattle away, especially since the North wouldn't allow for it. Now everyone's clamoring for it. Prices are going through the roof. If the railroad investors will pick up laying track," Barnett declared, "we could haul them all the way up instead of having to drive them. That would keep them a lot fatter."

"I thought there were issues with driving Texas cattle north," Laura's father commented. "Some problem with tick fever, as I recall."

"There's always some issue to contend with," Tyler said. "But desperation makes folks forget their issues. We've even heard tell of a man who's trying to build a stockyard city in the middle of Kansas. Guess time will tell if that comes about."

"I'm interested in ranching myself," Brandon said, surprising Laura. "As I was telling you, I grew up raising horses, but of late I've found more and more interest in beef. I suppose I would do well to talk to you more on the details of such a life."

"You'd be welcome to come up and learn the ropes, so to speak," William Barnett told him. "Cattle ranching is sure to be a lucrative business for as long as there are people. Even though we had lean times during the war, it wasn't for a lack of interest or need from the general population. Had the North not put embargoes on the South and refused to allow the sales, we could have easily continued selling cattle. I'm sure between the two of us," he said, motioning to Tyler, "we could teach you just about everything you'd need to know for ranching in Texas."

Laura was eager to hear Brandon's response, but just then Effie brought in the fish platter and the talk moved back to the food. By the time the dessert was set before them, Laura found the men far more interested in talking about the growth of Corpus Christi.

The men retired for a time after the meal and it was nearly an hour later before Laura saw anything of Brandon again. He threw her an apologetic smile as he walked into the front parlor where she was reading.

"Would you care for some company?"

"Of course. I was nearly ready to take up smoking cigars so that I could join you."

Brandon laughed. "There was very little smoking going on, so that might have been quite a shock." He took a seat beside her on the settee. "You look lovely tonight."

"I could be wearing a flour sack and you'd say that," Laura said, closing her book. "But thank you."

"I would pay good money to see you wear a flour sack," he said in a hushed whisper.

Laura looked at him in shock. "Mr. Reid, how positively scandalous you've become."

He gave her a look that suggested she'd started the scandal, then grinned. "Nevertheless, I speak the truth."

"Sometimes," Laura said, growing thoughtful, "I still marvel at how you came into my life. Who would have thought that such an ugly ordeal in the back alleys of Corpus Christi could have led to such a beautiful acquaintance? It was as if God Himself had a hand in putting us together—as if there were a purpose in it all. I suppose I believe there was."

Brandon's face took on a pained expression before he looked away. Laura wasn't sure what caused his discomfort but figured it might well be embarrassment at how he had acted that day so long ago. Then again, maybe she'd been too forward. Embarrassed, she decided to bring up her brother-in-law.

"I know you said there were men watching Malcolm. Is he still in town? I haven't been able to see Carissa in weeks, and we're sick with worry."

"As I told your father, Malcolm is still in town and returns to the house each evening. Those watching him have seen a woman fitting Carissa's description and believe her to be safe. Other than that, I have very little information about her well-being."

"If she's there, then I'm going to see her," Laura said, looking at the clock. It was nearly nine and she knew that Brandon and the others would soon be leaving. "Perhaps you can drive me over there now?"

He shook his head. "Your father said you would ask, but he didn't want me to take you. He wants a chance to speak to Malcolm first. I think you should allow him that."

"But Carissa might need me."

"If she does, your father will hopefully be able to learn that, as well. He would probably rather I not tell you this, but he plans to go there quite early in the morning. Give him that, Laura. Afterward, if Malcolm still keeps you from seeing Carissa, I will help you."

She looked at him for a moment, then finally relented. "Very well. But I am not happy about it."

He moved a little closer to where she sat and threw her a look that left Laura trembling. "Perhaps I can get your mind off the matter. At least for a few minutes."

Shaking her head, Laura laughed nervously. "Brandon Reid, what are your intentions?"

He laughed. "Well, that's something that I think we definitely need to figure out."

"You don't know what your own intentions are?"

"Oh, I know very well what I have in mind," he replied. "I'm just not sure you would approve of them."

He had her full attention. "Perhaps you should explain."

He leaned ever closer and reached up to caress her face. Without giving her a chance to protest, Brandon very gently kissed her lips. Laura felt a wave of warmth spread throughout her body. She had never been kissed by a man—had fully intended to never be kissed by anyone other than her husband. When Brandon pulled away, Laura's fingers immediately touched her lips.

The sound of the other men coming from her father's study caused Laura to stand rather quickly. Brandon chuckled and did likewise. Unable to look away, Laura peered into his blue eyes and marveled at the feelings he'd evoked. If he had asked her in that moment to leave with him—to go north never to see her family again—Laura was certain she would say yes.

What a very dangerous state of mind, she thought. *Dangerous and wonderful all at the same time.*

As planned, Father visited Malcolm the following day. And while the man had been cordial, he firmly suggested that as newlyweds, they needed their privacy. Determined to keep the peace, her father relented and remained silent about Malcolm's nonexistent job.

Though frustrated by Malcolm's control over Carissa, Laura felt a measure of relief as the colored troops were mustered out of Corpus Christi without any major problems. Laura had no way of knowing if the additional surveillance Brandon put on Malcolm had thwarted his plans, but she didn't care. There were no explosions of powder and no large number of soldiers killed. So long as Malcolm's devious and deadly schemes were set aside, Laura felt they'd gained a victory. What did not set well was the fact that they were still unable to see Carissa.

Finally one morning she simply announced to her mother,

"We're going to see Carissa," and pulled on her gloves. "One way or another."

They had the driver take them over in the carriage, just in case Carissa answered the door and wanted to return home with them. Approaching the dwelling, Laura could see that all of the curtains and shades had been pulled tight. She hardly gave the driver time to set the brake before she jumped from the carriage in a most unladylike fashion. Leaving the driver to assist her mother, Laura all but ran up the walk to the door.

She pounded the heavy wood with her fists, then reached for the knocker. "Carissa, it's Laura and Mother. Let us in." She continued to call and to pound for what seemed an eternity.

"Where could she be?" Mother asked, wringing her gloved hands. "She surely must be here."

Laura peered into the house, but it was impossible to see through the drawn drapes. "I'm going to try the door." She turned the knob easily enough, but something held the door in place. "It seems to be blocked with something," she said, looking to her mother. "Help me."

Both women put their bodies against the door and pushed, but nothing happened. Mother began to weep and Laura felt guilty for forcing her to come.

"Let me take you to the carriage. I'll get you settled, then I'll go around back and try that door."

Mother reluctantly agreed, but once they were halfway down the walk she stopped. "No, I want to come with you."

"Of course." As Laura turned them back toward the house, she saw the fluttering movement of the upstairs curtains.

"Look!" she said, pointing upward. "Someone is up there.

I'm certain of it. I saw the curtains fall back into place just now."

The two women hurried around the side of the house and made their way through the tiny yard to the back entrance. Laura tried the door and was relieved when it gave freely. She pushed it back and stepped into the house.

"Carissa Elaine Marquardt Lowe!" she called loudly. "We know you're up there. Please come down here!"

Laura pulled Mother with her through the tiny kitchen and into the short narrow hall. When they reached the stairs, Laura cried out again. "Carissa, Mother and I are coming up to see you."

"No." Carissa's voice was flat. "I'll come down."

The house was dark, so Laura went to the front drapes and pulled them back to let in some light. In doing so, they were better able to see Carissa as she made her way to the bottom of the stairs. Both Laura and their mother gasped at the sight.

"What in the world has happened to you?" Mother asked, rushing to her daughter.

Bruises covered most of Carissa's face. Forcing her focus downward, Laura also saw discoloration around Carissa's neck and shoulders.

"Malcolm did this," Laura said in a hush.

Mother looked at Laura as if she'd lost her mind. "What did you say?"

Carissa gently pushed Mother's hands from her face. "No," she said, almost sounding frantic. "I fell. I fell down the stairs. My heel caught the hem of my gown. It was just an accident." She looked to her mother and smiled. "See, I am fine. You know how easily I bruise. It's nothing, really." She waved her arms and took several steps. "See, nothing broken."

"When did this happen?" Laura asked.

"Oh, a few days ago. I could hardly go out in public like this," she said. "And of course, I didn't want you to see me this way. I know I look frightful. Why, the shock on your faces even now is enough to make me regret even receiving you."

"But you didn't receive us," Laura said, not buying a word of her sister's story. "You left us to break into your house. Speaking of which . . ." Laura turned to check the front door. There was a metal bar in place that had been affixed there to keep the door from being pushed open. "What is this?"

Carissa shrugged. "Malcolm worries about everything. It's just his way of keeping me safe. Honestly, you mustn't go on so. Shall I make tea?"

Laura shook her head. "No. You will go upstairs and get what things you need. You're coming home with us."

"Yes," Mother agreed. "You will do exactly that. You need my care."

"I am a married woman." Carissa's stance seemed a little less certain. "I can't just leave. Besides, Malcolm is away on business. He won't know what's become of me."

Laura stepped forward and took hold of her sister's shoulders. A cry of pain slipped from Carissa's lips and she immediately put her hand over her mouth. Laura stood up straighter. "I'll go pack your things. Mother, help Carissa to the carriage."

Laura went to the front door and threw off the metal bar. It was heavy, but she found that anger gave her unexpected strength. "Go this way."

She hurried up the stairs before Carissa could offer a word of protest. Laura found her sister's bedroom and quickly moved about the room, grabbing things she thought most necessary. She didn't worry about hats or gloves or hairbrushes. Carissa could borrow all of those things from Laura. Instead, Laura collected a couple of gowns that had been draped across the end of the bed. It looked as if Carissa had been mending them.

"Probably because he tore them," Laura muttered. Her rage drove her to kick a pair of Malcolm's trousers clear across the room. "Monster! What kind of man beats his wife like that?"

Laura headed for the stairs and very nearly lost her balance. Shifting the clothes, she took a better hold on the rail and for a moment doubt crossed her mind. What if Carissa was telling the truth? Maybe she had only fallen down the stairs. Maybe her embarrassment had caused her to plead with Malcolm to say nothing. It was possible.

"But not likely," Laura muttered and continued down. The man was violent. He'd committed murder, hadn't he? Brandon was certain he was responsible, and she had overheard Malcolm talk about blowing up Yankees.

Laura paused for a moment at the front door. She needed to calm her spirit and get control of her anger. She was allowing emotions to cloud her good judgment.

"Oh, Father God," she prayed aloud, "please let the truth be known."

❧

With Carissa safely installed in her old bedroom and their mother busy seeing to a tray of food, Laura questioned her sister.

"You have to be honest with me about this. I want to help you," Laura began. "I know you didn't fall down the stairs."

Carissa opened her mouth and then closed it again. Tears welled in her eyes. "I can't tell you."

"Yes you can. We're sisters, and you can tell me anything. I already know that Malcolm did this to you, so why not tell me why?" Laura gave an exasperated sigh. "Not that there is any good reason for beating your wife."

Carissa remained very quiet for several minutes. Laura waited, knowing that sooner or later Carissa would tell her the truth.

"I wanted to surprise Malcolm at work one day," Carissa began. She sounded very much like a little girl telling of a horrible fright. Her voice trembled and her hands shook as she continued. "I went . . . to the mill. I went there to . . . just . . . just see him and . . . walk home with him. I got there and . . . and the men were leaving so I asked them about Malcolm. And . . . and . . . ."

"And they'd never heard of him?" Laura asked, reaching for her sister's hands.

Lifting her surprised face to meet Laura's, Carissa nodded. "He doesn't work at the flour mill."

"I know. Father just learned the same thing."

Carissa shook her head. "I was so shocked—hurt that he wouldn't just tell me about his job. You see, I'd asked him many times about his work. He always got mad and told me to mind my own business."

"And he'd hit you if you didn't stop pestering him," Laura offered matter-of-factly.

Her sister was still unable to admit the truth. She lowered her bruised face and continued. "I went home, and he still wasn't there. I waited and it was very late before he finally showed up. I asked him where he'd been. He said he had to work late at the mill. I called him a liar."

Laura winced, imagining the man's anger at his wife's accusation. She gave Carissa's hands a gentle squeeze. "Go on."

"He flew into a rage like I've never seen. He wasn't even the same man. He threw things. He told me I was . . . was . . . a traitor to the South—that my family were traitors. He said he wished he'd never . . . married me." She sniffed. "I told him I felt the same way. I told him . . . I said. . . ." She pulled her hands from Laura's hold and covered her face. A muffled sob escaped.

Laura waited for what seemed an eternity for Carissa to continue. She didn't know what else to do. The very idea of someone hurting her was breaking Laura's heart.

Finally Carissa seemed to regain control. She straightened and drew a deep breath. "I told him I wished I were dead, and he said . . . he said that was one wish he could give me."

"Oh, Rissa," Laura said, using her sister's long-forsaken nickname. She tried to take Carissa into her arms, but her sister wouldn't have it.

"I'm sorry I couldn't tell you." She met Laura's eyes. "I can't tell Mother. She mustn't ever know."

"Keeping it from her doesn't change that it happened."

"No, but it will keep her from the nightmares you may well have once I tell you exactly what he did to me."

Laura felt her blood go cold. For a moment she wasn't sure that she wanted to hear any more. It was obvious that Malcolm had beat Carissa within an inch of her life.

Without warning her sister began to give the horrendous details of that night and of a beating that should have claimed her life. As Carissa spoke, it was as if the entire scene played out in Laura's mind. She could almost feel the blows—see the man's rage.

"I begged for mercy," Carissa said, finally coming to the end of her story. "I told him I would never question him again. I begged him, Laura."

"I'm so sorry." Laura realized there was nothing else she could say. No amount of comforting words would change what Malcolm Lowe had done. Nothing she could do would restore Carissa's innocence. For a moment Laura just sat shaking her head. One thing was for certain: Their mother could never know. The abuses heaped upon her sister that night were not the kind of thing you could repeat—especially not to one's mother.

"I guess you were right, Laura. I really didn't know Malcolm well enough to marry him," Carissa admitted. "I thought only with my heart and not with my head, and now it's too late."

"It's never too late," Laura replied. "You can just stay here. Father needs to know what has happened. He won't allow Malcolm to even set foot in this house."

Carissa shook her head vehemently. "No. Please. I do not want either one of them to know. You cannot tell them. You must keep this secret for me."

Laura didn't know what to say. How could she agree to keep such a secret? If she said nothing and Carissa returned to Malcolm, the next beating could very well claim her life.

For several minutes the two women just sat, staring at nothing. It wasn't until their mother returned with a tray of food for Carissa that Laura could even pull her thoughts from the tortures her sister had described.

"I brought you soup. Cook had some left from lunch." Mother placed the tray on Carissa's lap. "It's fish chowder—your favorite. I've brought you some of Cook's hush puppies too. They're cold, but the soup is hot. That's what took so long."

"Thank you," Carissa said, smiling at their mother. "I will eat it and then I believe I'll sleep. Honestly, you mustn't worry. I'm fine. Just tired."

Mother seems to want to believe this more than anything, Laura thought. She returned Carissa's smile and patted her on the head as though she were a small child.

"Very good. I believe I will take a nap myself." Mother smoothed the front of her gown. "Laura, a rest would do you good, as well."

"I'm sure it would, Mother," Laura said, unwilling to argue. But she seriously wondered if she would ever be able to rest easy again.

"Very good," Mother said. "I will see you both at supper."

Laura would have laughed at the absurdity of it all had the situation not been so grave. Once their mother had exited the room, however, she looked at Carissa.

"I will keep your secret on one condition. You must never . . . ever . . . go back to him."

Carissa toyed with a hush puppy, turning it over and over in her delicate fingers. "That could be a problem," she said in barely a whisper.

"Only for Malcolm," Laura declared, getting to her feet. "I'll put myself between you and him before I'll ever let him take you from this place." She thought for a moment of the investigation and how Malcolm was thought to have committed murder. She longed to tell Carissa of Brandon's suspicions, but something held her back.

She swallowed hard. "I'm sorry for losing my temper, but I am so angry right now I don't even trust myself. You are safe here," Laura said, taking a deep breath to steady her emotions. "That's all that matters. Eat your soup and rest. I'll check in on you later."

Laura didn't wait for Carissa to respond, but instead moved to the open door. "I won't sleep. I'll listen for you and if you need me, just call."

"I think I'm with child."

The words hung in the air. Laura couldn't imagine that she'd heard correctly. After the severe beating her sister had received, how could she possibly be pregnant?

"I know it seems difficult to believe, and perhaps it's not true. But I had my cycle just days before we married and I've not had one since," Carissa said. "I think despite everything that has happened . . . I'm going to have a baby."

19

Brandon arrived at the Marquardt house the next day. He had made arrangements the week before to take Laura out for a buggy ride, and he'd even managed to borrow a very charming two-seat basket phaeton with a fringed top. It was smaller than the last phaeton he'd borrowed; in fact, it was more of a ladies carriage and could barely contain his long legs. But he was certain it would delight Laura.

Jumping down from the buggy, Brandon secured the black gelding and offered the horse a bit of apple. "I shall return momentarily, and you shall see that Miss Marquardt is all that I declared her to be and more."

The horse gave a slight bob of his head but quickly went back to searching for more apple. Brandon gave in and palmed another piece of the fruit before heading up the steps to the Marquardt house.

Gaston admitted him on the first knock and Brandon was

surprised to find Laura already awaiting him in the music room. She seemed pale and not at all herself as she played a dark dirge on the rosewood grand piano.

"It's a beautiful day," Brandon declared. "Perfect for our planned outing."

Laura looked up and the palpable pain in her expression pierced Brandon to the soul. He studied her for a moment and frowned.

"What is it? Has something happened?"

She rose rather stiffly from the piano and extended her hand. "Please get me out of here," she whispered.

He didn't waste any time. Whatever was wrong would not be helped by remaining in the music room and asking questions. He walked her to the door, stopping only long enough for Laura to tie on a bonnet and wrap and then take up her gloves. She pulled them on quickly and gave him the briefest of nods.

A million questions raced through Brandon's mind as he assisted her into the phaeton. He wondered if Malcolm Lowe had threatened her. If that was the case . . . if the man had done anything to frighten her . . . Brandon would see he paid.

He went to free the horse and then climbed up beside Laura, taking his place ever so carefully—almost fearful that she might break should he get too close.

"I'm afraid this is a snug fit," he said in apology. "Not that I mind."

She said nothing but stared straight ahead as Brandon flicked the reins.

They rode in silence for well over ten minutes before Brandon decided he'd had enough. He directed the horse toward a sea-view park and found a place where he could stop the carriage.

"Laura, you have to tell me what's wrong. I can see that you're very upset, and I must have the reason."

She looked at him for a moment and nodded. "And I intend to give you the reason, because you're the only one I can tell."

He didn't like the way this was starting to sound. Reaching out, he grasped her gloved hand. "Then tell me."

Drawing a deep breath, Laura appeared about to speak, but then she simply exhaled. She did this three more times before finally beginning her story.

"My sister is at the house. We brought her home yesterday."

"She's left her husband?"

"Not exactly." Laura bowed her head and looked at their entwined hands.

Brandon wasn't about to let her drift into silence again. "Tell me what happened. Why did you bring your sister to the house?"

Laura met his gaze. "She was . . . He . . . beat her."

Brandon's eyes narrowed. "Beat her?"

"Very nearly to death." Her breathing came faster and in shallow little gasps. "He . . . he . . . is a monster. She . . . she only . . . she only . . . ."

Brandon could see she was starting to strain for air, and so he cupped her chin so she'd focus on him. "Breathe deep. Laura, do you hear me?"

She stared at him, wide-eyed and pale. Very slowly she did as he told her. At first Brandon wasn't sure she would ever draw a lungful of air, but finally, after several frightening moments, Laura finally seemed to calm.

"Does Malcolm know she's with you?"

Laura shook her head. "I . . . don't know. He wasn't there. Carissa said he . . . he was gone on business."

Laura slumped against him and began to cry. Sobbing long and hard, she cried for quite some time. When finally she slowed to little hiccuping sniffed whimpers, Brandon felt he could question her further.

With great tenderness, he dried her face with his own handkerchief. "I know this has been hard on you. I am so very sorry. What is your father doing about it?"

She shook her head and whispered, "He doesn't know."

"What do you mean? With your sister there—how can he not?"

"Carissa . . . doesn't want them to know. She told Mother and Father that she caught her heel in the hem of her dress and fell down the stairs. They believe her."

"But you didn't?"

She looked him in the eye. "I told you before that he was violent. I told you."

"Yes, I remember." He reached up and touched her cheek, but Laura pulled away.

"I was certain he'd done this to her," she continued. "I told Carissa so, and she finally admitted it. Then she swore me to secrecy."

Brandon knew that many a man struck his wife and generally everyone looked the other way. It was just one of those things that happened . . . with some people. He bit back an angry sarcastic remark about Malcolm's character. Laura was in no mood for his anger, righteous or otherwise.

"Why wouldn't she want your parents to know the truth?" he asked.

Laura shook her head. "She believes herself to be with child."

For a moment, Brandon couldn't speak. What could he say? A husband had full rights to his wife and children. The law would not intercede in most cases to protect a woman who had endured such treatment. To suggest otherwise to Laura would be a cruel thing to do. Laura was no fool—no doubt she'd already considered what type of legal recourses might belong to her sister.

"And Carissa said Malcolm is gone somewhere on business, so he hasn't tried to see her?"

Laura met his gaze. "No. Thankfully. I may have shot him had he come around."

The complete seriousness of her statement caused Brandon to feel a wave of cold run through him. "Laura, listen to me. You cannot take this matter into your own hands. Promise me you'll not go anywhere near Malcolm Lowe. I cannot allow you to risk your life."

"It's too late for that now, Brandon," she said in a quiet, even tone. "We have to find a way to stop him—to make him pay for all he's done."

"Revenge for your sister isn't what this investigation is about. It's about bringing a man to a fair trial. It's about proof and evidence that will reveal his guilt beyond a reasonable doubt. Laura, this cannot become a personal vendetta."

She gave a harsh laugh. "Oh, it's definitely too late to stop that now."

He took hold of her shoulders and turned her to face him in

the narrow buggy seat. "Listen to me. You have to be reasonable, Laura. Malcolm Lowe would just as soon put you in the ground as speak to you. If he would treat Carissa this way, just imagine what he would do if he found out you were trying to see him imprisoned."

"I don't care. He has to pay, Brandon." Tears formed again in her eyes. "God must punish him for what he's done to Carissa."

"And God will," Brandon asserted. "*God* will. Not you. Not me. You must leave this in God's hands, Laura. He hasn't abandoned us. He hasn't even abandoned Carissa. You need to trust that God will avenge this wrong on Carissa's behalf."

Laura said nothing, but neither did she turn away from him. A single tear slid down her cheek, and Brandon reached up to wipe it away. "The Bible says that God puts our tears in His bottle. I think I'll just keep this one for Him." Brandon pressed the damp finger to his lips.

"So we let him go on hurting her?" Laura asked. "We send my sister back into the arms of the man who tried to end her life for simply asking him about his place of employment?" Brandon watched as her eyes blazed with emotion.

"That's all it was, Brandon. Carissa had gone to surprise him at work and learned he had never been employed at the mill. So she asked him about it, and he beat her. Do you know that my sister prayed for death? She wanted to die. She wanted to leave this world and all the pain behind."

Laura squared her shoulders and looked straight ahead. "He did things to her that I cannot—will not—repeat. I had no idea a person could even think of inflicting such harm on another."

"But even so," Brandon said, keeping his voice low in hopes

of stilling her rage, "even so . . . you cannot change what happened. Your sister is safe for now. We will do what we can to see that she remains in the care of your family. I will do everything in my power to see that Malcolm is arrested. Even if we don't have all the evidence of what his current plans are and who his cohorts are, I will explain the situation to the general. We will take him into custody, and God have mercy on his soul . . . for he will likely hang. All I ask . . . all I beg of you, Laura, is that you would not have anything further to do with this situation. I no longer want your help in this investigation. I knew what I was getting myself into when I delayed my retirement to help in bringing Lowe to justice, but you didn't. Do not put yourself in harm's way for the hope of revenge. I love you, and I cannot lose you."

Laura was silent, and Brandon wasn't even sure she'd heard his declaration. When next she spoke, he was certain she hadn't.

"I will see him pay for what he's done. If that causes me grief or injury . . . so be it." She looked at Brandon and shook her head. "And may no one have mercy on Malcolm Lowe . . . especially God."

Two days before Thanksgiving the doctor confirmed Carissa's suspicion that she was indeed with child. She had healed from her injuries for the most part, although there were faint smudges of bruising still to be seen here and there. What hadn't been seen was anything of Malcolm Lowe. And then without warning, the day before Thanksgiving, he showed up at the house looking for his wife.

Laura was with her Father when Malcolm was announced. Her emotions had calmed considerably during the weeks of his absence, but her desire for revenge hadn't abated. She sat in silence watching Malcolm as he strode into the sitting room as though he hadn't a care in the world.

"I'm hoping that you might know where Carissa has gotten off to," he said, as though describing a kitten that had gone astray.

"She is here with us," Father replied, getting to his feet. "She has been recovering from her fall."

"Fall?" Malcolm asked innocently. "What fall are you speaking of? Is she all right?"

Laura wanted to get up and slap the look of concern from his face. Instead, she sat and coolly observed the man who had caused her sister so much pain.

"I had to go away on business. I had no idea she'd taken a tumble."

Father frowned, and Laura knew he was thinking "a tumble" didn't begin to account for the damage done to his daughter. Laura wanted very much to ask what kind of business had taken Malcolm away for so long, but she said nothing. It was as if they were all playing some sort of strange chess match—each waiting for the other to make a mistake.

Laura knew that her father had no idea that Malcolm had beat Carissa, but he did know that Malcolm had lied about his job at the mill. He would also have little respect for a man who was so unconcerned with his wife's welfare that he could be gone for weeks at a time and not let her know of his whereabouts.

On the other hand, Laura was more than aware of Malcolm's cruelty. She narrowed her eyes and stared at him as though he might grow horns and a tail at any moment. She had never before hated anyone, but now she hated this man. She could feel the anger boil inside her. It was all she could do to keep her seat.

She fought with her emotions and reasoning. The inner battle was fiercer than any she'd ever known. If she said nothing about the truth, Malcolm would reclaim her sister and take her home to dominate again. If she did say something, he might well deny it and then it would be Laura's word against his, for surely Carissa would say nothing.

"Yes, apparently she fell the very day you left," Father was telling Malcolm. "She suffered a great deal of bruising and pain. The doctor said it was a wonder she didn't lose the child."

"Lose the child?" Malcolm asked. "What are you talking about?"

"My sister is going to have a baby."

Malcolm turned to Laura, as though seeing her for the first time. His lips curled into a grin. "A baby. Imagine that? Well, this is a great day."

Father smiled. "Indeed it is. I thought perhaps you had already suspected the news."

"Not at all," Malcolm declared, appearing quite proud of himself. "I had hoped, of course. We both did. Carissa and I want to have a large family."

Laura feared all accountability and reason was lost, but her father surprised her. "And how will you support that large family, if I might be so bold as to ask? I know that you have not been employed by the flour mill, as you had once told me. And, since you have been quite willing to seek me out for support, I believe I'm entitled to an answer."

Malcolm bobbed his head up and down most enthusiastically. "Indeed. You are more than in your rights to ask me about that. See, I tried to get the job at the mill as planned, but it didn't work out. I was truly ashamed to admit my failings." His expression seemed to sadden. "It was hard for me to admit such a thing—even to myself. Still, I did not give up. I soon teamed with some of my friends from the war, and we decided to go into business together."

"What kind of business?" Father asked.

"Freighting," Malcolm replied without so much as a pause. "We've been bringing stuff up from Matamoros and Brownsville. That's why I was gone so long. I hadn't figured to be one of the drivers. I thought I'd be keepin' the books and arrangin' the jobs for the other men. But I was needed to drive."

Laura wanted to scream. How could this man lie so easily? How could he act as if he were innocent of the horrible things he'd done . . . and likely still planned to do?

Just then Mother and Carissa came into the room. Laura didn't know why her sister had bothered to join them. If she'd had any sense, she would have remained in her room and refused to see him. But of course, then she would have to reveal the truth to her parents, and she'd already made it clear that that wasn't going to happen.

"Carissa!" Malcolm exclaimed like a jubilant boy. "I just heard the news about the baby. I couldn't be prouder." He went to her and took her in his arms.

Laura watched her sister smile prettily and murmur something. The entire scene sickened her, and she no longer wanted to continue the game.

"If you'll excuse me," she said, getting to her feet, "I believe I'm beginning to feel ill."

"Oh, I do hope you aren't coming down with the grippe," Mother said, looking worried. "So many illnesses are going around since the weather turned chilly."

"I don't believe it is the grippe that afflicts me," Laura replied. "I only know that I must seek the solace of my room."

"I do hope you'll feel better by tomorrow," Father called out as she turned to go. "We have a wonderful Thanksgiving dinner planned and many guests who will join us. I know Brandon would be sorely disappointed should he not be able to see you."

Laura paused in the doorway and glanced over her shoulder. "I really have no thought past the moment, Father, but I will do my best to recover before tomorrow."

On Thanksgiving Day Laura refused to join the others for the celebratory dinner. She remained in her room accepting well-wishes and a tray of food that as of yet remained untouched. She hadn't really given thought to fasting and prayer, but found herself doing exactly that. In fact, she had never prayed harder in her life.

When Carissa's soft knock fell upon her door, Laura allowed her sister admission. Carissa came into the room and waited for Laura to close and relock the door before speaking. "I know you are unhappy with me, but no more so than I am with myself."

"I'm not unhappy with you," Laura told her. "I'm furious with your husband. If I have to sit across the table from him, I am almost certain I could not refrain from throwing my knife into his heart."

Carissa took a seat and motioned to Laura. "Please come over here so we might not be overheard."

"Secrecy isn't resolving anything," Laura said, though doing as her sister asked. "He will just go on hurting you. You do know that—don't you?"

"He promised he wouldn't," Carissa explained. "Now that I'm expecting a baby, he realizes his mistakes."

"Mistakes? You had to get in a family way for him to realize that it was wrong to beat you half to death? Please. Please do not excuse that man's behavior or I will be sick."

"Laura, you don't understand. He's my husband. I'm not happy that he's done these things, but I cannot shame the family by leaving him."

"So you'll just allow his abuses to continue? I pray not!" Laura declared, raising her voice.

Carissa frowned and leaned forward. "Please lower your voice. I don't want Carlita or anyone else to overhear us."

Laura folded her arms and fixed Carissa with a stern expression. "You are so naïve. You don't even know this man. He is . . ." Laura let the words trail off. How could she explain to Carissa that her husband was suspected of murder?

"I know that I cannot leave him. Mother would be mortified. And how would I explain it?" she asked, sadly shaking her head. "You alone are the only one who knows what's happened."

"And I would happily bear witness to all that I know. I would not leave you to face this on your own." Laura squared her shoulders. "I would do everything in my power to keep you safe. Do you not know that?"

She smiled. "I do. You have always been like that. I remember when we were much younger and your actions kept me from harm." She sobered. "But, Laura, you can't keep me safe any-more. No one can."

"No, I will not accept that," Laura replied. "I've been pray-ing for an answer. I know God will help us. I just don't know how."

"I don't think God cares in particular," Carissa said, her voice heavy with sorrow. "I have spent a lifetime ignoring Him, and I think now He is doing likewise."

"God doesn't work that way," Laura said, reaching forward to take hold of Carissa's hand. "You cannot assign human pet-tiness to Him. God does care, and He is willing to intercede. I just know it. We have to have faith. We have to keep hoping." The words were meant for herself as much as her sister.

Carissa got to her feet. "Please say nothing, Laura. I want to give Malcolm a chance to prove himself. I think he deserves that much."

"He deserves nothing," Laura said. "But I will not further your pain by speaking out."

"Thank you. Oh, and you should know that Malcolm has agreed that I might hold a dinner party for my birthday. I do hope you'll be there. It wouldn't be the same without you."

Laura shuddered at the thought of an evening in the lion's den. Nevertheless, she would not let Carissa face this alone. "I'll be there. I promise."

⌒

The night of November thirtieth was colder than anyone had anticipated. The drive over to the Lowe house chilled them with crisp sea breezes. Mother and Laura huddled under warm blankets while Father sat opposite them, doing his best to keep warm on his own.

At Carissa's small house, Laura was surprised to see new furnishings. Her prior visits had revealed very little in the way of accommodations, but now there was a new dining room table and eight matching mahogany chairs. There also appeared to be new china laid for the party.

"Malcolm was able to get this lovely set from someone who planned to move to Europe," Carissa explained, bringing in another chair so that they could accommodate their seven guests. "I positively love it, don't you?"

Mother fawned over the furnishings, telling Carissa they were of the highest quality. Laura, meanwhile, stepped back and tried her best to bury the feelings of hatred she felt. Malcolm looked quite smug as he stood talking to the other men, including Father. She had always thought her father an astute man—a good judge of character—but seeing him laugh with Malcolm made her question that judgment.

Before supper Laura didn't have an opportunity to speak with Carissa alone. When Malcolm wasn't holding her at his side, their mother was possessively clinging to her younger child. Carissa appeared happy, however, and this set Laura's mind momentarily at ease.

I mustn't allow my own bitter feelings to ruin things for Carissa. This is her birthday, Laura chided herself.

The dinner progressed in good order. There were two other couples present besides Carissa's family members. Laura was introduced to each husband and wife as friends of Malcolm.

"We absolutely adore, Carissa," Mrs. Parker said to Laura's

parents. "She is such a sweet young thing." The woman was probably a dozen years Carissa's senior. "We have all become dear friends."

The other woman, a Mrs. Beech, nodded in agreement but said nothing. Mother smiled and looked to Carissa. "The girls have always had many friends. I would not expect it to be otherwise."

Esther was on loan to help with the party and had done a wonderful job of serving. Cook had prepared the foods ahead of time, but left prior to the party so Esther had charge of the kitchen, as well. Laura breathed a sigh of relief that the party had turned out so well.

It was nearing the time for them to share in dessert when she heard her sister say something in response to someone's question. Laura braced herself for Malcolm's reaction.

"Malcolm doesn't share about his work," Carissa explained. "I honestly have no idea of what he does."

"It seems to me a wife should have an understanding of her husband's business," Father interjected.

"It's my belief that the woman of the house should refrain from interfering with such things," Malcolm countered. "Carissa knows full well this is my desire."

Father looked at his son-in-law oddly for a moment. "Is it necessary to such a point that she doesn't even know where you work or what you do?"

Malcolm's eyes narrowed. "In my house, we do things my way." He got to his feet. "I will see to it that more coffee is prepared." He went into the kitchen, and a moment later Esther hurried in to finish gathering plates from the table.

Carissa was frowning, but in such a way that others might have believed her only deep in thought. Fear bubbled up inside Laura, however. Fear that once they all left the party and went their separate ways, Malcolm would punish Carissa for her comment.

"I'll see if I can help," Laura said, getting to her feet. Carissa looked as if she were about to say something, but Laura ignored her and continued to the kitchen.

Once inside, Laura found Malcolm putting wood in the stove. He glanced up but only threw her a quizzical glance before returning his attention to the fire. Laura tried to steady her rapid breathing.

"What do you need?" Malcolm asked as he finally straightened.

Laura took three determined steps to where he stood. "I need," she whispered, "for you to stop hurting my sister."

He looked at her for a moment and shook his head innocently. "I have no idea what you're talking about."

"You know very well. You and I both know my sister did not fall down the stairs."

"Is that what Carissa told you?"

"She didn't need to say a word for me to know that you're hurting her. I've seen the marks."

He shrugged. "She's clumsy, that's all."

"She is not."

Just then Esther entered the kitchen with a stack of dishes. They halted their discussion until the woman returned to the dining room. Laura leaned in and pointed her finger at Malcolm.

"If you ever lay a hand on her again, I will expose you to

234

Mother and Father. I will do everything in my power, in fact, to see that you never see Carissa again."

He laughed. "You would come between a husband and wife? You would put asunder what God has joined? When did you acquire such authority?"

"I love my sister, and I will protect her," Laura calmly stated. "Touch her and you'll pay."

"Get in my way and you'll pay," Malcolm replied, leaning forward. "Do you understand?"

"You're threatening to hit me next?"

"Hardly. I don't need to hit a woman to control her." He smiled, and it chilled Laura to the bone. "I happen to know that you're teaching blacks to read and write. My spies tell me, in fact, that you go every Saturday to be with the Negroes, while telling your mother and father that you're doing Ladies Aid work. If you don't want me to reveal your secrets, then I suggest you rethink your words."

Laura could hardly believe he was attempting to threaten her. He was correct in saying she hadn't yet told her parents of her deeds, but it wasn't for a lack of desire. Laura wanted more than anything to get her father's financial support, especially now that five other adults had requested lessons.

She realized that if she yielded to Malcolm's threats, he would always find ways to control her. Laura shook her head. "Touch her, Malcolm, and you will be sorry."

Without another word, Laura gathered her skirts and headed back into the dining room. Carissa and the others looked at her for a moment, and she smiled. "I hope you don't mind," Laura said, looking to Carissa, "but I'd like to make a little announcement."

Malcolm came in behind her and made his way to his chair. "I've already spoken about this with my brother-in-law," she said, smiling. Malcolm frowned and took his seat.

"Well, do go on," Mr. Beech encouraged. "You now have our undivided attention."

Laura smiled. "Thank you. I know this may sound unusual, but I am soliciting support for what I perceive to be a most important endeavor. Esther, please wait a moment before you go."

The older woman looked at Laura with a worried expression. Laura motioned Esther to join her. "Several weeks ago," Laura announced, "I began teaching Esther to read and write. Not long after we started, she asked if I might help her two boys to learn, as well, and so I did. Now there are six women and four children learning to read and write. We meet once a week."

Laura looked to her father and mother. "I hadn't spoken of this because I knew you both would have worried over my safety. However, now that the plan is in place and going along so well, I'm hoping you might assist me. Obviously supplies are needed. Slates, chalk, books, paper, and ink pens. So many small items that we take for granted." She turned to Esther. "Thank you for allowing me to detain you."

Esther nodded and hurried back to the kitchen as if embarrassed. Laura looked to the faces of the people at the table and smiled. "Now that the war is over and the slaves have been freed, I believe it is our responsibility to help educate them. Without an education, the colored people lack the skills to better themselves and their families."

"I think it is an idea with merit," Mr. Beech said, nodding. He was closer to her father's age than Malcolm's, and if Laura

236

understood correctly, he had been Malcolm's superior in the army. "However, my concern is that this will cause the Negroes to desire more than their station in life will allow for."

"Such as?" Laura asked.

He considered the question for a moment. "Well, if we teach them to read and write, they will soon come to expect jobs of greater pay. Perhaps they will even press to attend universities."

"And why not?" Laura countered. "There are already colleges in the North that allow for this. Why would it not be fitting to encourage learning?"

"Knowledge can be very dangerous," Malcolm replied before anyone else. "I have to agree with the sarge. The darkies will soon be demanding admission to every job imaginable if we allow them more education."

"I hardly see that as a problem," Laura replied. "But nevertheless, the simple ability to read and write should be a right for all mankind—no matter the shade of one's skin. I have helped to teach Mexicans to read and write, and in turn have learned to speak their language. It has only served to benefit me."

"Well, while this conversation is quite interesting," Father said to Laura's surprise, "we want to remember that it is your sister's birthday, and that is the reason we are here." He looked to Carissa and smiled. "And what a happy day it is! Not only are you more radiant and lovely than ever, but God has blessed you with a child."

Carissa blushed and Laura could see that her mother was most uncomfortable with Father bringing up such a delicate matter. But no one rebuked him and soon everyone was busy eating cake and laughing.

Laura met Malcolm's gaze only once. He lifted his wineglass as if in salute to her bold declaration. Laura shook her head ever so slightly and turned away. The man was a threat to them all, and she would do whatever it took to assist Brandon so that Malcolm Lowe might be hanged.

Laura listened without interest as her mother talked on and on about the upcoming Christmas social season. They had received invitations from several people, and while the economy of the town and state was still not good, it was enough to know the war was behind them and this Christmas they could truly celebrate.

"We must have new gowns," she said, stopping for a moment to tap her chin. "I shall discuss this with your father immediately. Perhaps he will allow me to purchase something for Carissa, as well. After all, since we had the wedding party earlier, we can hardly be expected to host a Christmas gathering. Without that added expense, your father will surely have enough money to spare for new gowns and gloves. Oh, and maybe even a fashionable new hat. Wouldn't that be fun?"

She didn't wait for Laura to respond. "The Davis family is hosting a Christmas Eve dance," she said, putting aside her stack of invitations. "I'm so glad. A Christmas ball is always a magical experience. Why, I remember once when I was just newly turned out that one of the finest families held a Christmas ball, and that was where I fell in love with your father. It was a night of such wonders. . . . Perhaps it will be for you, as well. Perhaps your Captain Reid will propose."

Laura looked at her mother in surprise. "I have given you no reason to think he might. Has he done something—said something?"

Mother gave a light laugh. "Goodness, Laura, it isn't as though the rest of us can't see what's going on. The man adores you and you are clearly besotted with him. My only question is *when* you two will marry, not *if*."

The idea of marriage to Brandon Reid thrilled Laura to the very core of her being; however, the problems with Malcolm had stolen much of her joy in even imagining wedded bliss. Malcolm's heinous behavior had, in fact, taken almost all of Laura's focus. Even when she was working to teach Esther and the others to read, she couldn't help but wonder if Malcolm and his men would use violent means to see her stop.

"I think the atmosphere will be much improved by all of us delighting in the holiday season. I've already arranged to have Carlita and Esther retrieve the Christmas decorations from the attic. I thought this year we might even have a Christmas tree like the von Blüchers' always have. What do you think?"

"Do you suppose Carissa will be there?"

"Be where?"

"At the Christmas ball," Laura said, forgetting about her mother's idea of a German tree. "You were talking about having

Father buy her a new gown. I just wondered if you really thought she would attend."

"And why not? She won't yet be in her confinement. I doubt she'd even be showing, so I think it would be perfectly fine for her to be in attendance. Besides, if she has a new gown, Malcolm will no doubt want to show her off." Mother got up from her chair. "I believe I'll go speak to your father right now." Her mother darted from the room without another word. It was as if the only thing of import in Mother's world was having new dresses made.

Sighing in exasperation, Laura picked up a book she'd been trying to read and opened it to where she'd left off. For nearly half an hour she immersed herself in the challenges of poor Jane Eyre. Mr. Rochester had lied to Jane about his marital state, and the poor girl very nearly wed a married man.

Laura frowned at the tragic deception. Jane had fallen in love with a man who had not only lied to her, but had continued the falsehood very nearly at the cost of her innocence. Men could be so barbaric in their thinking. How could one ever consider such actions acceptable? But then again, how could Malcolm Lowe believe hitting his wife to be a reasonable response?

Laura thought instead of Brandon, of his gentle spirit and kindness toward her. He had been faithful to call on her and send little notes of encouragement since her teary carriage ride. She had to admit that Brandon was all that she could hope for in a husband. His sacrifices prior to and during the war had made him a hero in her eyes. But the stories he told her were never given to praise himself. Brandon shared the past in a way that either brought God glory or spoke in admiration of someone else.

He's such an honorable man, she thought. So unlike Malcolm. Malcolm didn't care about putting his wife in danger. He only thought of himself.

She got up and walked to the piano, thinking she might like to practice a bit on some new Christmas pieces when something Brandon had said to her came to mind.

"Do not put yourself in harm's way for the hope of revenge. I love you, and I cannot lose you."

She clutched at her throat. "He said that he loved me." Had she remembered correctly?

Laura struggled to remember the conversation word for word. She closed her eyes and pictured them sitting in the buggy.

His words were impassioned, and she recalled that he said he no longer wanted her help in the investigation. Again his declaration brought a lump to her throat. *"Do not put yourself in harm's way for the hope of revenge. I love you, and I cannot lose you."*

"He loves me," she murmured. How in the world had she missed that?

Laura sat down to consider what she should do. Perhaps Brandon was waiting for her to say something about the declaration. Perhaps upon reflection, he regretted his announcement. How could she bring up the subject without appearing brash?

But then another part of the conversation echoed in her head. *"I knew what I was getting myself into when I delayed my retirement to help in bringing Lowe to justice. . . ."*

Something about that statement seemed oddly out of place. Brandon hadn't delayed his retirement to bring Lowe to justice. He hadn't even known there was a problem with Malcolm until

Laura had shared the information she'd overheard the night of the wedding. Or had he?

She bit at her lower lip and tried to recall her first encounter with Brandon. In the alley, he had thought her to be a trouble-some Southern belle who was abusing his men. Later at the party her parents held, Brandon mysteriously arrived as a guest. He was surprised to find her there, as well—surprised even more to learn of her family's Union support.

"Miss Laura," Esther said as she entered the room, "yar father wants to see ya in his study. He say for ya to come right away."

Troubled for reasons she couldn't yet put a finger on, Laura got to her feet. "Thank you, Esther." She hoped the churning of her stomach wouldn't be made worse by whatever her father wanted to discuss. It had been three days since Carissa's party, and he'd said nothing to her about her announcement to teach reading and writing to the Negroes.

Making her way to the study, Laura spied the open door and stepped into the room. "You wanted to see me?"

Her father nodded soberly and pointed to a chair. "Please sit with me. I have something I want to discuss."

Laura did as he told her, sitting prim and proper on the edge of a large leather wingback. "I suppose this is about my an-nouncement at Carissa's birthday party," she said, hoping to just get the topic on the table.

"Indeed it is," Father replied.

"First, please let me say that I did not take on this endeavor to disrespect you, Father. I simply saw a need—one that I felt confident I could meet."

"I'm not angry, Laura. I wish you would have told me sooner, and that you wouldn't have put yourself in such grave risk by going into the colored part of town."

"But Jesus went where the sick people were," Laura said with a weak smile.

Her father nodded. "But Jesus was a man—and the Son of God." He smiled. "Even so, I want only to keep you safe—not forbid you to continue, as you might imagine."

She felt her body relax a bit although she remained on the edge of her seat. Father came from around his desk and took the chair beside her. "I believe in your project, my dear, and I do want to help."

"I was worried that you might not, since our previous conversation some time ago was not at all favorable."

Father eased back in the chair and crossed his legs. "It's true that I was less than supportive. I'm afraid it was simply bad timing for me. I'd recently listened to several friends who were speaking of the problems they were enduring because of the slaves being set free. These were good people, Laura. They were good to their slaves."

"Can one truly be good to a person they claim to own?" she asked.

"I suppose not," he replied. "Even so, the government was making a great deal of trouble for my friends and it tainted my thoughts that day. I hope you'll forgive me."

"Of course." Laura leaned forward. "I hope you'll forgive me, as well. I rarely have gone against you, and I felt quite worried about keeping my actions from you and Mother. As I said, it was never done as an act of defiance, but rather one of love."

"All is forgiven," her father assured. "Now, however, I believe we need to make plans. I delayed in speaking to you until I could figure a couple of things out. First, I have a location in mind where you might continue lessons. There is a small house on the edge of town near the colored section, but not in it. I believe it would be a suitable and safe place to arrange classes. If you agree, we can go take a look at it later today."

"I would like that very much."

"Second, I have spoken with some of my business associates, and we are arranging for tables and chairs, as well as the supplies you mentioned."

"They know, don't they, that there can be no charge to the students?" Laura asked. "Some of these people are living twenty to a shack and have no money. They are barely existing as it is, and schooling isn't something they can afford."

"They understand, my dear. We all do. I suppose for those of us with a conscience, we accept the responsibility and realize that it is by our hand and permission that the black man and his family were not allowed to receive a proper grounding in education. I can honestly say that I bear deep shame over this thought, but I also realize shame will not change the problem. A man might feel a great many things, but action is still required to prove the heart."

Laura thought her father very wise. She also thought of Brandon's declaration of love. He might feel love for her, but he hadn't taken any action to truly prove his heart in the matter.

Her father smiled and continued. "So I propose that we work together. In fact, I would also like to find a young man who might assist you. Do you suppose that Mr. Reid might be interested?"

"For what purpose?" Laura asked.

"So that black men might also learn to read. I cannot allow for my daughter to teach men, and that is not negotiable."

Laura understood and had already turned away two such requests. "I completely agree." She thought for a moment. Working with Brandon would be something akin to wonderful; however, she knew he had spoken of starting a ranch. She frowned. Hadn't he told her that he would have great difficulty ever working in the confines of a school?

"Since we are only meeting on Saturdays, Brandon might be willing to help—at least so long as he's here in Corpus Christi. I know he has other . . . irons in the fire, so to speak. But perhaps if you were the one to ask him, he would agree."

"Very good. I'll speak to him as soon as an opportunity presents itself. I would feel quite safe knowing you were in his care."

She thought of Brandon's words of love once again and smiled. "I would, too."

Malcolm felt as if people were watching him all day long. It seemed wherever he went, someone was off to the side, reading a newspaper or just whittling on a stick. They always seemed to refuse to look directly at him, and that made Malcolm even more suspicious.

He walked into the house at half past eight and smelled the faint aroma of food. At least Carissa had thought to fix him something to eat. Malcolm made his way into the kitchen and checked the warming receptacle. A covered plate awaited him. He took it and the coffeepot and went to the table.

"I'll get you a cup and some silver," Carissa said, startling him with her silent approach.

He spun around in his nervous state and all but lunged for her. Stopping himself, Malcolm drew in a deep breath and gave a curt nod. He sat down at the table and tried to steady his nerves. Nothing was going right. First they'd had unexpected delays in getting enough black powder, and now there were other problems with ammunitions and blasting caps. His intent to kill off a good number of the colored troops had been thwarted when they'd mustered out of the city in November. Now Malcolm wasn't even sure they could carry through with their plans to create havoc on Christmas Eve. Nothing was working in his favor, and now . . . now he was certain someone was following him.

"I hope you had a good day," Carissa said, putting the cup and silverware in front of him.

Malcolm took up the coffeepot and poured himself a cup. "It was fine."

"I had another cooking lesson," Carissa said, pointing to the plate. "Esther came over and helped me learn how to cook pork chops and gravy. I hope you like them."

"Is there any bread?" he asked.

She nodded and returned to the kitchen. Malcolm hated her hovering over him. He hated most everything about her these days. She was trying overly hard to be sweet and it irritated him to no end.

Carissa brought a loaf of bread and a knife and put them both beside her husband. She took a seat across from Malcolm and started to reach for the knife. "Would you like me to slice it? You seem very tired."

He grabbed a hunk of bread and tore it off rather than cut it. "And you're very annoying."

She frowned and straightened in her chair. "I was just trying to show some concern, Malcolm. I know you're working hard . . . at whatever it is you do. I just want you to know I appreciate your efforts."

He sopped his bread in the gravy for a moment, and then looked at his wife. "Is that your way of tryin' to get me to talk about my job again?" He purposefully lowered his voice to sound menacing. "Because if I thought you were startin' that again, I'd have to deal with it here and now."

"You know better than that," Carissa said, seeming to lose some of her patience. "I was just trying to be nice."

"Be nice somewhere else."

"You don't want me to keep you company while you eat?"

He pounded his fist on the table and almost laughed at the way she jumped up from the chair. "No. I don't need company, and I don't need your questions. Get on out of here. Go to bed. That's where you can do me the most good."

Carissa looked at him for a moment. "I know I've said it before, but you've changed. I thought you loved me . . . loved being with me. We used to have fun together."

"And now we got a baby on the way and a town full of Yankees who don't seem to know when it's time to go home," he said, picking up the knife to cut into the pork. He took a bite and found the flavor to be exceptional. Another time he might have given her a compliment, but not now. Not with her asking stupid questions and pestering the life out of him.

"Are you sorry that we're having a baby?" she asked.

He could hear the sadness in her voice and instead of soften-ing him, it only served to make him angry. In one move, Malcolm was on his feet. He raised his hand, almost forgetting the knife he held. Carissa's eyes widened, and she backed up several steps.

Malcolm lowered his arm. "Now, get out of here like I told you. I'm hungry, and I don't intend to listen to you nag me."

A sob broke from somewhere deep in her and Carissa turned and ran. Malcolm wanted to be sorry that he'd made her cry, but he wasn't. At least if she was scared and crying, she wasn't here talking and whining.

He sat back down and finished the meal. The person he was really angry at wasn't even Carissa. It was her sister. Laura had caused him no end of trouble. Every time she stuck her nose in their business, Carissa got mouthy and pushy. No doubt she'd been visiting her sister today.

There was also the problem of Laura's beau. Reid was an absolute mystery to Malcolm. He'd tried on several occasions to get information on the man, but it was as if the lines had been cut. No one seemed to even know where he was living at this point. What kind of man was so paranoid he kept his bed and board a secret?

All of this, combined with Malcolm's plans against the Yan-kee oppressors, made him more than a little paranoid himself. He knew he'd been followed that evening. He could feel eyes watching him, and it only served to stir his rage. Malcolm didn't like folks in his business—especially now that the stakes were so high.

He pushed back the empty plate and got to his feet, then blew out the lamp and waited twenty minutes in the dark. He hoped that if anyone were watching the house, they'd figure he went to bed.

At the end of his wait, Malcolm pulled on his hat and slipped out the back door. He needed to see Jed Lanz and make sure that he'd rounded up enough men to help with tomorrow's workload. He saddled his horse and rode toward town, making sure to stop before getting too close to the city. He tied off the animal and decided to walk the rest of the way. If he were being followed, it would be harder to track him afoot. Not only that, but if he remained mounted, there was always a chance the animal might be recognized. His dapple gray was a very dark color with a shocking white mane. Folks were bound to know to whom the horse belonged.

Heading down an alley, Malcolm kept to the shadows. He'd gone no more than a block or two, however, when he heard the unmistakable sound of footsteps. He stopped. The footsteps continued but grew more distant. Malcolm picked up his pace. He'd be glad when they got this job done. Once they managed to blow up the Union headquarters and kill off half the command, the war would be back in full swing. At least in Corpus Christi.

He heard it again—footsteps. Malcolm gritted his teeth and shoved his hand deep into his coat pocket. Closing his fingers around the wooden grip of his pistol, he breathed a sense of relief. The piece was like an extension of his hand, and Malcolm always felt better when he had a gun at the ready.

Stepping cautiously to the main road, Malcolm hurried across the street before weaving through a series of alleys. Lanz lived near the poorer white section of town by the water, but Malcolm wasn't very familiar with the neighborhood shortcuts.

Coming at a dead run from the alley onto a main thorough-fare, Malcolm turned left and slowed his pace. If someone had been following him, he was sure to have lost them by now. He breathed deeply and felt his heart slow. He smiled to himself.

You're getting mighty nervous for someone who knows what he's doin', he told himself. He very nearly laughed at his fool-ishness when someone popped out from the corner of a brick building just ahead. Malcolm came up short at the sight of the tall man. The dim street lighting gave a face to his fears.

"You." Malcolm scowled. "Are you followin' me, Reid?"

Brandon Reid cocked his head to one side and smiled. "Why? You need following?"

22

"I'm so glad Mother thought to have this gown made over and let out," Carissa said, giving the skirt a quick twirl. "Goodness, but I feel like the belle of the ball. This plaid has always been a favorite of mine."

Laura was glad to see Carissa so happy with the dress. It was probably the only thing she'd been happy about since the night of her birthday party. She said very little about her life with Malcolm, but to Laura's relief she'd not seen any more bruises on her sister's frame. Still, that didn't mean there weren't bruises where no one could see.

"You look beautiful," Laura told her sister. "And I'm so glad you decided to come with Brandon and me tonight. I don't think you'll regret it."

Carissa sobered a bit and shrugged. "I was desperate to be out of the house and doing something other than staring at the walls. I am so often alone that I have even taken to reading."

She laughed. "Which you know has never been a pleasurable pastime for me. Although I must admit it keeps me from being too lonely now."

Hearing a knock, Laura turned to Carissa. "Sounds like Brandon has arrived early." She quickly glanced at her reflection in the mirror that hung over the fireplace mantel. Her buttery brown hair was perfect. Carlita had pinned it up on one side and allowed long sausage curls to drape down the other. She'd trimmed the arrangement with gold ribbon and pearls, and Laura felt like a queen. Perhaps Brandon would propose tonight.

She frowned. The nagging concern over his honesty with her continued to haunt Laura. She'd not had a chance to really ask him about his investigation of Malcolm. She tried to push the worry aside, however. Tonight the three of them were going to attend a Christmas party at the Sondersons'. The revelry of the season was muted by a lack of money and supplies for most people, but nevertheless, the Christmas spirit lived.

When Gaston entered the room, it was Tyler Atherton and not Brandon Reid who followed. "Miss, you have a guest. Mr. Atherton."

Laura went to greet him while Carissa turned to the mirror in order to rearrange the ribbons in her hair. "Mr. Atherton, what a nice surprise."

"The pleasure is all mine, Miss Laura. Goodness, but you look as pretty as a plum."

She smiled. "Thank you. I love the holidays and find that the colors suit my mood." She glanced down for only a heartbeat at the maroon velvet gown that had been trimmed in black. It was an older gown of her mother's, but one that had been remade for Laura. The seamstress had done a marvelous job and Laura doubted anyone would even remember the dress in its updated appearance.

"Look, Carissa," Laura said, "Mr. Atherton has come."

Carissa nodded at the man. "You are most welcome here, sir."

"Just call me Tyler, please. I can't abide formalities."

"Tyler it is," Laura said. She wasn't one to easily cast aside proprieties, but the holiday spirit put her of a mind to do so. "Our father isn't home, so if you were hoping to see him, I'm afraid you will be disappointed."

He looked down at his black suit and then back to Laura. She wasn't sure, but he appeared rather nervous. "I actually came to see you. I realize you're courtin' Mr. Reid, but I wondered if you might accompany me to a lecture being given at the Episcopal church. I know it's short notice, but I only heard about it myself this day. They're having someone speak on Christmas traditions and I thought it might be of interest to . . . you."

Laura was surprised at the invitation. Since he knew she was courting Brandon it seemed inconsiderate that he should invite her to go out with him for the evening. Even so, she couldn't be angry with him. He seemed so sweet and sincere.

"I'm sorry, Mr. Ath . . . Tyler. We are just now waiting for Brandon to arrive and escort us to a Christmas party." She saw the disappointment on his face and quickly went on. "However, we would be quite happy for you to accompany us. There's plenty of room in the carriage, and I know the family wouldn't mind at all if we were to bring an out-of-town guest."

His expression brightened. "I'd like that. I guess I'm feeling a little out of sorts being so far from home."

"I've not had to experience that myself, but I know it would sorely grieve me to be away from family during the holidays."

Carissa muttered something from behind Laura. Turning, she could see that Carissa was searching for something. "What's wrong?"

"Oh, I've lost an earbob. Goodness, but I can't imagine where it might be. I can't go to the party with just one."

"Why don't you go upstairs and borrow a pair of mine," Laura said. "Brandon will be here any moment. Let Carlita know so that she might look for the earring while we're gone."

Carissa nodded and hurried from the room. Laura turned and asked Tyler, "Will you have a chance to be with them for Christmas? Do they live far from your ranch?"

"My family relocated to Dallas, and I hope to see them on my way back. The ranch is to the north of Dallas, but isn't much just yet. The Comanche burned most of it to the ground, and we've been building a little here and there. It's comin' along, but hardly suitable for women. My ma and sister are quite happy in Dallas, so I doubt they'll ever want to go back to the ranch. My grandpa might, but he's gettin' old, so it's hard to say. And to answer your question about Christmas—well, I came down to fetch those two bulls Will and I purchased, but I'm hopin' to reach Dallas in time for Christmas dinner. So long as those beeves aren't too bent on misbehavin'." He grinned. "Be a whole sight easier if there were a train I could just load them onto. I guess I'll have to content myself with the fact that we can take them by ship to Galveston."

"I did hear that plans are in the works for a rail line," Laura stated, recalling something her father had said earlier. "As I understand, the government is eager to get Texas settled. They are encouraging folks to move west, despite our occupation of troops. Even so, Father tells me that the Federal Army in our city has mostly been as a show to the French, who are interfering in Mexico. I suppose they're concerned with that threat more than with building railroads."

"You are a very smart woman," Tyler replied. "No doubt you are correct. Frankly, given talk of some Texans, I think the government might even be a little worried that we'll take Texas back."

Laura considered that thought a moment. "Do you think that's even possible?"

"Anything is possible," he said with a shrug. "After all, they didn't reckon it was possible for Texas to be a Republic or a state to begin with. Folks figured this would stay a part of Mexico. This war changed a lot of people." His expression sobered. "A lot of folks will come here to forget what happened back east, and those that already lived here will want to put the past behind them, as well."

"As if that is even possible," Laura said, shaking her head.

Gaston shuffled into the room once again. "Mr. Reid," he announced.

Brandon stepped around the older man and stopped to admire Laura in her holiday finery. "You are without a doubt the most beautiful woman in all of Texas."

Tyler laughed. "I'll second that."

The two men exchanged a glance. "Tyler, good to see you again," Brandon said, extending his hand. "Have I interrupted something important?"

"Well, I had stopped by to see if your gal would come with me to a church lecture. Nothing untoward, I promise you." He held up his hands and grinned at Brandon's look of surprise. "But Laura has invited me to come along with you two and her sister. Would that be acceptable to you? I don't wanna be steppin' on any toes."

Brandon shook his head. "My toes are quite safe. Is Will with you?"

"No, he has his wife and her young sister and brother to watch over, so I suggested what with Christmas around the corner, he ought to just stay home. Especially now. He's gonna be a pa."

"That's wonderful news," Brandon said, smiling. "Well, with or without him, you are most welcome to join us."

"In that case," Tyler said, looking at Laura, "I accept."

The party was just the thing to divert Laura's attention. She enjoyed the lively conversations and was delighted when she heard of families who were moving back to the city. With the onset of the war, the population had gone from several thousand to several hundred practically overnight. It gave Laura much joy to imagine Corpus Christi being restored.

The Sondersons had done their best to arrange the house in a festive manner. There were brightly colored stars hanging from the fifteen-foot ceilings and dozens of lighted candelabras positioned around the room. Mrs. Sonderson had brought in wagonloads of the dark red *flores de noche buena*, or poinsettias. The room was a delight to behold—like a lighted garden under the stars.

For a time, Laura lost track of Carissa. The last she'd seen her sister she had been talking with a couple of her old friends. But as more minutes passed with no sign of her, Laura started to worry about her sibling.

Beginning an earnest search, Laura finally spied Carissa sitting alone in a corner of the room's alcove. She looked so sad—weary. Laura wanted to believe that the expectant mother was simply tired. She thought about going to her, then stopped. The last thing she wanted to do was to hover over Carissa, smothering her like their mother was wont to do.

Laura turned instead to a table laden with wonderful food. Brandon quickly joined her and offered to arrange her plate. Laura agreed and pointed to some little pieces of toasted bread. The Sonderson cook had decorated them with a variety of meats and cheese, and Laura suddenly felt quite hungry.

"I hope you didn't mind my speaking with Mr. Sonderson. He had asked me some questions about Indiana, and I wanted to accommodate him."

"Not at all," Laura said.

"I was kind of surprised that Mr. Atherton came to call on you," Brandon said, helping her to find a place where she might sit and eat.

"No more so than I." Laura took her seat. "Jealous?" she asked with a grin.

Brandon handed her the plate and grinned. "Incredibly."

"Well, there's no need. I have eyes only for you," she said, batting her lashes like a simpering belle.

Laughing, Brandon straightened. "I am relieved to know that. Otherwise I might have had to call Mr. Atherton out. Dueling has long been frowned upon, but I'll do what I must to defend my place." He let the words fade as he turned to go.

"And exactly what place might that be?"

Laura's question caused him to stop and turn back to face her. He gave her a mischievous wink. "I suppose we shall have to better explore that query at another time."

By the time Laura finished eating and participating in a few guessing games, she thought it might be best to see if Carissa was ready to leave. She was growing tired of the noisy crowd and figured Brandon and Tyler might well desire an excuse to depart. Laura located Carissa much in the same place as she'd spied her earlier.

"Are you feeling unwell? We can return home if you are."

Meeting Laura's eyes, Carissa shook her head. "No. I suppose I'm just reflecting. This time last year we were still at war, and yet I was happier then."

Laura touched Carissa's arm. "I know things are difficult."

"He frightens me, Laura."

She didn't have to ask whom Carissa was talking about. "You were so right . . . about everything. I wish I'd listened to your cautions last summer. I know I've made a grave mistake in marrying Malcolm, but there is nothing to be done about it now." She looked across the room at the festivities and tears came to her eyes. "I want so much to be happy. To rejoice in my new life and the baby . . . but I can't."

"But God is here to help you," Laura told her. "You only need to turn it all over to Him."

"I know that's what you believe. I'd like to believe it myself, but I can't. It's just impossible."

"Can't or won't?" Laura asked in a gentle tone. "I find myself often declaring a thing impossible, especially when I don't want to put forth the effort to try."

"But I doubt God would make possible a divorce," Carissa said matter-of-factly, "and that is the thing I most want. Forgive me for saying so, but it's the truth."

"There's nothing to forgive, you silly girl. I love you and I only want you happy."

"I never imagined Malcolm would act in the manner he has—completely ruthless—always angry. The man is a complete stranger sometimes."

Laura realized the time had come to tell Carissa the truth. She had to give the woman hope or she might well fall into even deeper despair. "There are some things you should know."

Carissa looked at Laura. "Such as . . ."

"I don't want to go into it here, but suffice it to say, there are things Malcolm has involved himself with that are . . . well . . . illegal."

Carissa laughed in a harsh way that suggested she knew all about it. "Malcolm does whatever Malcolm wants. He doesn't want me knowing anything about it, and he's gone out of his way to make that abundantly clear. So legal or illegal, I won't confront him."

Laura nodded. "I would not want you to. But this is something you need to know. It may well give you hope of redemption."

"How could it?" Carissa asked. "My redemption can only come in his demise."

"Exactly." Laura knew her words were coldhearted. "We'll speak more of it when we return home."

"No. Tell me now. Please."

Laura considered her request for a moment. What could it hurt? "Malcolm is involved in a great many things that will most likely see him imprisoned or hanged."

"Hanged?" Carissa gasped. She put her hand over her mouth as if the whispered word had been shouted.

"I've wanted to tell you about it for a long while now, but I didn't want to hurt you. I knew you loved Malcolm."

Carissa lowered her hand to reveal a dejected expression. "I don't think I've ever even known what love is. At least not the kind of love a man and wife should know. I always dreamed of the tenderness and kindness that I saw Mother and Father share, and at first Malcolm seemed to offer that. Now all I have is anger and bitterness."

"Malcolm is a criminal—possibly a murderer. I think you're entitled to feel anger at his deception."

Carissa pressed her hands together almost as if she were going to pray. "I suppose that your words shouldn't surprise me. I've suspected that Malcolm was up to no good. He wants no questions asked and refuses to account to anyone for his time and money. Father told me he feared gambling was Malcolm's main means of providing for me, but I dare not ask him."

"No. Play the role of a complaisant wife for now. I don't want you hurt. Don't give him any reason to hit you again. If he feels safe and cared for, then perhaps he'll drop his guard and Brandon and his men can take Malcolm and his cohorts into custody before they kill anyone else."

Carissa looked at her sister in disbelief. "Malcolm has killed someone? I mean, I know he killed in the war . . . but murder?"

Laura nodded slowly. "Remember those soldiers who were killed in their beds last May? Brandon believes Malcolm and his men were at the bottom of it."

"Brandon is involved? When did that happen?"

"Apparently while he was in the army. Brandon's actually still working in conjunction with them. I really don't know much else," Laura said, realizing how much it bothered her.

For a minute Carissa said nothing, and when she did speak, it pierced Laura to the heart. "I'm so afraid."

"I am, too. Mostly for you. Why don't you come back to the house and stay with us?" But Laura shook her head before Carissa could even speak. "I suppose that wouldn't work, would it? Malcolm would be more than a little suspicious if you left him."

"Why don't you come stay with me?" Carissa suggested. "I will tell Malcolm that I'm not feeling well—that the pregnancy is starting to cause me trouble and I need to rest more. It's true enough. I keep having fainting spells. I'll tell him that I've asked you to come and be my companion and see to my needs."

Laura thought about this for a moment. "I'll speak to Mother and Father about it," she told Carissa. "They might have an even better idea. No matter what, we have to make sure that Malcolm doesn't get suspicious about what the authorities are doing. You have to keep this a secret no matter what. You do understand, don't you?"

"Of course." Carissa sounded greatly offended. "I'm not a child."

Brandon watched Laura cross the room to join him. Mesmerized by the sway of her skirts and the graceful glide of her walk, Brandon knew he could no longer wait to claim her as his own. It irritated him that Tyler Atherton would dare to ask Laura out for the evening, but perhaps it was Brandon's own fault. After all, he had not put a ring on her finger, nor made any pledge to do so.

"I've been looking for you," Laura said. "I wanted you to know something."

"I have something I want to tell you, as well." He took hold of her arm and maneuvered through the crowd to a much less occupied parlor. Swinging her around to face him, he smiled. "So what did you want to say?"

Laura glanced at the other people in the room. They seemed occupied with a game of charades and were not likely to listen to their conversation. Nevertheless, she lowered her voice. "I told Carissa about Malcolm."

Brandon leaned closer to Laura. "Do you think that was wise?"

"I do. She's so miserable. I felt I had to give her some glimmer of hope that this might all end soon. She feels so trapped and discouraged."

"And how did she receive the news?"

She turned her heart-shaped face to his. "She was rather surprised that Malcolm's deeds included murder, but otherwise, she didn't seem too astounded."

"And will she be able to keep from saying anything to Malcolm?"

"I believe so. Carissa and I have shared secrets through the years, and while I've known Carissa to be flighty at times, I've never known her to break her word."

"Yes, but secrets have a way of slipping out."

Laura's expression grew guarded. "You mean like when you told me that you'd been involved with Malcolm's investigation since before you retired from the army?" She asked the question so matter-of-factly that Brandon almost wasn't sure he'd heard correctly.

"What do you mean?"

"When I was so upset that day during our buggy ride—when you told me you no longer wanted me involved with getting information from Malcolm—you also mentioned that you knew what you were getting into when you delayed resigning from the army."

Brandon remembered his words and winced. He had actually hoped that she might have forgotten that part of his declaration. Since she'd said nothing about his words of love, he'd honestly thought she had. "I said other things, too, as I recall."

Laura nodded. "Yes, you did, although I was far too upset at the time to appreciate them."

"And now?"

"Before I answer that, I need to know something. Obviously you were involved in trying to get evidence against Malcolm before we became acquainted. You deceived me."

He sighed. "It was never my intention."

"Nevertheless, that is what happened."

He heard the sadness in her voice. "I am sorry," he said. "I didn't want to deceive anyone. I was following orders."

Laura looked confused and Brandon wanted to kiss her and make her forget all that had happened. For months he'd worried that this exact thing would occur, and now he was angry with himself for not just bringing the subject to her attention himself.

"I want to know," she said seriously, "did you court me as a means to get closer to him? Was I nothing more than a pawn in this bizarre game of chess?"

Brandon shook his head and took hold of her. "No. I have worried all along that you would think that, should the truth come out. I can even have you talk to my former commander, because I told him the same thing."

She pulled away from him. "So you knew it didn't look good. You knew that I or someone else would have a reason to question your actions."

He led her to the far side of the room and drew her down to sit with him by the window. "Laura, please listen to me. I swear to you that Malcolm Lowe has nothing to do with our courtship. I meant what I said that night." He paused and touched her cheek with his hand. "I love you. I'm completely smitten, and you can rest assured that when I'm with you, Malcolm Lowe is the furthest thing from my mind. Please forgive me. None of this was ever meant to hurt you."

Laura shivered slightly under his touch, but Brandon couldn't be entirely sure if it was from pleasure at his declaration or the burden of her sorrow. She bit at her lower lip, and Brandon thought she'd never looked quite so vulnerable. Did she not believe him? Did she honestly think he'd paid her court for no purpose but to catch a criminal?

He tilted her chin up and gazed into her eyes. "Laura, listen to me. I have never loved any woman as I love you . . . and I never will again love another."

"I want to believe you," she said in a whisper.

There was a single tear in her eye, and Brandon felt a rush of guilt that he had put it there. "Then do. I pledge it before God, and you know how seriously I take my faith. I would never make such a pledge before my God and King were it not so. My love for you is second only to my love for Him. Please believe me. Please forgive me."

Laura closed her eyes for a moment, and Brandon thought perhaps she would break into tears. He wondered if he should escort her to a more private place, but had no idea of where that might be. The seconds ticked by, and finally Laura opened her eyes and fixed him with a smile.

"I forgive you. You have given me a wonderful Christmas gift, so let me return the favor. I love you most dearly. I have never given my heart to another, and never will." She shivered again, and this time Brandon had no doubt it was due to the emotions of the moment. "I would forgive you even if I did not love you so. . . . However, I beg you to never deceive me again."

"I promise you that I will endeavor to always be truthful. My motives were pure, even if they appeared otherwise."

She seemed to relax a bit. "You have no idea how afraid I've been these last few days."

"Afraid?"

"Yes. Afraid that you didn't really care for me as much as I thought." She twisted her gloved hands together. "I knew I'd lost my heart to you, but then I felt a fool for doing so."

He lifted her hand to his lips and kissed her fingers. "You are no fool, Laura Marquardt. In fact, you may very well be the most intelligent woman I've ever known."

She laughed. "So it's my mind you're fascinated with. I should have known."

Brandon chuckled and kissed her forehead. "Your mind, of course. But more importantly—your heart. You have held possession of that part of me for some time, Miss Marquardt. Very nearly from our first encounter."

"When you yelled at me?" Her dark brow rose ever so slightly.

"I did not yell. I was merely firm."

"And bossy and opinionated. You didn't even let me explain myself." She moved back on the settee and folded her arms. "Is that how you always deal with matters of importance?"

"I believe in obedience to authority," he said, folding his arms, as well. "And you might as well know that I will probably have other moments of bossiness and opinionated firmness should we take our courtship further."

"Somehow that doesn't surprise me." Laura raised her fan and drew it slowly across her cheek, allowing it to fall fully open.

"Another language lesson?" He grinned.

"Indeed."

She got to her feet, but Brandon pulled her back. "Well? You know I am hardly fluent in fan."

Laura laughed. "It would do you well to learn a few Southern customs. But I shall take pity on you." She drew the fan open as she pulled it across her cheek. "This means I love you." She met his gaze, and Brandon lost himself in the warmth of her eyes. "And I always will."

Laura could scarcely draw a breath when she left Brandon's side. She had never been in love before now, and the feelings and wonder of it all very nearly brought her to tears. How glorious it was to be in love and have that love returned.

She caught sight of Tyler and her sister and immediately sobered. Carissa looked ill, and Tyler was helping her to the door.

Laura quickly joined them, Brandon right behind her. "What's wrong?" she asked.

"Your sister got too hot. She's feeling faint, and I thought perhaps some fresh air would do her good."

"I have a better suggestion," Laura said. "I think we should return home. Carissa, I know you planned to have me join you at your house, but it would be best if you were to remain with us tonight. If you get worse, the doctor is only a short distance away. I'll have one of the grooms ride over to your house with a note, just in case Malcolm returns from his trip tonight."

"Let me get your wraps," Brandon said, leaving Laura with her sister and Tyler.

Laura maneuvered toward the front door with Carissa close behind. "I am so sorry you have taken ill."

Carissa shook her head. "I am fine. From time to time I feel a little faint. The doctor has assured me that it often happens in my condition." She flushed and glanced at Tyler. "Excuse me for mentioning such a delicate matter."

"No apology needed," he assured her.

They reached the door and the butler had just opened it when Carissa turned to look at Tyler. "I am so very sorry," she said in a gasp and promptly fainted.

Laura gave a little shriek but quickly recovered as Tyler caught Carissa before she could fall to the ground. "Please bring her outside. The fresh air will do more to revive her than anything else."

She motioned their driver to bring up the carriage. He hurried from where he'd been chatting with some of the other men while Laura turned to meet Tyler's worried expression. "She's to have a baby."

"I figured as much. Do you think she's all right?"

Laura nodded as Carissa started to come around. "She'll be fine. Let's just get her to the carriage."

Carissa opened her eyes and looked confused. Then she seemed to become fully aware of Tyler's hold on her and her whereabouts all at once. "Oh . . . goodness . . . oh . . . put me down."

"Tyler is going to carry you to the carriage first," Laura insisted.

Brandon arrived just then with their things. The driver pulled up to the foursome and quickly reined back on the horses. "Whoa now. Whoa."

"Stay there," Laura commanded the man as he started to set the brake. "We can manage." She opened the carriage door and stepped back, and Tyler climbed the step without difficulty.

Laura felt a hand on her elbow and Brandon pulled her toward him. "What was that you were saying about going to stay with Carissa?" he asked to her surprise.

"She's afraid," Laura replied, then turned to join her sister. Brandon stopped her. "Of course she's afraid. You should be, too. You cannot go there and stay in the same house with that madman."

Laura felt a surge of anger. "Do not tell me what I might do where my sister's safety is concerned. Malcolm would never dare lay a hand on her while I am there."

The grip on her arm tightened. "Malcolm Lowe doesn't care if you are there or not. He will not be thwarted by your presence. If he chooses to hurt his wife, there is very little you can do about it."

Laura leaned closer in order to whisper. "I will not let her be alone. She cannot be sent back to that house and the danger that it represents without help. My parents have no idea of Malcolm's abuse. And even if they were to know, I seriously doubt they could do or say anything that would change the situation."

"But you think you can?" he asked in disbelief.

"Laura, are you coming?" Carissa called weakly from the carriage.

"I am," she replied and looked hard at Brandon.

"We will discuss this further when we arrive at your home." Brandon helped her into the carriage, then took a seat beside Tyler.

Laura arranged her sister's cloak around her shoulders and drew her close. "We'll have Carlita get you tucked into bed as soon as we get back. I'll have Esther bring you up something warm. Would you prefer milk or tea?"

"Tea, I think," Carissa said and sighed. "I apologize for ruining an otherwise perfect evening."

"Bah, you didn't ruin anything," Laura replied.

"She's right, you know," Tyler said in a good-natured manner. "It wasn't that perfect. There wasn't a single sprig of mistletoe anywhere to be found. And believe me, I looked."

The foursome laughed at this, and Laura was grateful for the way it broke the tension of the moment.

After the short drive home, Laura allowed Tyler to help Carissa to the door, then asked Brandon to assist her inside. She turned to Tyler and smiled. "Thank you so much for all you've done. If you are still in town tomorrow, I would be pleased to have you join us for dinner—say around twelve thirty?"

"I would love to, but I have plans to be on my way. Thank you, however. I won't forget your kindness, and the next time I'm in town, I will happily take you up on the offer."

Laura nodded. "I'll call for your horse."

"Don't bother. I know the way to the stable. I'll retrieve him myself. Good evening." He gave the briefest bow.

Laura hurried inside and found Mother already fussing over her younger daughter. She deposited her wrap and gloves with the butler before turning to find Brandon watching her most intently. "I suppose we might as well discuss this now."

"I think that would be wise."

Moving back the pocket doors to a small sitting room, Laura took up a lamp from the hall table. Once she'd lit another in the sitting room, she replaced the lamp and took a seat. Brandon came and sat down beside her.

"You know that Malcolm is dangerous. I'm not exaggerating that fact. If he has in mind to harm Carissa—he will most likely have no problem hurting you, as well."

"But what am I to do? Carissa can't face him on her own. She's far too delicate."

"Then get the doctor to recommend she stay here. Take the man into your confidence and let him know that Malcolm hits her. Tell him that you need him to insist Carissa remain here with women who can tend to her needs."

Laura thought for a moment. It might work. The doctor was a longtime friend of the family, and Laura knew she could trust him. "I suppose I can do that." She let out a long sigh. "I know I cannot keep her safe forever." She turned to Brandon with a pleading look. "Please, please get the necessary evidence and put that man behind bars, where he cannot hurt her. Please, Brandon."

He nodded and took hold of her hands. "I will. I will see that he is apprehended as soon as possible. Just remember—if we don't manage to get the proper evidence against him, Malcolm could well go free. Then things will truly get ugly."

A trembling started in Laura's knees and spread throughout her body. She was terrified of what might happen. The very thought of Malcolm being arrested only to be set free had never crossed her mind. "Oh, Brandon, God alone can see us through this."

He nodded. "You speak the truth. God has the only means to see justice done. We must trust Him to watch over the entire affair and reveal evil where it has its hold."

⁓

After Brandon left, Laura hurried upstairs to check on her sister. Their mother had finally gone to bed and Laura could see that Carissa was far from being sleepy.

"Do you want to talk?" Laura asked.

Carissa nodded. "Did you send a note to Malcolm?"

"Yes. I had it sent soon after we arrived. Brandon reminded me before he left." Laura sat on the bed beside her sister. "He also had a good idea. He suggested that I speak to the doctor and let him know of how Malcolm mistreats you. He believes, as do I, that the doctor will keep our confidence. We can have him suggest that you need to stay here due to your condition—that you need to have the care of someone in case you faint again."

Carissa met her sister's gaze. "And he doesn't want you anywhere near my house for fear of what Malcolm might do to you."

Laura thought to deny Carissa's comment, but decided against it. "Brandon said that if a man will beat his wife— threaten the mother of his unborn child—he would have no trouble hurting me. I suppose that his statement is true enough. That's why I'm begging you to allow me to speak to the doctor. I will go first thing in the morning on the pretense of bringing him here. I will tell him what he needs to know. Are you agreed?"

Carissa placed her hands on her still slim belly. "I am. Let us see if we can arrange this without Malcolm causing either of us further harm."

24

It was easy enough to get the doctor to agree to Laura's request. He had no patience for men who hit their wives and promised to keep Carissa's secret. He also spoke directly to Stanley Marquardt, suggesting that Carissa needed to remain with her family in order to be properly cared for. Laura and Carissa exchanged a look of relief.

"I don't believe she needs to be bedfast," the doctor explained. "However, due to her penchant for fainting it would be dangerous for her to be alone."

"I completely understand," Father replied. "Of course she shall remain with us. I will let her husband know the situation when he returns to town."

The doctor nodded, then gave Laura a quick smile. "I believe I've done all that I can here. Don't hesitate to send someone for me, however, if there is a problem."

Once he'd gone, Laura gripped her sister's arm. "We should

go to the house and get your things before Malcolm returns." She looked to their parents. "I can go with Carissa. She can sit and point to what needs to be retrieved."

"Take Esther with you," Father suggested. "That way you'll have additional help."

"That's a wonderful idea, Father. Thank you."

Carissa and Laura rose in unison, but it was Carissa who spoke. "I'm so sorry to bring this on you. Thank you so much for allowing me to stay."

"Don't be silly," Mother replied. "This will always be your home. We want you and the baby to be properly cared for."

Within the hour Laura and Carissa walked through the back door of the young bride's house. Esther followed with a couple of carpetbags. There was no sign of Malcolm, and the note that had been delivered the night before remained on the kitchen table.

"Apparently he's still gone," Laura said, looking around the small room.

"We'd probably best get right to it," Carissa declared. "I don't have any idea of when he'll return."

Laura directed Esther to go upstairs with Carissa. "Start the packing and I'll be up shortly. Carissa, don't waste any time."

"What are you going to do?"

A thought had crossed Laura's mind only seconds earlier. "I'm going to see if there's any evidence we can take that might make the case against Malcolm."

"He has an office, but he keeps it locked," Carissa said, pointing down the hall.

"A skeleton key would most likely work," Laura said. "Have you one?"

"Yes—in the drawer just over there."

Laura went and rummaged through the contents until she found the key. "This should work. You go ahead and get your things. Hurry."

Esther and Carissa understood the urgency and rushed from the room. Meanwhile Laura made her way to the locked door of Malcolm's office. She hesitated for a moment. What if Malcolm came home while she was in his office?

"I have to try," she whispered to no one.

The key easily did the trick and she entered the room without further delay. Unable to see very well, Laura pulled back the drapes and went quickly to Malcolm's desk. The newspaper from nearly two weeks earlier was still sitting on the edge of the desk with a pen and inkwell, but otherwise the surface was clean.

Laura pushed back the chair and opened the center drawer. She took out a handful of papers; nothing there looked overly important. Shoving them back, she went next to the side drawers. The first two revealed a variety of items. Several books, a few letters, and writing paper. Digging deeper, Laura found a bottle of whiskey and shook her head. It only surprised her that he'd bothered to try to hide it.

The bottom drawer proved to be locked. There was no evidence of a key anywhere. Laura pulled at the handle again, but the drawer refused to budge. Just then, she remembered a time when she'd managed to get some pieces of clothing caught in her dresser drawer. Carlita had resolved the problem by removing the drawer on top.

Laura went back to the second drawer and pulled it all the way out. It was heavy and she very nearly spilled the contents as she wrestled it to the top of the desk. Once this was done she glanced to see if she'd gained access to the bottom drawer. She had. Her heart picked up its pace a bit as she reached into the darkened hole.

Her search uncovered two small rolled maps and invoices for black powder. There were also several pages of handwritten notes, but Laura didn't take the time to study them. She collected everything from the drawer and glanced around the room to see what she might put the papers within for transport. Seeing nothing suitable, she merely tucked them inside her snug jacket and secured the middle drawer in place.

Once she'd reached the hall, Laura relocked the door and went in search of her sister and Esther. The two women were just coming down the stairs when Laura was about to start up. She could see that the carpetbags now bulged as Esther struggled to heft them.

"We got everything we could," Carissa declared.

"Then let's get out of here," Laura instructed. "I found enough evidence that I believe Brandon's superiors will have little trouble convicting your husband."

Carissa's eyes widened. "Truly?"

They'd reached the kitchen and Laura was about to reply when she heard the sound of horses and men talking. She glanced out the window. It was Malcolm and five other men.

"He's here, and he has friends," Laura said, turning back to her sister.

"He will know we're here because of the carriage," Carissa said, shaking her head. "What are we going to do?"

Laura looked at Esther. "Leave the bags, Esther." She reached into her jacket. "These papers must reach Brandon. Do not give them to anyone else. Leave by the front door and don't let yourself be seen. Brandon may be at the army headquarters, so try there first. When you find him, let him know what's happened—just in case we don't make it home."

Esther's eyes widened. "I don't wanna leave ya here alone."

"It's the only way," Laura said, pulling the woman through the house. "Carissa and I can tell Malcolm why we've come and how the doctor wants her to be with us because of the baby. If he's not suspicious we will be able to get to the carriage and start for home before he can realize that I've taken his papers. Now go."

She pulled the metal bar from its place as Esther stuffed the papers inside the bodice of her gown. Laura all but shoved the woman through the front entrance. She had barely closed the door and replaced the bar when she heard her sister greeting Malcolm and the others.

Making her way casually to the kitchen, Laura reached for the carpetbags. "If you're sure this is everything . . ." She stopped talking and smiled at Malcolm. "Oh, we're so glad you're home. I'm sure you read our father's letter."

Malcolm frowned. "What letter? And what's with those bags?"

Laura acted as though it were nothing more important than a Sunday school outing. "The doctor wants Carissa to stay with us. Given that you are so very busy and often travel, he felt it important to her health. You see, she keeps fainting. It's because of her delicate condition, of course."

The men seemed rather put off by the subject, but Laura

continued. "The doctor felt that Carissa needed other women to tend to her needs, and we knew you'd understand. See there on the table? We sent you word last night. Carissa was with me when she passed out. It might have been quite tragic if I'd not been there."

Malcolm looked at the letter and then back to his wife. For a moment Laura felt sure he would fight her on the idea, but to her surprise, he simply nodded. "I think that would be a good idea. Carissa should stay with you—probably at least until Christmas. My work should settle down by then, and I'll be able to arrange a housekeeper for her."

Laura smiled. "How grand. Well, then let us be on our way. Carissa, I'll just put your things in the carriage."

"Thank you," Carissa said in a barely audible voice. Laura feared her sister's nervous state might well give them away.

"Just a minute," Malcolm said as Laura moved toward the door. He motioned to the men standing there. "One of you take those bags to the carriage for her."

A tall, scruffy-looking man at Laura's right reached out and took the bags. "I got 'em, boss."

Malcolm's gallantry surprised Laura, but she struggled to maintain her composure. "Thank you."

Malcolm gave his wife a nod and headed for the hall. "I have to get something in my office, and then we'll be on our way, as well. I probably won't see you again before the first of the year."

"Do . . . be . . . careful," Carissa said.

"Come along, sister. You're starting to look pale again. I don't want you fainting." Laura took hold of Carissa's arm and all but dragged her toward the back door. She wanted to run, knowing they'd have very little time to get away before Malcolm was able to learn the truth about his papers.

"We should hurry," she whispered to Carissa.

Laura had just assisted Carissa into the carriage and was hurrying to the other side when Malcolm appeared at the back door. "Ladies, I need to show you something before you go."

Laura turned and forced a smile. "She's really tired, Malcolm. Can't it wait?"

He smiled, but his expression was cold and sent a chill down Laura's spine. "No. It can't wait."

Carissa hesitated, and Laura felt at a loss as to what to do. She had been relieved to get out of the house and into the open. There weren't any other houses in the area, but she somehow felt safer being there than inside the house with those men.

"Carissa."

The single word was a command.

Laura looked to her sister and nodded, not knowing what else to do. "I'll come with you," she said in a hush. Taking hold of Carissa's arm, Laura helped her from the wagon. Together they walked back to the house.

"What is it you wish for me to see?" Carissa asked.

Malcolm took hold of her and pulled her away from Laura. "Come with me, and I'll show you." He glanced at Laura. "You too. I think you'll both find this interesting."

Laura trembled. *Dear Lord,* she prayed. *We need your help. We need your protection.*

She followed Malcolm and Carissa back into the house and through the kitchen. Laura had a horrible feeling in the pit of her stomach when Malcolm stopped at the room where he kept his office. Pushing open the unlocked door, he did nothing but stand there.

Carissa looked to Laura and then to her husband. "What is it? What do you want me to see?"

"I thought you might like to see how nice the sunlight is."

Carissa frowned. "We were just outside, Malcolm. I could see the sun there."

Laura felt as though she might be the one to faint. She'd forgotten to refix the draperies. Malcolm had known without ever needing to search his desk that someone had been in his office. She frantically searched her mind for an excuse—some reason that he might accept for her having been there. Of course, once he found his papers missing, he would blame her no matter what.

"It is lovely," Laura finally said, forcing the words. "I can see why you have your office here."

He glared at her. "I keep the drapes closed. Someone opened them." He narrowed his gaze at Laura. "I don't suppose you'd know anything about that?"

"Why should I?" She did her best to sound unafraid. "I had no reason to be here. I've been helping Carissa with her things." Laura prayed he'd believe her and let them go before searching his desk.

"I see," Malcolm replied. He toyed with the fountain pen on his desk before moving around to the other side. For a moment he paused, and the tension only mounted. Laura looked behind her, wondering if they might make a run for it, but Malcolm's cohorts were blocking the hall. Malcolm slowly leaned down and unlocked the bottom drawer.

"Hmm, I suppose you don't know anything about my papers, either." He straightened and fixed Laura with a hard look.

"You're being rather obscure, Malcolm. What papers are you talking about?"

"The papers I keep in this drawer." He eyed Laura with a withering look.

Laura stood her ground and feigned surprise. "Well, since the drawer was locked, I suppose no one would have knowledge of the contents."

"The office was locked, too, but someone still managed to get inside."

At this, Carissa looked at Laura and then to her husband. "I'm not feeling well, Malcolm."

He laughed. "I'm sure you aren't." He motioned to one of the men. "Joe, go get those bags from the carriage. I have a feeling I'll find what I'm looking for in them."

Laura stiffened. She knew they wouldn't find the papers there, but she had no idea what Malcolm's next move might be after that. He had no way of knowing that Esther had come with them, but when he couldn't find the things he was looking for, Laura knew he would be determined to know the truth. Would she be able to refrain from admitting her guilt? What if he decided to torture her? Worse yet, what if he threatened to hurt Carissa?

In less than a minute, Joe was back with both bags. He tossed them on the desk and Malcolm immediately poured the contents from each. Laura clutched Carissa's hand and squeezed her sister's fingers.

Malcolm shuffled through the clothes and then looked back to the two women. "Where are they?"

Laura shook her head. "Malcolm, we haven't a clue what you're talking about. However, your wife is ill and needs to rest. Now, if you are done with this game, I suggest you help me get Carissa to the carriage."

"You two aren't going anywhere until I get those papers. If you've hidden them in this house, I will find them."

To Laura's surprise Carissa stepped forward. "Malcolm, you keep this office locked. How is it that you could possibly think we've taken anything? Perhaps we've been robbed."

Malcolm laughed. "And the thief just happened to relock the office door before leaving with nothing of value? Those papers aren't good to anyone but me. Unless, of course, someone was of a mind to turn them over to the authorities."

Laura struggled to keep up the pretense. "Why would the authorities care?"

"You two play a good game, but I'm not convinced." He came around the desk so quickly that Laura nearly stumbled as she stepped backward. "Take hold of her," Malcolm said to the man nearest Laura. He did so with an ironclad grip that dug painfully into Laura's arms.

Malcolm took Carissa in hand and searched her for any sign of his papers. "Where are they, wife?"

"I don't have them, Malcolm," Carissa said, shaking her head. "And please don't be so rough with me. Remember my condition."

"I don't care about your condition," he said, shoving her aside. He looked at Laura. "Maybe you're hiding them. Do I need to tear every stitch off you in order to search them out?"

"You wouldn't dare," Laura countered.

"Wouldn't I?" He reached out and yanked her jacket open. The buttons tore from their place and fell to the wood floor.

"Malcolm, stop!" Carissa cried out. "We don't have them. We sent them away."

Laura swallowed hard as Malcolm's expression turned to granite. He turned very slowly, and then delivered a slap across Carissa's face that sent her backward into the arms of one of the men.

"Where?"

"They're gone and have been for some time," Laura said, trying to pull his attention back to her. He would no doubt kill Carissa if given the chance, and she couldn't allow that to happen. "If you want them, you'll have to let us go. The papers are safe—for now. But if we don't return immediately to the house, our father will send soldiers for us."

Malcolm raised his hand to strike her, but Laura merely stared him down. He held off and drew a deep breath. "It would appear we have a little problem." He walked back to his desk and sat down. For several very long minutes, he said nothing.

Laura's heart pounded so hard she felt certain everyone in the room could hear it. She longed to run, but knew the impossibility of it. She prayed that Esther had gotten safely away and that the papers would soon be in Brandon's hands. She prayed that he would come to their rescue . . . but worried that it wouldn't be in time.

randon arrived at the Marquardt house shortly after noon. Laura had encouraged him to come back for dinner that day, and he was glad to oblige her. But he was greeted with the worst possible news.

"The girls went off this morning to collect Carissa's things. Esther went with them, and I expect them back most anytime," Mrs. Marquardt told him.

Brandon was unable to hide his displeasure. "Why would you allow them to do such a thing?" He hadn't meant to chide her in such a manner. He realized from what Laura had said previously that her parents didn't know of Malcolm's violence. "I mean, the luggage would probably be far too heavy for them."

"Esther has a strong back, and Laura insisted they would be fine. Now, would you like to join me? I was just about to partake of some dinner. Cook has made a wonderful shrimp gumbo.

She procured the recipe from her sister in New Orleans, and I must say we all delight in it."

Brandon didn't want to upset the woman, but he felt strongly that he should go in search of Laura and her sister. "As delectable as that sounds, I must decline. I only stopped by for a few minutes. If you'll excuse me, I'll take my leave. Please let Laura know, however, that I will return this evening."

"Oh, I surely will," Mrs. Marquardt said. "Do come for supper, Mr. Reid. We will be most happy to have your company."

He nodded and turned for the door. "I thank you, Mrs. Marquardt."

Gaston had no sooner closed the door behind him when Brandon spied Tyler Atherton riding toward the house. He wondered if he might convince the man to aid him in searching for the women.

"Atherton, I thought you were to be on a ship bound for Galveston this morning," Brandon said. He quickly untied his horse and mounted.

Tyler nodded and Brandon rode up to face him. "There were some problems with delivery. The bulls should be here tonight, and I'll leave in the mornin'."

"Well, I wonder if you might ride with me just now. I have a problem, and I would like to solicit your help."

Tyler looked at the house. "I came to see how Mrs. Lowe was feeling, and Laura invited me for the noon meal."

Brandon tried not to show his irritation. "Look, neither woman is currently here. In fact, they may be in some danger, and I'm wondering if you would assist me in finding them."

"Danger? From what?"

Considering the situation for a moment, Brandon motioned to the street. "Ride with me and I'll explain."

Atherton glanced once more at the house, then nodded. He moved his bay to follow after Brandon's mount. "What's this about, Reid?"

"I know you fought for the South, Atherton, but there are problems afoot by some of your former Confederates, and it stands to claim a great many lives. The lives of Laura and Carissa may well be in that count. What I want to know from you is whether you can take a stand against the men you once fought alongside."

Tyler didn't hesitate. "If the women are in danger, I'll fight General Lee himself. Now, what's this all about?"

Brandon urged his horse to a quick lope and Tyler did likewise. "Carissa's husband is suspected of having killed Union soldiers."

"I did that myself," Tyler admitted. "Don't like to dwell on it, but it hardly makes me a criminal."

"You didn't kill them after the war was over and while they were asleep on their cots—did you?"

"Lowe did that?"

Brandon motioned that they were going to take the road to the right to avoid going directly through town. "He did. We were going to nab him on those counts when we uncovered additional plots that he was involved with. In fact, he's most likely leading the entire business. Laura overheard something about a plot to blow up Union soldiers. It seemed Lowe had plans to kill as many of the colored troops as possible. We got this information to our superiors and they in turn mustered the troops out of the city. We'd hoped it would put an end to Malcolm's plans. We thought perhaps he would hesitate to kill white troops, but it didn't seem to matter. We suspect he's now planning to kill hundreds—we just can't be sure of where or when."

"And you think the girls are somehow involved—in danger?"

"I'm hoping they aren't, but they went this morning to retrieve Carissa's clothing and other articles and bring them back to the house. See, Carissa's husband has a heavy hand, and Laura said her sister has grown quite afraid of him. Apparently Laura convinced Carissa to stay with them at the Marquardt house. They left this morning and still haven't returned. Mrs. Marquardt felt certain they would have been home in time for dinner."

"But you think Malcolm has them?" Tyler asked.

"If he came home while they were there, he might well have lost his temper. Malcolm may have returned at any time. Carissa said that much last night when we were riding to the party. You might remember she said that Lowe had been gone for some time, and she thought he would surely be back that evening or the next. Now, that doesn't necessarily mean there's a problem, but since the girls haven't made it back, it does bear checking into."

"I agree," Tyler said, nodding. "Glad I can help."

Twenty minutes later they arrived at the Lowes' house. There wasn't a sign of anyone. The girls and the Marquardt carriage were nowhere to be found. Tyler knelt on the sandy soil and looked at the tracks while Brandon rushed to the house. He pounded on the front door for some time, then took himself to the back and knocked on it, as well.

When no one answered, Brandon tried the handle and found the door opened easily. He stepped inside. "Laura?"

There was no sound at all. His voice filled the sparsely furnished space of the kitchen. "Laura! Mrs. Lowe! It's Brandon Reid."

Still nothing. He decided to go through the house, but upon investigation found that no one was there. He felt his brows furrow. The only road out here was the one they'd come in on. If the girls had returned to town, he and Tyler would have seen them.

He made his way back outside and found Tyler squatting in the middle of the road, thirty yards away. Brandon waved and called to him. "What did you find?"

Tyler straightened and motioned. "What's down that direction?"

Brandon walked toward Tyler shaking his head. "I don't know. I would imagine the beach. We aren't that far from the water."

"They drove the carriage that way and about five or six horses followed. The tracks are deep enough I'm guessin' the mounts had riders. At least most of them."

"There's no reason for Laura and her sister to do that," Brandon said, going for his horse. "My guess is that they were forced to go that way. Come on."

He swung up into the saddle, not even bothering to use the stirrup. "Can you keep tracking them?"

Tyler nodded. "So long as there's light and a good wind doesn't blow the sand around too much." He pulled his horse along. "I'll stay on foot for now and we'll see what we can find." Handing his horse's reins to Brandon, Tyler smiled. "It'll be a sight easier for me if you take my mount."

"Certainly." Brandon wrapped the reins around his saddle horn and followed slowly behind Tyler as he gave special attention to the ground.

But they'd gone only about half a mile when the road split into not two but three different narrow trails. Worse yet, the carriage was sitting at the side of the main road, and there was no sign of the women.

"Riders went down all three paths," Tyler declared. "Apparently they were afraid of being followed."

Brandon urged his horse down one of the paths for a few minutes, but saw nothing. Returning to Atherton he shook his head. "Where could they have gone?"

"I couldn't say. You probably know this land better than I do."

Brandon nodded. He'd had some time on Mustang Island, which was just a short distance from this place. Could they be headed there? He didn't think that was likely, but then again he didn't know Lowe or his companions. The island might well be the place they were storing their gunpowder and other supplies.

"I think we're going to need some help. Let's get back to town so that I can speak with General Russell. If we're going to capture these men and see the women to safety, we're going to need the army's help."

Laura and Carissa found themselves tied to chairs inside a ramshackle building not far from the water's edge. It was nearly nightfall, and Laura was starting to worry that Esther had been unable to find Brandon and deliver the papers. Surely if the woman had found him and told him what had happened, Brandon would have come in search of her and Carissa.

Across the room at a small table, Malcolm sat while his men stood gathered round. Laura could hear most of what was being said, but from time to time her brother-in-law would lower his voice enough that she couldn't make out all the details.

"Laura, what are we going to do?"

"I don't know," she whispered.

They'd been there now for some time and Laura's arms hurt from where the ropes bit into them and bound her to the chair. Her hands were tied at the wrist, as were Carissa's. The place smelled of black powder and other things that Laura couldn't identify. She wasn't even sure she would have realized that the kegs they sat amongst were black powder had they not been stamped as such.

"We'll have to do it tonight," Malcolm declared. "Since those two decided to stick their pretty little noses into my business, we can't afford to wait any longer."

"What'll we do with them, boss?" one of the men asked.

"I've given that some thought," Malcolm replied and got to his feet. He looked at Laura and then Carissa. "I've a feeling that no matter what I do, you two are gonna be bad luck for me." He looked back at his men. "We'll have to kill 'em."

Laura gasped. "You would kill the mother of your unborn child? You'd kill your baby?"

Malcolm rolled his eyes. "Merciful days, woman. You are as daft as you are nosy. I only married your sister in order to get at your father's money and friends. I don't care a thing about her or that brat she's carryin'."

Laura looked to Carissa just in time to see her sister's expression change from fear to anger. "I should have known you were incapable of love," she accused Malcolm. "I should have figured that out a long time ago."

He laughed. "Yeah, you probably should have, but you were too busy being the little belle of the ball. I've never known a woman as stupid as you."

Carissa winced as if struck, but Laura turned on Malcolm in hatred. "My sister isn't stupid; she merely has a big heart. It can hardly be her fault that you deceived her and she believed. When a person loves another, they want to believe the very best of them." She thought of Brandon and his confession to having been involved in Malcolm's investigation long before she'd mentioned his plans. She wanted to believe only the very best about him.

"It's easy to fool a fool," Malcolm countered. He turned back to the men. "We'll move out tonight and set the explosion to go off around two in the morning. That way the soldiers will be asleep, and they won't be changin' the guards for a while."

"And them?" one of the men asked.

"We'll take 'em along and put them square in the middle of things. They wanted so much to be a part of it all, so we'll accommodate them," Malcolm replied.

Carissa began to cry softly. Laura longed to go to her and hold her close. She gave a desperate search around the room, hoping that she'd overlooked something that might aid them. The men's attention was on whatever drawing Malcolm had on the table. Laura tried once again to pull her wrist through the tight bindings. It seemed as though she could feel a little give, but not enough.

"Now, get those wagons loaded," Malcolm instructed, stepping away from the table. "Pack them just like we planned. If you don't distribute the weight evenly, we're likely to get stuck in the sand. Get everything set and don't leave anything to chance. We'll only have one opportunity to make this work."

The men grunted their approval and walked from the shack. Malcolm turned to the women once more and dragged his chair over to where they were sitting. Turning the chair, he sat on it backward and leaned against the frame.

For a moment all he did was stare at Laura and Carissa. His penetrating gaze was unnerving, and Laura finally had all she could take. "What are you going to do now?"

He shrugged. "We're loading the powder," he said, giving a sweeping motion with first his left and then his right arm. "If I thought I could trust you two, you'd be out there helping."

"Malcolm, this is a horrible thing you are doing," Carissa said, looking at her husband. "Please, if I've meant anything good to you . . . please let my sister go."

Giving a brief laugh, Malcolm slapped his thigh. "You do say the most ignorant things. I ain't gonna take my orders from no woman."

"I'm your wife, Malcolm. I have your child growing inside me." She sounded stronger and more self-assured than Laura had thought possible. "I'm begging you to reconsider."

He cocked his head to one side for a moment. "I did as you asked, and I'm still convinced my way is best." He laughed again. "Now I'm goin' to go help my men. The sooner we're loaded, the sooner we can get out of here."

"To go where?" Carissa asked.

Malcolm's expression caught between a smirk and a look of self-satisfaction. "Well, you little ladies enjoy yourself. Oh, and if you do happen to get free, which I seriously doubt you can accomplish, I want you to know something. It's ten miles back to town. Ten miles of dangerous paths, and you won't know where you're going. It's dark—and believe me, there's more than me to contend with out there."

Fixing his gaze on Laura, Malcolm scooted the chair closer. "You know, you always were the smart one of the bunch. Never could abide that kind of thing in a woman, though. Made me glad that your sister was just willing to arrange flowers and clean house."

Carissa went pale and Laura felt her anger stir. "Malcolm, did it not ever dawn on you that those papers will explain everything to the army, and they will post guards around all of the necessary locations? I mean, I didn't take the time to read your papers, but even I can figure that one out."

"I wasn't foolish enough to note the locations—or to even sign my name to them. I drew maps and designed how we would set the powder, but I'm good at this. I know better than to leave anything around that could be found by snoopy little girls."

"They watch you all the time, Malcolm," Laura warned him. "You'll never get away with this."

Malcolm struck her with the palm of his hand before Laura even knew what had hit her. She reeled backward and heard Carissa yell something at her husband. The room swam, and Laura thought for just a moment she might pass out.

Lord help us, she prayed, fighting for consciousness. *Please, Lord, send a deliverer—send us help.*

Malcolm was laughing, and Carissa continued to argue with the man. "You had no reason to strike her, Malcolm. I can't believe I ever thought you to be an honorable man."

Laura's eyes strained to focus, and she saw Malcolm scowl at Carissa. "My honor died on the battlefield for anyone or anything but the South. That's where my honor lies, and that's what I'll go on fighting for." He got to his feet. "Now, like I said, I'm going to go see to the loads. You two, try to have a pleasant time." He laughed as though he'd told a great joke and made his way from the tiny shack.

Carissa looked at her sister and shook her head, tears streaming down her face. "This is all my fault. You warned me not to marry him so quickly. You tried to convince me that I wouldn't be happy, but all I could think about was the wedding and the banquet afterward. I wanted so much to be a beautiful bride and have all my friends gathered round. I was so blind, Laura. So blind. And now you'll pay for my mistakes."

"Unless God has other plans," Laura said, trying her best to smile. Her cheek still ached from Malcolm's slap.

"You still believe in God—even now?"

"Especially now," Laura replied. "I couldn't get through this without Him."

"And you think God is really listening to your prayers?" Carissa asked.

"I'm certain of it."

"And you aren't afraid?"

"I didn't say that. I wish I could tell you that because I believe God is in control, that I never fear life's circumstances. But I do. I'm terrified. I know that God is still with us, however, and I'm learning little by little that this is enough. That He is more than able to meet my needs."

"I'm so scared, Laura." Carissa bit her lip and closed her

eyes. "I want my baby to live. *I* want to live." She opened her eyes again and met Laura's gaze. "I want you to live. Can God do that? If I pray to Him . . . will He listen?"

"He listens to the prayers of the faithful and repentant. If you repent of your sins and ask Jesus to be your Savior—He will. He will come into your heart and forgive all of your sin."

"And we'll get out of this without getting hurt?" Carissa asked hopefully.

Laura wanted to tell her yes, but knew that would be a lie. "I don't know. I don't know what God has planned in any of this. I don't know how the devil will strive to interfere. I only know that God is faithful, and we can trust Him to never leave us nor forsake us. That's really all that matters, Carissa. If we die without Him, we are lost. If we die with Him, we are saved no matter what."

"But I'd rather live," Carissa said. A sob caught in her throat.

"Then put your trust in Jesus. I promise, you won't be disappointed. He will deliver us, Carissa. I'm certain of it." And for the first time since they'd been taken hostage, Laura truly was certain. She had an uncanny feeling that God had already made provision for their deliverance.

"We're going to be all right, Carissa. We're going to be all right."

26

"But where could the girls be?" Mrs. Marquardt asked her husband.

"I hate to say this," Brandon told them, "but I believe your son-in-law has taken them hostage."

Stanley Marquardt looked at Brandon, quite confused. "But why?"

Throwing a glance at Tyler, Brandon nodded. "Laura has been helping me to get information on him. We knew Lowe was responsible for the murder of several soldiers. Remember the killings last May?"

"Of the black soldiers?" Marquardt questioned.

Brandon nodded. "We have proof that Malcolm headed that up. He has a team of former Confederate soldiers who are helping him carry on the war."

Mr. Marquardt couldn't have looked more shocked had Brandon hit him in the face. He glanced at his wife before he asked, "And what did Laura have to do with this?"

"We were slated to take Malcolm into custody when Laura overheard him talking about his plans to blow up Yankee soldiers. We delayed his arrest hoping that we could catch his cohorts. We have been watching Malcolm and have managed to identify some of the men. When I learned about his abuse of Carissa—"

"What abuse?" Stanley Marquardt cut in.

Remembering what Laura had said about her parents' ignorance of Malcolm's true nature, Brandon knew the time had come to reveal the truth. "Your daughter didn't fall down the stairs at home. Her husband beat her within an inch of her life. Laura figured this out and forced Carissa's confession."

Mrs. Marquardt raised her hand to her mouth and stumbled a step backward, while Stanley Marquardt's face turned beet red. He cursed, something Brandon had never heard the man do before.

"I'm sorry to be the one to have to tell you, but apparently Malcolm has been hitting her on a regular basis."

"Oh, our poor girl," Mrs. Marquardt moaned.

"Perhaps you should sit down," Brandon suggested. She didn't even argue, but sank into the nearest chair.

"Tyler and I have been searching for the women and believe Lowe and his men have them. We have an idea of where he took them, but I've arranged for some soldiers to assist us. I only stopped here long enough to let you know what was happening."

Just then a commotion rose at the front door. Gaston was arguing with someone, but the decidedly female voice would have nothing to do with his protests.

"I gots . . . to see . . . Mr. Brandon. It's a . . . matter of life and death."

Brandon and Tyler turned as Esther made her way into the house. She was holding out some papers and looking to Mr. Marquardt in apology. "I knows . . . the workers . . . don't use the front door . . . but this be important." She was panting, and Brandon could see that she was covered in sweat despite the cool temperature.

Mr. Marquardt reached for the papers, but Esther pulled them back. "Miss Laura said these was for Mr. Brandon and nobody else."

Brandon stepped forward before Marquardt could protest and took the papers. "Where did you get these, Esther? Where's Laura?"

"That Mr. Malcolm . . . he done took her and Miss Carissa. He and his men come jes afore we could leave. Miss Laura, she find these papers in Mr. Malcolm's office. She say for me to get them to ya, but I watched for a time and I saw the men take Miss Carissa and Miss Laura in the carriage. Then I go to town to search for you."

"We found the carriage," Brandon told her, "but the ladies weren't there."

Brandon looked through the papers quickly and unrolled the maps. To anyone else it might have been questionable, but Brandon easily recognized the layout of the army's main supply headquarters. There were notes and arrows pointing in a variety of directions from that building.

"Do you know where Malcolm took the girls?" Marquardt asked.

Esther shook her head. "They headed out the old north road, but I don't know where they be bound."

"Thank you for getting these to us." Brandon looked to Tyler. "It looks like they plan to set off a dozen separate explosions. Lowe means not to just wreak havoc; he means to start another war."

"What can we do?" Marquardt asked. "How can we help the girls?"

Brandon drew a deep breath. "I'm going to need you to take these to General Russell at the Ironclad House. Tell him I sent you and that he will need to put the troops on full alert. Security must be of the utmost strength in case we cannot get to Lowe and his men in time. Tell them the main area appears to be the HQ supply house. From there, I can't be sure, but my guess is that Lowe intends to set enough charges to blow up as many soldiers as possible. He may intend to set fire to the supplies and get the men working to put out the fire before setting off a larger explosion. Mention is made of setting fire to another location—looks like the Ironclad House. I don't have time to study it all, but he will."

"I'll take my horse and go right now," Laura's father said. He looked to Esther. "Thank you for what you've done." He locked his gaze on Brandon. "Please bring my daughters back to me." He darted from the room without waiting for Brandon to reply and headed toward the back of the house.

Mrs. Marquardt wept softly into a handkerchief, all the while rocking back and forth in her misery. Brandon looked to Esther. "Take care of Mrs. Marquardt, would you? Tyler and I will go find Laura and Carissa."

Esther nodded. "God bless ya, Mr. Brandon. God bless ya."

❦

Laura knew the hour was late. Darkness engulfed them as the men moved her and Carissa to the wagons. Malcolm was giving the final instructions to his men, and Laura could see from the glow of two lanterns that the wagons had been fixed with two teams of horses each.

"You aren't going to get away with this," Laura told Malcolm as he made his way to where she stood between her captors.

"I already have. If your thievery had done any good, we would have already had to deal with the army. I don't believe your people were able to make heads or tails out of my notes, and therefore our plan is secure."

"You go on thinking that then," Laura said, "but leave Carissa and me here. Like you said, it's nearly ten miles to town. It will take us all night to walk it."

Malcolm laughed. "You're both going with us. You're our guarantee."

"What do you mean?" Laura asked.

"Well, should anyone get sight of us and decide to cause trouble, we'll have you and Carissa to make them think twice."

"So you're going to hide behind a couple of women, is that it?" She shook her head. "Somehow that seems fitting for you."

He raised his hand to slap her again, then halted. "Put her in the first wagon. Put her up front with you," he told one of the men. "Then put a barrel of black powder at her feet."

"I'll keep Carissa with me," he said, smiling. "After all, she is my beloved wife."

Carissa surprised Laura by spitting in Malcolm's face. Laura would have applauded the effort, but Malcolm backhanded

Carissa with such force it knocked her to the ground. Malcolm kicked her hard in the legs.

"Guess you'll never learn, will you?"

"Stop it!" Laura screamed. "You brute! She cannot bear your cruelty."

"Then she oughtn't to have spit on me." Malcolm wiped his face, then reached down and yanked Carissa back on her feet. "It's probably best you die in this fracas, otherwise you wouldn't have lived long anyway."

A shot rang out and one of Malcolm's men cried out in pain. Before anyone could react, Brandon Reid called out.

"You're surrounded, Lowe. You've got nowhere to run."

Malcolm pulled Carissa in front of him and drew his Colt revolver. "If I were you, I'd back off, Reid. I have the women, and I'm not afraid to use them. If any more shots are fired, I'll send us all to kingdom come. These wagons are full to the brim with black powder."

Carissa struggled against her husband, and Laura fought to escape the hold of her guard. The man only laughed and hoisted her over his shoulder.

"You need to let the women go," Brandon countered. "The army knows all about your plans. There's an entire regiment dedicated to nothing but capturing you and your men. We have the road secured all the way back to town, so there's no way for you to escape. It'll go a whole lot easier on you if you just give up now."

"Ha!" Malcolm snorted, climbing into the wagon and dragging Carissa with him. "No Yankee ever went easy on a Reb. You know that better than anyone. I'm not listenin' to anything you have to say, Reid. My men and I are taking this powder and leaving. You try to stop us, and the women die. I'm no fool. I have men waiting for us in town. If we fail to show, they'll come to our assistance, so it's best you call off your Yankee army and admit defeat."

Laura cried out when her captor threw her roughly atop the kegs just behind the wagon seat. "You sit there and hold on to my shoulders—that way you'll be a shield to my back. You let go, and I'll put a bullet in you myself," he sneered. "Not in a place that will kill you, but it'll sure make you wish you were dead."

Knowing she had to buy some time, Laura did as she was told. It was difficult at best to find a comfortable way to sit on the kegs. She felt as if her breathing would be cut off by the angle of her body and the tightness of her corset. Nevertheless, she maneuvered herself into a somewhat workable position and took hold of the man.

Brandon had said nothing for several minutes, and Laura wasn't at all sure what was going on. She tried to pray—tried to focus on what she might do to escape, but nothing was coming to mind for either effort.

Finally, just when she'd begun to worry Brandon and the men had gone, he spoke. "Look, Lowe, you can't hope to get away. If you hurt the women, you're dead men. It's that simple."

"The way I see it," Lowe said, drawing Carissa across his lap, "I'm the one with the most firepower. Not only that, but I got something you want."

It was a standoff. Laura bit her lip to keep from crying out or saying anything that might distract Brandon or the other men. If she could just remain completely still, perhaps even the driver would forget her presence.

God, help us, please. It was the only prayer she could pray.

After another few minutes, Malcolm spoke again. "I'm losin' my patience, Reid. I want you and your men to leave right this minute. I want you headin' all the way back to town. If I so much as see a shadow movin', I'll shoot one or both of these women. And just so you know I'm serious, I'll start with Laura."

"Fine. We'll go."

Laura felt as though Brandon's words had knocked the wind from her. Go? How could they just go?

"Move out now and ride hard," Malcolm demanded. "Move out and don't even think of trying to ambush us. I know this area better than you could ever hope to. When we come down that road, it'd better be deserted."

Malcolm addressed his men then. "Once they've been gone ten minutes, we'll move out."

For what seemed an eternity, Laura and the others held their position. Laura felt the damp chill cut into her body. Her knees ached from the way she'd pinned them beneath her, and her back felt afire. She longed to know that her sister was all right, but there was no hope of that just now.

When what seemed like far more than ten minutes had passed, one of the men called out to Malcolm. "We gonna get out of here, boss?"

"Indeed. Dismount and take the women. Make your way to the boats."

Laura pulled away from the driver as he turned to take her in hand once again. She fought him, but he was much too strong and in a matter of seconds had her off the wagon and back over his shoulder.

Fear gripped her like a wild animal. She felt a sense of frantic confusion. Brandon would expect them to head down the road; any ambush or countermeasure would be planned for that very thing. He wouldn't know about the boats. She hadn't even known about them.

Her captor came alongside Malcolm, who was foisting Carissa off to a man on his right. "Bind them both good and tight and throw each one of them into a different boat. We'll split up and get out of here. Head to that cove I told you about. We'll meet up there and decide what's to be done."

"You want to just leave this stuff here?" one of the men questioned Malcolm.

"We don't have a choice. They'll be setting an ambush up for us on the road. Leastwise if Reid is even half as smart as I think he is, that's what I'd do."

"You can't hope to get away from here," Laura said. "If they were able to follow you here, they know all of your hiding places. Brandon is no fool."

Malcolm turned on her and yanked her head up and back so hard that Laura saw stars. Her back was bent painfully back toward her captor's head and all the while Malcolm seemed to twist his fingers deeper into her hair.

"Sister, dear, I will take special delight in closing that mouth of yours once and for all. You may think you know exactly how this is going to play out, but you don't. See, I'm a man who learned early on in the war to never count on anything going as planned. I was more than prepared for Reid's little stunt here tonight. Believe me, I'm far from worried about how this is going to play out."

"You should be worried," Laura said despite the pain. "Brandon will stop you. I know because I've been helping him these last few months. I know things about you and your plans, and Brandon knows even more. You haven't fooled anyone. They know all about your hiding places. They know about your contacts. They'll soon have all of you in jail."

"If they do," Malcolm replied without emotion, "it'll come at the cost of your life."

❧

Brandon waited in the darkness with Tyler and two other soldiers. They'd sent the others ahead a ways to hide additional teams of four all along the road to town. He knew they would have to let Lowe make the next move, but it was hard to wait. The man was an animal, and he would kill Laura and her sister with very little provocation.

"It's been nearly fifteen minutes," Tyler said, using a match to check his watch. There wasn't so much as another sound except for the distant wash of waves upon the shoreline.

Brandon had a bad feeling about all of this. When twenty minutes passed, he felt they'd been had. Getting on his feet, he decided to leave his horse and make it on foot back to the shack.

"If we go by way of the beach," he told Tyler, "we can sneak in from behind."

"I'm with you."

Brandon turned to the two soldiers. "Go find the others and make your way back on the double-quick. Stay in the shadows and keep hidden. Don't let them know you've returned. They have to be there—there's no other way in or out."

"Except for the water, sir," the younger of the two soldiers interjected.

Dread washed over him. The idea of Lowe and his men leaving by sea had never entered Brandon's mind. What a fool he'd been!

He didn't wait any longer but headed for the beach at a dead run. If the man was right, Malcolm had already had twenty minutes to make his escape.

This time not only were Laura's hands bound, but her ankles and knees, as well. Her captor—the same man who'd carried her from the wagon—now dumped her without care into a small boat. Laura fell hard and barely kept her head from smashing against the wood. She muffled a cry of pain and hurried to scoot away from the man. It was next to impossible, however. She really could do very little but wriggle, and that wasn't getting her anywhere very fast. The man only laughed at her efforts, further aggravating Laura. She supposed the same was being done to her sister, but because of the darkness she couldn't tell.

"You must be a grief to your mother," Laura told the man as he yanked her into place.

"My mother is dead," he replied in a growl. "Now shut up."

Two men climbed into the boat with her, while another two pushed the small launch into the water. The two men near her took up oars while the man who had tied her climbed in just as the boat slipped into deeper water. Laura wanted to call out to Carissa but feared what might happen if she did. Malcolm was in no mood for discussion, and he might hurt Carissa if she tried to answer Laura's inquiries.

Praying came hard. Usually in times of need, Laura had found talking to God to be the easiest thing in the world, but just now her tongue seemed tied. They were being taken away from Corpus Christi. Brandon would surely follow, but would he come in time?

I don't know why this is happening, God. Don't you see? Don't you care? We need your help. Laura closed her eyes and tried to still her spirit. Her questions wouldn't resolve anything. *Lord, I don't understand, but I'm trying hard to trust you. Please give me courage.*

"Halt!"

Laura heard the voice and knew it was Brandon calling from the shore. She couldn't see him, but his presence made her smile. Malcolm seemed less delighted.

"I thought I told you I'd shoot these women if you didn't leave," Malcolm yelled back.

"I made the mistake of thinking you were a gentleman," Brandon replied. "Instead, I find I'm dealing with a coward who hides behind the skirts of women."

"I'll hide wherever it serves my purpose." Malcolm laughed. "And you know full well I'm no coward."

"Then return the women. We'll let you be on your way if you'll set Laura and her sister free."

"You hold no power now, Mr. Reid. On land you may have

had half the army at your command. But here on the water, I feel quite comfortable. Farewell."

Laura heard him order the men to double their efforts and pick up the pace of rowing. She felt a moment of despair and tried to loosen the ropes on her wrists. Her skin burned painfully as she fought the binding. It was no use. She wasn't strong enough to budge the hemp.

She stopped as she caught the sound of Carissa crying. It pained her so much to know her sister was suffering at the hands of that madman. She wanted to scream at him to leave Carissa alone but knew it would do no good.

Dear Lord, please intercede on our behalf. We have no hope but that which is in you. She prayed this over and over, taking comfort in the words. *Our hope is in God,* she reminded herself. *God never fails.*

A sound caught her attention. The disturbance obviously drew the attention of the men, as well. "What's that?" one of them called out.

"Sounds like a steamer," someone answered.

Laura strained her eyes to see in the moonlit waters. Around the bend she saw a dark form rise like a beast from the waters. Lights along the rails could soon be seen. The small ship advanced much faster than the men could row, and to Laura's surprise was upon them before they knew it.

Malcolm was cursing a stream of obscenities when the ship's captain called down. "This is Captain Clairmont of the United States Navy. You will return to shore immediately or be fired upon."

"We have hostages," Malcolm returned. "Two women. We

won't be forced to shore, and if you try, I'll throw them overboard one at a time. Starting with this one."

Laura could make out her sister's form in the boat some ten feet away. Malcolm lifted her in his arms. "What's it to be?" he called out.

"You have no hope of escape, Mr. Lowe. We will block your way for as long as needed."

Fear for Carissa overtook any fear Laura might have felt for herself. Carissa couldn't swim—even if her hands and feet had been unbound. Not only that, but the water would be terribly cold—nothing like the tepid warmth of summer.

"Looks like you're gonna go swimmin'," one of the men said, taking a firm hold on Laura's arm. He laughed and pressed his face to her neck. "Pity too, you smell so sweet and all."

Laura jerked away, but he held her fast and laughed again. "You ain't gonna go nowhere until I say so."

"This is your final warning," the captain called again. "Return to shore and surrender to the troops there."

By now, Laura could see some lantern light coming from the shore. They were probably no more than ten yards away and the forms of men were taking shape.

Malcolm seemed uncertain what to do. Laura could hear his men questioning him, asking for directions . . . but he remained silent. Without warning, he stood in the boat. "You want the women—you can have them."

Then she heard a splash and Laura screamed as her sister sank in the black water. A shot was fired and then another. Laura's captor took hold of her and threw her overboard without warning. The first shock of cold water took her breath, and then the heavy hold of the sea began to drag her downward. Laura fought with all of her might to reach the surface. By doing a strange little waving kick of her legs, she was able to come to the surface momentarily, but then the water again dragged her downward.

She heard the shots being fired and knew the men were battling for their lives. No one would have time or the ability to rescue her and Carissa. Reasoning left her and despair permeated her soul. She was to die. Die in the black waters of the Gulf—never to be seen again. Once more she fought to wriggle her way to the surface and barely broke the water for a breath. Her efforts were futile, however. She couldn't fight the pull of the water.

The last bits of air escaped her lungs, and Laura fought to hold her breath. She felt the black cold hand of death tighten its grip around her. She thought of her family and of Brandon. If she were to die, it would be with his image fixed in her memory.

Something pulled at her hair. She felt the persistent tugging even as she drew in a mouthful of water. Someone had come to rescue her—but it was too late.

Laura opened her eyes briefly, certain she'd be staring into the face of God, but instead she found herself facedown on the shore—the taste of sand in her mouth. Someone was pressing hard against her back and she was coughing and sputtering as if she'd never get the water out of her lungs. She began to shiver, shaking so hard that her teeth chattered between the coughing spells.

Without any gentleness, she was rolled to her back and lifted into strong arms. "Laura! Laura, don't you die on me," Brandon was demanding.

She smiled and closed her eyes. "Wouldn't think of it," she murmured.

When next she opened her eyes, Laura found herself in her own bed. She frowned for a moment and wondered at the horrible images of guns, black powder, and water. So much water. Had it been a dream?

She rose slightly, surprised that two lamps burned full on the bedside tables. A man knelt beside the fireplace and stoked the fire with a poker. Rubbing her eyes, Laura shook her head. What had happened? The events of the night came back in a rush. Malcolm had taken her and Carissa hostage. She tensed as the man rose from the hearth and turned.

"You're finally awake," Brandon said, the relief in his tone evident.

Laura looked at him in confusion. "What happened?"

"You very nearly drowned." His expression still held a look of worry. "How do you feel?"

She fell back against the pillow. "Weak. Tired—more tired than I've ever felt before."

"Nearly dying will do that, I've heard." He sat on the chair beside her bed and took hold of her hand. "The doctor believes you'll make a full recovery, although there is some concern of pneumonia."

Laura closed her eyes, unable to resist the pull of her weariness. Then an image of Carissa came to mind. She tried to sit up, but Brandon put his hands on her shoulders.

"Just rest," he commanded.

"But my sister . . . Carissa," Laura demanded. "Where . . . what happened to her?"

Brandon pushed her back against the pillows. "She is fine. Tyler got to her in time. Your mother is passing back and forth between your two rooms. I had to fight quite fiercely to be allowed to remain here with you. However, I finally convinced your father."

"He's usually very reasonable," Laura said, finally allowing herself to relax a bit. If Carissa was safe—that was all that mattered.

"Especially since I asked him if I might have your hand in marriage."

Her eyes widened and the fog in her head seemed to clear just a bit. "You . . . asked . . . him . . ." She fell silent and Brandon chuckled.

"I did. And better still, he said yes." Then his voice became husky. "But before I can marry you, Laura, I need to know that you won't be inclined to any more foolish acts. You went to your sister's house after I specifically told you not to." Brandon reached out and tenderly touched her cheek. "When I thought you might not live, it very nearly killed me. I don't want to lose you, Laura."

She pressed her hand against her cheek. "I know. I was foolish," she finally admitted. "We should have waited for you or for someone to come with us or go in our stead. I'm sorry."

He leaned forward and kissed her forehead. "And it won't ever happen again, right?"

"What? Putting my life at risk?" Laura questioned. "Because if that's what you're asking, I cannot agree."

Brandon pulled back. "And why not?"

"Because, my dear man, life is a risk. How can I marry and give you children without risking my life? How can I endure the sicknesses and needs of those children without some risk being involved?"

He let go a heavy sigh. "I know you're right, but I only want to keep you from harm. I love you more than life, Laura, and when I thought I might lose you—I couldn't bear it. I want to marry you and grow old with you. I want to know the pleasure we'll share as husband and wife, and to raise a family of our own."

"Then you'd do well to ask me," she said matter-of-factly.

He laughed and let go his hold on her. Getting to one knee beside the bed, Brandon reached up and took hold of her hand. "Will you do me the honor of accepting my hand in marriage?"

She felt tears threaten, but smiled anyway. "I will."

Brandon got to his feet and leaned down to take her in his arms. Lifting her, bedcovers and all, he whirled her in a circle, then pulled her even closer and kissed her with great passion.

It was a little like drowning all over again, Laura thought for a moment. Just as frightening in some ways, but far more pleasurable.

The next day, Laura didn't awake until well into the afternoon. Finding herself alone, she got up and donned her robe before making her way to Carissa's room. She found her sister sitting by the window in her nightgown, staring through the glass.

"Carissa?" She didn't so much as blink, and so Laura touched her shoulder. "Carissa."

Her sister looked up and shook her head. "Malcolm is dead."

"Brandon told me. I am sorry. Sorry mostly that he turned out to be the kind of man he was. Sorry, too, that you have to bear this."

"The doctor said only time will tell if the stress of this ordeal causes me to miscarry," Carissa replied, putting her hand to her stomach. "For now, the baby lives—or so he believes."

Reaching for the ottoman, Laura pulled it alongside her sister's chair and sat. "I hope that brings you some comfort. You've already been through so much . . . but know that I'll always be here for you. Even when I marry."

Carissa looked at her oddly. "So he has finally asked?"

Laura smiled. "He did, and I said yes."

Her sister nodded. "I'm glad. I want that for you. Brandon is a good man and has proven himself over and over. Malcolm was nothing but bad."

"Brandon loves the Lord and that makes all the difference in how he conducts himself. Had Malcolm been a man of God, his anger might not have led him into sin."

"I think I understand that now," Carissa said, looking back to the window. "I've been praying . . . a lot. I know that what you told me about trusting God was right. And for once . . . I yearn to know more."

"One of the most important things to know is that God loves you, and He will never leave you." Laura reached out and gently pushed back her sister's long hair.

"I've been so foolish," Carissa said with a sigh. "I am a stupid woman, just as Malcolm told me."

"No! No, you are not! You've made mistakes, that's all. You

trusted your heart, but we all do at one time or another. Sometimes it turns out well and sometimes it does not. But putting your trust in God first is what is most important. You will see, Carissa: Life will be so much better knowing God's truth and love. I promise you that much."

Carissa met her eyes and sighed. "When is the wedding to be?"

"We haven't yet set the date, but it will be very soon. Neither of us wants to wait."

"But I thought you were opposed to short engagements. I remember you were quite adamant on that when I was to marry," Carissa said. "You said it was important to know a man, and now I realize just how right you were. Perhaps you and Brandon should delay, as well. After all, you have known him even less time than I knew Malcolm."

Laura considered her sister's words. "Would it make you feel better if I did?" She wasn't sure why she asked the question, but for some reason it seemed important.

Carissa remained silent for a long time. Finally she shook her head. "No. I think it would only make me feel worse. You and Brandon may have only been together for a short time, but you have one very important difference from my situation."

"What do you mean?"

"You both love and trust God. You have a faith that will see you through many bad situations. I didn't have that."

Laura patted her arm. "But you do now."

For several minutes Carissa said nothing. Laura thought to leave, but then her sister piped up. "And I suppose you will go far away—back north to his family?"

Laura shook her head. "No. That's not the plan. Brandon

and I spoke long into the night. We want to start a school for the former slaves. A free school. Hopefully we can get support from the local churches, and maybe in time even the state will help to fund it. But for now, Father is calling in favors from his friends. It won't be a full-time venture, however. We're also going to purchase some horses. Brandon's father raises them, and we can start our own herd here in Texas."

"Horses and a school. How like you." Carissa smiled.

"It will be very simple—at least to start," Laura replied, "but already I feel God's approval. It's a little like touching the sky."

Her sister looked at her oddly, but Laura only laughed. "I'll explain it later. For now, you need to help me plan my wedding."

March 1866

On a beautiful spring Saturday, Laura donned her mother's wedding gown and pledged her life to Brandon Reid. The tiny church was filled to capacity with friends and family. There was more than a little showing of the Federal blue uniform as Brandon's friends filled the groom's side of the church. Laura held only the highest regard for the men who had worked so diligently to save her and Carissa.

Standing before the pastor now, Laura couldn't help but think over the past year. The war had ended, and life in Corpus Christi would be forever changed . . . her life would be forever changed. She marveled that so much could be accomplished in so short a time.

Brandon slipped a simple gold band on her finger and whispered words of promise. "With this ring I thee wed, with my body I thee honor, and with all my worldly goods I thee endow."

Laura met his gaze and lost herself momentarily in the promise. She had promised her life to this man—to love him and honor him, to obey him and care for him. He'd given her the same pledge and the moment was forever etched in her heart.

"Let us pray," the pastor declared. "Father, we ask your blessing upon this man and his wife. May they always seek your face and know your grace. May their love be strong enough to weather any storms of life, and may you bless their union with children who will grow to love and devote themselves to your service. In Jesus' name, amen."

"Amen," Laura whispered.

The pastor gave Brandon a smile. "You may now kiss your bride."

"I've looked forward to this all day," Brandon said. He pressed his lips against hers in a rather chaste kiss. Pulling back just a bit he winked. "I'll finish this later."

She felt her cheeks flame but ducked her head so that no one else would see. No doubt there would be enough teasing as it was—after all, they'd broken with protocol and tradition to marry quite quickly. Tongues would already be wagging.

At the Marquardt house a grand reception entertained most of the town well into the afternoon. Laura felt exhausted from the day's events and longed only for a chance to be alone with Brandon. Brandon's friends, however, had other plans. They constantly worked to keep the couple apart, amused at the frustration they were causing.

More than once Brandon disappeared from the gathering altogether, only to reappear sometime later searching the crowd for her. At one point, Laura even spied the men throw a gunny-sack over her groom's head and take him in hand.

"Mercy, but these men are bent on wreaking havoc," she told Carissa.

"It's all in good fun," her sister countered. "Just be glad they're leaving you alone."

When the clock struck five, Laura went upstairs to change clothes. She had worried all day about causing harm to her mother's gown and was relieved to at last change into her own clothes. Carlita awaited her in the bedroom.

"You are a beautiful bride," she told Laura. "I am so happy for you."

"Thank you," Laura said, waiting for Carlita to undo the buttons down the back. "I felt quite beautiful. I think Mother's dress would make anyone feel so."

The buttons were finally undone, and Laura stepped from the seventeen yards of white satin and lace. The fashion was out of date, but for Laura, it was a perfect choice for the ceremony. When Laura requested to wear her mother's wedding gown, Agatha Marquardt had burst into tears, declaring it the dearest thing Laura might have asked of her.

"Where is Mr. Brandon taking you tonight?"

Laura accepted a dark blue traveling skirt and a shirtwaist from Carlita and smiled. "We have a reservation at the hotel. Then tomorrow we're to take a ship to New Orleans. I'm so looking forward to it. I've never been there, but Brandon has and says it's a city of wonders."

Carlita finished helping Laura dress. "You will be happy, I think. Mr. Brandon is a good man."

"He is," Laura said, smiling. She checked her reflection in the mirror.

"I can fix your hair again," Carlita offered. She reached up to tuck a few stray wisps back into place.

"No," Laura replied. "I have no desire to keep Brandon waiting. I only hope he's been able to rid himself of those pesky friends. They seem determined to keep us apart."

She stepped into her button-top boots and waited while Carlita secured them. Laura couldn't contain a nervous giggle. "I can hardly believe this day has come." She hugged her arms to her body.

Carlita finished with the boots and went back to the care of the wedding gown. "I will miss you."

Laura went to retrieve a small hat and her gloves. "But you'll have Carissa and a new baby to help with before long."

"Sí, it will be good to have a baby in this house. Maybe you will soon give us another one."

"Perhaps," Laura said. "But only God knows when that will be." She pulled on her gloves. "How do I look?"

Carlita glanced up from her work. "Lovely."

Laura headed for the door. "Now to find my husband and if necessary, force him from his friends and this place." She giggled again at the thought of manhandling Brandon away from the soldiers.

She made her way down the stairs and smiled as Esther met her at the bottom. "Don't forget to remind Father about ordering that list of supplies for the school."

"I won't." She returned Laura's smile. "Ya is the prettiest bride they ever was. Mr. Brandon's gonna be mighty proud to show ya off in N'Orleans."

"No prouder than I'll be to have him at my side." Laura could see there were a great many people in the front rooms. "Have you seen him?"

"He said iffn I saw ya I was to tell ya that he gone to the stable. Ya's suppose to meet him there. Jes don't let nobody else know, else they might wanna stop ya."

Laura suppressed a light laugh. "Such intrigue. Thank you, Esther." Music was starting up, and Laura knew the guests would soon be busy with dancing and the buffet supper. She leaned close to Esther. "Tell Mother and Father I bid them good evening."

Hurrying from the house via the back door, Laura was glad that her father had thoughtfully put in lighted torches for the guests. There was still enough daylight left, but already shadows were dancing on the lawn. Laura gave it one quick final glance. The day had truly been perfect. She all but ran down the walkway to the stables and had nearly reached the door when she heard a noise to her left.

Thinking it was Brandon, she stopped and turned, only to have a gunnysack forced over her head. Brandon's friends had apparently extended their games to include her. Laura gave a scream, but the sack muffled the sound. She fought with all her might, but the captor threw her over his shoulder without a word and very nearly knocked the wind from her.

"Let me go," she gasped in protested. "Let me go now!"

The man held her fast, however, and without so much as a grunt, mounted a horse. He shifted Laura in his arms to sit across the horse in front of him. She tried hard to pull away, but he refused to let her go and kicked the horse into action instead.

Laura thought for certain she would fall from the horse. With the sack down over her arms, she had no ability to even hold on. Brandon would be livid when he found out what had happened.

The horse slowed and the sounds of the party and city faded away. Laura tried to relax and think about what she would do, but when she heard the faint sounds of the water lapping against the shore, she could only think of the night Malcolm had taken them hostage. She shivered.

The rider seemed to notice and halted the horse. Then very quickly the sack was pulled from her head. Laura swung her hand upward to strike the man.

"Don't—it's me." Brandon took hold of her hand to block the hit.

Laura strained to see him in the dark. "You? How could you?" She didn't want to be angry, but the memories of Malcolm's attack fed her fear. "You nearly scared me to death. What kind of man are you to terrify your bride?"

Brandon laughed and pulled her close. "It was the only way I could get to you." He kissed her cheek and Laura calmed a bit. "I don't think our so-called friends were going to ever let us leave."

Laura shook her head. "You could have told me. I would have come quietly."

"Well, to be honest, I have a surprise." He directed the horse ahead another twenty or so feet and stopped. "Hold on." He slid back in the saddle and positioned Laura to be able to grip the horn. Stepping from the horse, he then reached up and pulled her into his arms.

Ahead of them, a small cottage awaited in the glow of sunset. Brandon easily carried her the distance and put her down only once he'd stepped across the threshold into the darkened house.

In a moment, he struck a match and Laura waited in silence as he lit a single lamp. The light showed a simple room, hardly bigger than Laura's bedroom at home.

"Where are we?"

"My place," Brandon said with a grin. "Or should I say, our place. At least tonight."

Laura looked at him in surprise. "In all this time, I never even knew where you were staying."

"You never asked," he said, putting his hands on either side of her face. He lowered his mouth to hers and kissed her with great longing. "Ah, Laura, how I love you," he whispered against her ear.

Laura wrapped her arms around him and sighed. "I love you, too. I never thought this day would come. I thought the war had taken all of the good men away. Instead, the war brought me the best."

Brandon lifted her in his arms once again. "I could say the same thing."

"Then you don't mind that you wound up with a sassy Southerner who questions authority?"

He laughed and tightened his hold on her. "I'm very good at teaching men how to obey authority. Surely it can't be that hard to train one woman."

Now it was Laura's turn to laugh. "Oh, Mr. Reid, you know very little about women. But fear not, I will be a very good teacher."

Brandon eyed her with a raised brow as if she'd introduced a challenge. "Then let the lessons begin."

TRACIE PETERSON is the bestselling, award-winning author of more than 80 novels. Tracie also teaches writing workshops at a variety of conferences on subjects such as inspirational romance and historical research. She and her family live in Belgrade, Montana.

Visit Tracie's Web site at *www.traciepeterson.com*.